MITO

Also by this Author

Mystery/Suspense:

Looking Over Your Shoulder
Lion Within
Pursued by the Past
In the Tick of Time
Loose the Dogs

Young Adult Fiction:

Breaking the Pattern:
Deviation
Diversion
By-Pass

Between the Cracks:
Ruby
June and Justin
Michelle
Chloe (Coming in 2017)

Medical Kidnap Files
Mito
EDS (Coming Soon)
Proxy (Coming Soon)

Stand Alone
Tattooed Teardrops
Don't Forget Steven
Those Who Believe
Cynthia has a Secret
Questing for a Dream
Once Brothers
Intersexion

MITO

PD WORKMAN

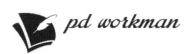

ISBN: 9781988390277

Your symptoms may be invisible.

But you are not.

Acknowledgments

I wish to personally thank the following people for their contributions and knowledge and other help in creating this book:

Beta readers, Hazel Grusendorf, Cindy McGrath, and Lisa Lamoureux.

Jim Grusendorf for editing.

CHAPTER ONE

IT WASN'T THE FIRST time in his life that Gabriel had woken up in hospital. He'd been in and out of hospitals as long as he could remember. But his head was thick and sluggish, and he couldn't remember what had happened. He looked around for his mother. Keisha would tell him what had happened and why he was there again.

She wasn't there. There was a visitor chair pushed against the wall beside his bed. That seemed like an odd place for it to be. Keisha would pull it out and push it as close as she could to his bed so that she could hold Gabriel's hand and look into his face. That's what she always did. She might leave his side to go to the restroom, or get coffee, or talk to a doctor, but it wouldn't be for long, and she would sit beside him again when she got back. Why wasn't her chair close to the bed?

A nurse came in. She had a flowered smock, and her stethoscope was pink. She had blond, curly hair, and a broad red face.

"Oh, you shouldn't be awake," she commented, seeing Gabriel's eyes open. She flipped through his chart for a moment; then she prepared a syringe to inject into his IV.

Gabriel tried to clear his throat and talk to her before she could finish the injection. She pushed the plunger slowly and glanced aside at him as he grunted.

"There, now. This will put you back to sleep," she told him. "You're going to be just fine, Gabriel."

He wasn't able to raise his voice before the whirling darkness swallowed him up.

When Gabriel awoke again, he was dizzy and nauseated. He tried to sit up a little, hoping that it would help him to regain his equilibrium. He listened to the hospital noises. A patient yelling down her hall. A young female voice, tones strident, very angry. The tired voices making announcements over the PA system. Footsteps and wheels up and down the corridor. It was all familiar, but that didn't reassure him. The chair beside him was still empty.

A nurse came in. The same one as before. For an instant, Gabriel thought maybe he should play possum. If she didn't know that he was awake, she wouldn't drug him back to sleep again. But there had to have been a reason that they had wanted him to be asleep. They would explain it.

He cleared his throat and tried to wet his dry, sticky mouth as she approached him again.

"Where's my mom?" he croaked.

"Everything is just fine, Gabriel. You need to stay calm and relaxed so that you can get better, okay?"

"But I want to know." He looked at his body for signs of injury. Had he been in a car accident? Maybe Keisha had been hurt too. Maybe she was also in hospital, in a bed somewhere close by. Maybe she was badly hurt. "Please tell me why I'm here."

"You're here to get better. You need to listen to what we tell you so that you can get better."

"But where is my mom?" Gabriel raised his voice insistently.

"You need to calm down. Just stay relaxed, everything will be all right."

"It's not all right!" Gabriel looked at the untouched visitor's chair. "I want my mom!"

The nurse shook her head, frowning in disapproval. She injected another syringe into his IV.

"Don't do that!" Gabriel shouted. "I want to talk to the doctor! I want to know what's going on!"

"Go back to sleep. Everything is fine."

Gabriel didn't know how long he had cycled between sleeping and waking. Whenever he was awake, he felt nauseated, and muscle cramps racked his limbs. He was confused, sometimes not able to remember what was going on, and sometimes remembering the nurses and being put back to sleep again. He was exhausted just from lying in bed, unable to get up or to think straight. He stopped asking questions about why he was there or where his mother was. Whenever a nurse came in, he just closed his eyes and pretended to be asleep.

A doctor and a nurse came in and talked at his bedside. He knew that one was a doctor, not because he was a man, but because of the authority in his voice and the nurse's subservience to him.

"How's our young Mr. Tate coming along?"

"He seems to be calming down. He's less agitated when he wakes up. Not so confrontational."

"Good. How are his vitals?"

The nurse made a *tsk* sound. "Up and down. His body is still adjusting to the withdrawal of all the medications he has been on. I'm afraid it's going to be a while before we have any kind of baseline."

"Well, continue with the demedicalization protocol. There's no way of telling what he really needs until we can see how his body behaves without any intervention. His system has been poisoned for too many years."

"It would be easier if we could get his cooperation."

"You know that's not likely. Just continue with what you've been doing."

"Yes, doctor."

They walked back out of the room, rustling papers and talking in low voices. Gabriel opened his eyes a crack to watch them go.

He wanted to stay awake, but a headache throbbed in the back of his neck. Even the painful cramps in his legs were not enough to keep the darkness from closing in again.

CHAPTER TWO

WHEN GABRIEL REGAINED CONSCIOUSNESS next, the chair had been moved and was occupied. He breathed a sigh of relief at first; but raising his eyes, he quickly realized that the chair was not occupied by his mother. She still wasn't to be found.

Instead, sitting in the chair was a girl around Gabriel's own age. A bit younger, maybe fourteen, dark straight hair, dark eyes. Hispanic. Was Hispanic the right word? He couldn't remember whether it was more polite to say Hispanic or Latino. Not 'them Mexicans' or 'dang illegals', like Mr. Murray next door said. Not that she really looked Mexican. Her skin wasn't very dark. But he was pretty sure she wasn't Caucasian. He felt a bit of kinship with her right away. There wasn't a high population of non-whites in the valley, so Gabriel's black skin stuck out like a sore thumb.

"Hi!" the girl greeted. "I'm Renata."

He just looked at her, his lips parted slightly, not sure what to say. She was another patient, obvious from her blue gown and plastic wristband. But he wasn't sure what she was doing in his room. He looked around to see if they were sharing the room. The hospital didn't usually mix genders in rooms, but with overcrowding, sometimes they had to for a day or two. It was better than being stuck in a hallway.

"This is where you say, 'Hi, Renata. I'm Gabriel,'" the girl pointed out.

Gabriel looked back at her mischievous smile. He tried to smile back with the right amount of warmth. Finding his tongue took a few minutes, the silence drawing out awkwardly.

13

"I'm Gabriel," he echoed, lips and tongue thick and uncertain.

"Nice to meet you, Gabriel."

He looked to see if she was holding out her hand to shake, even though he wasn't sure that he could find his own hands right now. But she wasn't. Her arms were folded tightly across her chest in a closed-off gesture, in spite of her friendly voice.

"Mito?"

"What?" Gabriel was taken off guard.

"I said, have you got mito?"

So few people had even heard of mitochondrial disease. He'd never known another patient with it. People just looked baffled if you said you had it. Like you had two heads.

"Yeah," Gabriel said. "How did you know?"

"It's sort of the specialty around here."

"Really?" Gabriel studied her, looking for something familiar in her face or body. He could never sit like she was, with her feet tucked under her. It would hurt too much. The thought brought his attention back to the muscle cramps in his legs, and he wanted to rub them. But first he'd have to sit up, and he didn't think that he could manage that. Renata was looking at him expectantly. Gabriel's words came out slowly. She was going to think that he was stupid. "You have mito?" he asked.

"Yeah. Is this your first time here?"

Gabriel looked around the room. "At the hospital? No."

"In this ward. In psych."

Psych? Gabriel tried to push himself up, but his body was too weak and wouldn't cooperate. Why would they put him in psychiatric? He was sick in his body, not his head.

"Psych?" Gabriel's voice was hoarse and squeaked up and down as if his voice were just changing. "I'm not in psych! I'm not crazy!"

She grinned. "None of us are. At least, none of us think that we are."

Gabriel tried to reach the call button for a nurse. "Why would I be in psych?" he protested.

"That's where they put you when you're first apprehended. Because it's secure. And because they can use chemical restraints."

He managed to reach the button and pressed it several times. "Apprehended?"

She raised her eyebrows and laughed at him. "You're pretty new at this, huh? Apprehended, amigo. Stolen. Kidnapped. Taken away from mommy and daddy."

"No!" Gabriel protested. He tried to comprehend what she was saying. Taken away? Put into psych like a crazy? Chemical restraints?

A nurse came into the room at a leisurely pace, scowling. "What's the problem, Mr. Tate?" She saw Renata sitting beside the bed. "Miss Vega, you know better than to bother the other patients. Out of here. Go on."

Renata didn't move. "I can talk to him if I want to."

"You are bothering him."

"He doesn't know why he's here. I'm just filling him in."

The nurse's eyes were dark. She looked at Gabriel, assessing him. Then back at Renata. "Out, Renata. Do I have to call an orderly?"

Renata uncurled herself from the chair and got up. She smiled at Gabriel and gave him a conspiratorial wink.

"Now," the nurse insisted, reaching out to hustle Renata along.

Renata avoided her. "Don't you touch me," she warned. "I'll scream bloody murder."

The nurse watched Renata walk out. She shook her head. "Don't you listen to anything Renata Vega has to say," she warned Gabriel. She moved the call button just out of his reach and tucked the sheets around him, making it more difficult to move. She slid the visitor chair back against the wall again. "Renata has a lot of issues."

"She said this is the psych ward."

The nurse didn't confirm or deny it. "Try to get some rest."

The nausea had turned to a relentless pain in his stomach. The headache had grown worse, which he wouldn't have thought possible. He started to shiver, chilled down to his bones. The nurse had pulled the call button too far away, out of Gabriel's reach. He inched his body over on the bed, trying to get close enough to grab it. It was like crawling across the desert, starving and parched, the distance impossible. He finally managed to touch the cord and knocked it off the side table. But he managed to keep a hold on the cord. He pulled it up.

Gabriel pressed the button, but no one came for a long time. He pushed it a few more times. Nurses didn't like it if you pressed it more than once. It irritated them. But Gabriel needed help. Eventually, a nurse shuffled in, covering a yawn. Gabriel glanced the other direction and saw the dark window. It was night.

"What seems to be the problem?" she asked, approaching Gabriel's bedside, but looking at the IV instead of at him.

"Blood sugar," Gabriel had difficulty pushing the words past his chattering teeth. "Hypoglycemia."

She was in no hurry to do anything. She took his wrist and felt his pulse. Tapped the electronic thermometer in his ear to check his temperature.

"What makes you think your blood sugar is low?" she asked.

"Headache. Nausea. Cold. Know how it feels," Gabriel insisted. Did she think that he would just make up something like that?

"You are a bit cold," she acknowledged, looking at the thermometer and writing it down on his chart. She went to the skinny cupboard and pulled out a blanket, which she spread over him.

"Hypoglycemia," Gabriel insisted. "I need a snack."

She sighed and rolled her eyes. She walked out of the room without a word. Gabriel's chest tightened. Why wouldn't she help? If his blood sugar got too low, he could be in real trouble. Keisha would tell them. She'd get it straightened out. But where was she? Gabriel sniffled, trying to hold back tears, but there was no one to see him cry and he didn't know what else to do.

The nurse returned with a blood glucose monitor. Her eyes went to his face. "You're a big boy," she snapped. "Quit your blubbering."

Gabriel sniffled and tried to stop the tears while she lanced his finger and checked his sugar level. She made a noise and shook her head. "Why is your level so low? You should be stable on IV."

She had apparently come prepared, though. She pulled a vial and syringe out of her pockets and prepared it for injection into his IV.

"I should have a snack," Gabriel repeated. "Better than just sugar."

"It's the middle of the night. I'm not getting you a snack. You're not getting babied here."

Gabriel sniffled. "I'm not being a baby."

She raised an eyebrow at him. "No? Then stop complaining. A grown boy doesn't need night time feedings. You don't have diabetes; there's no reason for you to be hypoglycemic."

Did she think that he wanted to be hypoglycemic? That he was just looking for attention? He couldn't control his blood sugar by his attitude.

"I have mitochondrial disease," he told her.

She waved his argument aside. "Plenty of kids who come through here do and *they* don't have low blood sugar. That's no excuse."

Gabriel was silent as she injected the sugar into his IV. He closed his eyes and waited for the warmth that would tell him it was working.

In the morning, Gabriel was shaken awake by another nurse. She had dark hair and eyes and gave him a brief smile.

"Breakfast time," she announced. Gabriel saw the plate on the rolling dinner tray. "Do you want some help sitting up?"

Gabriel shifted his weight. "Yeah."

She adjusted the head of the bed so that it was higher, propping him up slightly. She leaned him forward to adjust his pillows, then pushed him back again. She wheeled the tray to position it over his lap and took off the cover.

"There you go, bud."

Gabriel looked down at the pancakes and eggs with whipped cream and berries. "I have allergies. Special diet."

"Sorry, no special treatment here. Everybody gets the same."

"But I'll get sick."

"You're in a hospital. But I don't think you will. I think you'll be just fine." She gave him a determined smile. "Won't you?"

Gabriel frowned, confused. Like the nurse the previous night, she was acting like he was in control of how his body reacted. It wasn't his choice to have food allergies. He couldn't decide whether he was going to have a reaction or not.

"How severe are your allergies?" she persisted. "Are you going to go into anaphylactic shock and die?"

"No… but I'll get sick."

"We'll see." She patted him on the shoulder. "I think you'll be just fine."

She turned and walked back out of the room. Gabriel looked down at the plate of food. He knew that he needed to eat to keep up his energy and keep his blood sugar stable. But Keisha always made sure that he had safe food, and he didn't know what he was supposed to do about not being given food that he knew wouldn't make him sick. If he didn't get safe food, how was he going to manage his illness?

"Knock, knock!"

Gabriel looked up at the cheery greeting. Renata stood in the doorway, grinning at him like they were best friends. Gabriel was happy to see someone other than a nurse, and Renata seemed to have more answers than anyone else, so he gave her a smile that he hoped didn't look too forced and beckoned to her to come in. Her face lit up and she bounded over to the visitor chair.

"They've got you on solid food today," she observed, scraping the chair across the floor to a comfortable vantage point. "That's good news."

Gabriel nodded. "Controls my blood sugar better."

He cut off a piece of egg with his fork and looked at it.

"Then why do you look like someone just shot your mother?" Renata laughed.

Gabriel grimaced at the mention of his mother. Where was Keisha? Why wasn't she there at his side? "I'm just…" he put the sliver of egg in his mouth and chewed it slowly. "I'm allergic to stuff… I don't want to get sicker…"

Renata rolled her eyes and sat down in the chair. "Don't tell me about food allergies. Look at this." She pulled her gown open and Gabriel averted his eyes. Renata laughed. "I'm not flashing you! Look!"

He slid his eyes over to her reluctantly, his face getting hot. Renata held her gown to the side so that her belly was bared. She had some kind of tube going into her stomach. She pulled the gown back together again.

"I can't eat anything by mouth. Had a tube since I was a toddler. And there's only one formula that I can take without throwing up. How would you like that?"

Gabriel shook his head and took another bite. He scraped the whipped cream off of his pancakes and took a tentative bite. "That would really suck."

Renata nodded cheerfully. "It does. They're not very good at feeding you here. Hopefully, they'll get you out of here and put you under Dr. Markey's supervision before too long."

"Dr. Markey?"

"Markus De Klerk. I like to call him Dr. Markey. But I wouldn't recommend you do; he hates it. He's the big boss over at the Lantern Clinic. That's where they send all the mito kids."

"*All* of the mito kids? But mito is rare."

"Yeah, well, they're well-paid to find them and get them into Markey's research program."

Gabriel's stomach was not happy with him eating so slowly. It let out a long, loud growl that made both of them laugh; Gabriel in embarrassment, and Renata with glee.

"Why would anyone pay to get us into a research program?"

"We're like gold for the drug developers. They pay millions."

"Millions?" Gabriel repeated doubtfully.

"Millions. They pay millions just for keeping the program full. That doesn't include all the rest of the kickbacks going around. How else would they get everyone to agree to kidnap us?"

Gabriel sandwiched a piece of egg between two pieces of pancake and swirled it around in the syrup—which he was sure was flavored corn syrup rather than maple syrup, but it still tasted really good. Keisha was so hardline about only giving him food that was good for his cellular metabolism, and not letting him have junk food that would just make him more tired. He didn't get pancakes for breakfast. And when they did have pancakes, they were heavier, wholemeal pancakes, with fruit and no syrup.

"I wasn't kidnapped," he said.

"No? Why don't you tell me what happened, then?" Her eyebrows arched up, as if she really were curious what he had to say about it, but didn't expect him to tell the truth. Kind of like the way that he would talk to a little kid that he knew just stole a soda at the corner store, knowing he was about to tell a whopper.

"I…" Gabriel tried to remember what had happened. The events leading up to his being in hospital were a blank. Where he should have memories, there were none. "I don't remember."

"It's the drugs they've got you on," Renata sighed and leaned back. "Chemical restraints often cause temporary short-term memory loss. Which is one of the reasons that they use them. Makes it easier to control you, if you don't even know who you're supposed to be fighting against, or why."

Gabriel watched her as he ate the rest of the first egg. If this was the psych ward and the nurse who said that Renata had a lot of problems was right, then she could be completely bonkers. Chemical restraints? Kidnap? She was completely crazy.

"When they wean you off, you'll start to remember," Renata said. "Some of it, anyway."

Gabriel said nothing. Maybe if he just ignored her ravings, she would give up and go find someone else to talk to.

"What's the last thing you remember before coming here?" Renata asked. "There must be something. School? Supper? A visit to a doctor?"

"I don't know..." Despite himself, Gabriel was drawn in by her questions. He wanted to remember. He had been to the hospital plenty of times and he didn't always remember how he got there, but this time it was different. Everything was different. "I did school work... I don't remember supper... We did go to one doctor's appointment. Well, nurse, I don't think we saw the doctor..."

Renata nodded encouragingly. "What was the schoolwork? Do you remember? All of the details. What subject was it? Do you remember going to school, or just doing homework?"

"I homeschool... because I can't really manage school... I don't know. I remember doing history. Underground railway. Really interesting..."

"Yeah, I'm sure. So did you go to the doctor after the history lesson? Or before?"

"I don't know..." Gabriel rubbed his forehead, then put down his fork and rubbed both temples. "I need to sleep."

"You're not going to finish that?" Renata gestured to his breakfast.

He would have offered her the rest, but she'd already said she couldn't eat anything. "Smaller meals are better for blood sugar. I'll have more later, in a couple hours."

Renata shook her head. "Is it good cold? They'll take it away if you don't eat it."

Gabriel rested his head back. "I need to sleep."

"Okay," Renata agreed. She moved the tray out of the way where he wouldn't bump it, and touched the syrup with the tip of her finger, then touched her tongue to it. She closed her eyes, savoring the single drop.

"I'd like to eat pancakes someday."

Gabriel was groggy, but feeling a little more like himself, when one of the nurses awoke him to take his vitals. Gabriel rubbed his eyes. He was still sitting most of the way up, with the head of the bed raised. He was quiet while the nurse took his pulse and temperature.

"Why am I here?" he asked, as she pumped up the bulb of the blood pressure cuff.

"You're here to get better," she said, and her lips pressed together in a long, thin line, signaling that it was time for him to be quiet.

"Why? Where's my mom?"

"Shh." She listened to her stethoscope as she released the pressure valve. She made a note on his chart. "Your pressure is high," she noted. "You need to stay calm and quiet so that it will go down."

"Then tell me what's going on."

She blinked at him. "Nothing is going on. You've been in hospital before. We're just trying to get you stable."

"That's a lie! Where is my mom? Why won't you give me my meds or the right food? That will make me sicker!"

She made a calming motion. "Shh. There's nothing to get upset about. Sometimes, you need a med vacation to get everything straightened out and working again. We need to make sure that they have you on all the right things. I'm sure your mom would be here if she could be, but there are strict rules during the intake period."

Gabriel opened his mouth to speak. She held up her finger and shook her head.

"The more cooperative you are, the sooner you'll be through the initial phase and will be able to see her again."

Gabriel closed his mouth. It didn't make any sense that his mother wasn't allowed to visit. Keisha was the one who took care of him. She was the one who knew all the medication protocols, and the food that he should be eating to be as healthy as he could be. She was the one who had done all the research and could tell the doctors what was the best for him.

As she wrapped up the blood pressure cuff and put it back in the little cage mounted to the wall, Gabriel had a tiny awakening of memory. The nurse that he had seen before his arrival at the hospital. The dark, distrustful look in her eye. She had not been happy with Keisha. Gabriel had thought that she would be delighted that he had been able to put on some weight, and had a little more energy than usual. But she hadn't been. She'd been angry with Keisha about all the research that she had done.

"You are not a doctor," she had snapped. "Knowing how to use Google does not entitle you to a degree. You need to follow the protocols that you've been given, not choose your own."

"But it's helping!" Keisha pointed out.

"You could be causing irreversible damage. You must follow the doctor's protocols."

CHAPTER THREE

EXHAUSTED, GABRIEL RUBBED HIS legs, trying to soothe the muscle pain. But he was still so weak and sick that his arms tired quickly. He could only rub his legs for a few seconds before he was overwhelmed by fatigue. He rested for a minute and tried again, almost crying with the pain and exhaustion.

When he rang for a nurse, she just shook her head at the suggestion that he needed a painkiller.

"We've withdrawn all unnecessary medication," she said crisply. "Growing pains and muscle cramps do not qualify as needing painkillers. You're just going to have to put up with it."

"It hurts," Gabriel tried to keep a sob out of his voice. "You don't know how much. Please…"

"I understand that you've been given whatever you think you need in the past. That's just what has landed you here. I'm sorry, but I'm not allowed to give you anything. It might help to rub them or walk around a little bit. I don't want you wandering, but if you want to walk around the room to loosen up your muscles, that's just fine."

"I'm too tired."

"Then I can't help you."

"Can you rub them?" Gabriel begged. He reached down to massage his painful muscles again, but gave up at the stretch and burn in his arms and shoulders. He flopped back down on the bed, frustrated and furious, tears escaping the corners of his eyes.

"No. I have other things to do. Now good night, Mr. Tate. You should be trying to go back to sleep."

She marched back out of the room. Gabriel stared at the black window. Everyone else must be asleep, so why couldn't the nurse rub his legs for a few minutes? What was she so busy with? What trumped patient care?

He had an urge to get up and follow her. Maybe she was in the middle of a card game with the other nurses. Or she was in an exciting part of her latest paperback. He wanted to catch her, call her out for thinking that her own comfort was more important than helping him. But that would mean getting out of bed, and he didn't think that his legs would support him. He had no idea what they had done with his braces.

There was a soft whisper outside his door and Gabriel looked up. With just a rustle of clothing, her bare feet making no sound on the tiled floor, Renata peeked in.

"Hey," she whispered. "I saw Nurse Ratched in here. Are you okay?"

Gabriel wiped at the corners of his eyes. "What are you doing up?"

"I don't sleep. Not much. And they've messed with my cocktail, so I haven't slept in three days." She sat on the edge of the bed instead of pulling over the visitor chair. Gabriel tried to pull his legs away from her. They were so tender that even just Renata's weight sinking into the mattress made them hurt more. "So? Are you okay?"

"My legs hurt."

She was staring at him. Gabriel couldn't see her very well in the dark, and he wondered whether she could see him at all. Dark skin in a dark room, and she had just come in from the brighter hallway.

"What can I do?" she asked.

"They won't give me anything."

"No." She put her hand over his left shin. He could feel the warmth of her hand through the sheets. "What if I rub them? Would that be better or worse?"

"Better."

Without further discussion, she started to rub his legs. Her touch was tentative at first. She barely touched him and moved very slowly. She gradually increased the pressure, focused on Gabriel for his reaction.

"Good? Is that too hard?"

"No. Good."

Gabriel closed his eyes and tried to relax, the pain finally lessening. Renata was quiet for once, just massaging his aching muscles. Gabriel was almost asleep when she stopped.

"Mmm. Keep going," he encouraged.

"Can't," Renata whispered.

He realized that she was breathing heavily. Opening his eyes, he saw her leaning over, supporting herself on her elbows, almost prone.

"Renata?"

Her breathing took on a labored whine, sort of a cross between a wheeze and a sob. Gabriel was alarmed.

"Renata? Are you okay?"

"Fine." Her words were forced. "Just tired."

She had mito too. She was in better shape than Gabriel was, but he'd been exhausted after mere seconds of rubbing his muscles. She'd been working on them hard for ten minutes. She hadn't slept in days. She was in no shape to be providing massages.

"I'm sorry. I wasn't thinking." Gabriel tried to reach her hand. "I didn't mean to kill you!"

She giggled. Gabriel managed to reach her shoulder. She was drenched in sweat. Gabriel held his hand over her shoulder for a minute. "I'm sorry..." He let go and pressed the call button for the nurse.

It was the same one as had come before. Nurse Ratched, Renata had called her, but Gabriel didn't think that was really her name. It was some kind of nickname; only he didn't get the joke.

"What's going on here?" the nurse demanded, peering at them through the dimness of the room. "Renata? What are you doing in here?"

"She was helping me," Gabriel tried to explain. "But she tired herself out."

"Get up," Ratched told Renata, tugging on her arm. But Renata continued to slump over, wheezing. "Stupid girl," Ratched complained. She moved around the bed to retrieve a wheelchair. She brought it to the side of the bed and set the brakes. "Come here. Into the chair," she instructed. She pulled on Renata until the girl slid off of the bed and into the seat of the wheelchair. "Back you go. Maybe this will teach you to quit wandering around at night."

"Doubt it," Renata offered between rasping breaths.

Ratched snorted.

"You should give her something to sleep," Gabriel suggested. "She said she hasn't slept in three days!"

"You can't believe anything that comes out of this girl's mouth," the nurse advised. She bent over to release the brakes. "She's already had an evening sedative. She shouldn't have any trouble sleeping." Ratched gave the wheelchair a little shake for emphasis as if Renata were a recalcitrant child. "If she'd just respond to her meds like a normal person."

"Nu-uh," Renata said, her voice mischievous in spite of her labored breathing.

Gabriel couldn't help smiling as Renata was wheeled out of the room.

Gabriel had repeatedly rung for a nurse to help him to the restroom, without any sign that they were listening to him. He knew that he couldn't wait much longer, and slid out of bed onto wobbly legs. With the IV pole for support, maybe he could make the few steps to the bathroom on his own. The nurse who had removed Renata the night before hadn't returned the wheelchair to his room.

Gabriel's legs shook with fatigue as if he'd been running or hiking all day. Standing up reduced the muscle cramps a little, but also increased the urgency to get to the toilet. His bowels shifted and cramped, pains shooting up his side and back.

Three steps were all he could manage before one knee buckled, and the other wouldn't be far behind. Gabriel tried to lower himself to his knees with care, but partway there, it was like his leg had been kicked out from under him, and he was face-first on the floor, barely managing to catch himself before his teeth hit the tile.

There was no getting back up. Gabriel continued to combat-crawl along the floor, but his arms were exhausted, and his IV was getting tangled up, pulling on the needle in his vein. One of the nurses finally made an appearance as he sobbed, in reach of the bathroom door, but unable to get up to open it.

"What are you doing?" she screeched, diving at him.

Gabriel took a few breaths, trying to steady himself before speaking. "Gotta use the john. Stomach hurts."

She was a short, stocky woman with a brightly-colored flower smock. Some of the nurses would have insisted that they couldn't help Gabriel up, but she swooped in, hauling on his free arm to put it over her shoulder, grabbing him around the waist, and pulling him to his feet.

"Ring for help and then wait," she told him, maneuvering him into the bathroom.

"Couldn't wait," Gabriel insisted, barely managing to hold his bodily functions in check until she had him on the toilet. He held his arm across his stomach, sucking in his breath, as his bowels loosened and emptied in a loud, foul-smelling torrent.

He was embarrassed, but at the same time glad that he'd made it. He'd rather she was standing there wrinkling her nose than complaining about having to clean him up after he'd fouled himself and the bed.

"You've pulled out your IV," she said, pulling on the needle that just barely hung onto his arm. She produced a piece of gauze and pressed it over his arm while she removed the needle the rest of the way. "Hold that."

Gabriel held the gauze in place, rocking back and forth with the waves of intestinal cramps.

"What's wrong with your stomach?" the flowered woman asked, scowling down at him.

"The food. I have allergies."

She sighed in exasperation. "Why didn't you tell anyone that?"

"I did. They said just eat it and don't get sick."

She rolled her eyes heavenward. "There's got to be a better way for De Klerk to sort out the malingerers."

Gabriel repeated the word. "Malingerers?"

The nurse busied herself with tying off the IV.

"What does that mean, malingerers?"

"Look it up. Are you done?"

Gabriel shook his head.

She pursed her lips. "Are you going to be okay if I leave you alone for a couple of minutes?"

"Yeah. For a bit."

"There's a pull-cord," she gestured to it. "Call if you need help. I'll be back in just a few minutes. Don't go anywhere."

Gabriel grimaced. "I won't."

* * *

It had been a couple of days since Gabriel had seen anyone other than nurses. There didn't even seem to be any doctors supervising his care, which didn't feel right. He always liked the safe, cared-for feeling that he got from a doctor checking in and reassuring him that everything was under control, and he was going to be home soon.

Gabriel hadn't realized how much he would miss Renata if she weren't poking her head in a couple times a day. He wondered if she had gone home without saying good-bye. Without Keisha there to help keep him distracted with books, lessons, gossip about the neighborhood, and the latest news from his father overseas, the days dragged on interminably long. No books, no TV, no one to visit with.

So he was overjoyed when the shuffle of slippers brought Renata back in for a visit. She wasn't looking well. Usually, she had on only her hospital gown, with bare feet, and fairly skipped into the room. But now she seemed weighed down by the slippers and a dingy white terrycloth robe wrapped around her slim body. Her eyes were dark hollows, almost bruised.

"Hey, are you okay?" Gabriel worried. "Come sit down." He patted the mattress next to him.

Renata shuffled the rest of the way into the room, and perched on the bed next to him, slouching down with an exhausted sigh.

"What's wrong?"

"Messing around with my meds," Renata explained. "Chemical…" she trailed off, losing her train of thought.

"Why are they doing that? You were doing okay before."

"Control. They gotta control me."

"Is it because of what I said? That you weren't sleeping? Did you get in trouble for coming in here?"

Renata shook her head. "They're always trying to sort me out." She gave a weak grin. "But I'm like nothing they've ever seen before."

"Me neither," Gabriel agreed in admiration. Despite whatever they were putting her through, Renata was still a fighter. Still unbroken.

She smiled and put her hand over his.

"Once they get your meds fixed, will you be going home?" Gabriel asked. "Or to that other clinic?"

"Lantern," Renata reminded him of the name. "It's not residential. So I'll go back to my foster family."

"Foster family? So you're not with your real parents?"

"Nope. A kidnappee, like you."

"I wasn't kidnapped."

"I thought you didn't remember," she challenged.

"Well…" Gabriel tried to wrap his mind around it. "It doesn't make any sense. Why would someone kidnap me and bring me here? They'd get caught. And what would they get out of it?"

"Shove over." Renata nudged Gabriel with her hip. He moved over an inch, not sure what she wanted. She stretched out beside him, balanced precariously on the edge of the mattress. Gabriel moved over a couple more inches. A hospital bed was not built to hold double occupants, but he and Renata were both pretty skinny and it worked. Renata sighed and closed her eyes, her body relaxing and molding against his. "They don't get caught," she explained, "because they do it inside the court system. Right up front where everyone can see."

"Do what? That's not kidnapping."

"You take a kid away from his parents for money, that's kidnapping."

"*Who* does?" Gabriel demanded, completely at a loss. She really was crazy.

"The doctors and the social workers. It's all part of a conspiracy. To get us into foster care and into research programs like Lantern, for money. It's a booming business."

"Who gets money? Why would they get money for taking us away from our parents?"

"Doctors get money for getting kids into research programs. Or they do it to cover up their mistakes before parents realize and sue them. And DFS gets money from the federal government, for every kid they apprehend. Thousands of dollars a month for every kid."

Gabriel blinked and shook his head. "Money to care for them. That doesn't go to the social workers."

"Yeah? Who pays their salaries? You ever hear how much money foster parents are given to take kids? It's nothing compared to what the feds pay out. Chicken feed. So where does the rest go?"

"We need social workers to keep kids safe. Kids who are abused."

"That may be some administrator's grand plan," Renata agreed. "But there's more kids abused in foster care than in their own families. They're taking kids out of safe homes and putting them into unsafe ones." Renata took Gabriel's silence for dissent and forged on. "For money! The more money the feds pay, the more kids Social Services finds to take away."

"No…"

She turned onto her side to look at him, propping her head up with her elbow. "You're skinny and sick, but you don't look like you were neglected or abused at home."

"No. I wasn't!" He was aware that his tone was defensive.

"And yet, here you are." She stared at Gabriel, letting him think about it. "You know they're not letting your mom see you. They couldn't do that if she was still your guardian."

"What?" Gabriel sat up partway, looking at Renata. His heart raced, and there was a stabbing pain in his chest. Keisha wasn't his guardian? "What are you talking about?"

"Think about it, dopey. Why isn't she here? She decided to go on a vacation? Pop over to Disneyland and ride the roller coaster by herself for a few days?"

"No!"

"Then why isn't she here?"

"Because… they won't let her."

"Yeah. Exactly. But they couldn't stop her from seeing you if she was your guardian. Right? A hospital can't do that. Only a court can do that. And only if they sever her rights."

Gabriel's head whirled. He let himself flop back down on the pillow. He felt sick. And scared. And like crying. "She'd go to court. She'd get it straightened out. They can't just take kids away from their parents for no reason."

"Oh, they have their reasons. She'll fight, but she won't win."

"How do you know that?"

"I've been around. It's the rich guys that win in court, and trust me; DFS has got the money on their side. Your mom hasn't got a chance."

"A judge will see—"

"A judge will see what the social worker feels like reporting. And if they're kidnapping kids, you think they're going to tell the truth?"

"It's not kidnapping," Gabriel insisted.

"Call it whatever you like. They took you away from your family. Why?"

"I think..." Gabriel hesitated to tell her anything, but she was his only friend, the only one he could confide in. "I think it was something to do with my mom figuring out what would help me... This nurse I saw before I came here..." He saw her face in front of his eyes. Eyes angry and accusing. Furious with Keisha for taking care of him. "She was mad about mom changing my diet. Giving me supplements and stuff."

Renata nodded sagely. "That would do it. You can't do naturals instead of drug trials. They don't get paid for that."

"But... I wasn't part of a drug trial."

"Yet. Who was the nurse?"

Gabriel searched his memory. "I don't know... Maple? It made me think of—"

"Birch?"

That was it. Birch. "Yeah."

"I like to call her another name," Renata offered. "Just change one letter..."

He frowned at her for a moment, picturing the word in his head and trying out different substitutions.

"Come on," Renata encouraged. "Use that brainpower. B... I..."

"Oh!" Gabriel's face burned. "I get it." He was flustered, embarrassed. "How do you know her? You've met her?"

"She works here, at the hospital. With Dr. Seymour. Dr. Seymour has privileges here, but her main job is at Lantern. She funnels kids from the hospital to Lantern. So Birch at the feeding clinic, and other nurse practitioners in other programs, they push kids through to Seymour... to keep the program at Lantern full."

Gabriel shifted uneasily, thinking back. "She was mad at my mom. I don't remember very much. I couldn't understand why she'd be mad, when I'd put on weight. That was the whole point of the program..."

"But you didn't follow the program, did you? So she decided that your mom was medically negligent."

"But I gained weight... that's not negligence. When we followed the program exactly, I lost weight."

Renata rubbed her eyes, making a tired noise. "She woulda got you either way. You follow the program and lose weight, and she says your mom is neglecting you because you're losing weight. You don't follow the program, and she says your mom is putting your life in danger by not following the program."

"That doesn't make any sense."

"Where are you, Gabriel? And where's your mom? Tell me I'm not making any sense."

One of the nurses came in with Gabriel's supper plate and found Renata asleep on the bed beside him, snoring away. She was Asian, one of the nicer nurses, and she laughed when she saw Renata. She went back to the door and called out into the hallway.

"She's in here!"

As she set Gabriel's plate on his table, one of the bigger nurses and an orderly came in.

"She shouldn't be in here," the nurse declared. Gabriel wasn't sure whether the comment was aimed at him, or someone else. Or no one in particular. She grabbed Renata by the arm and shook her. Renata stopped snoring but didn't wake up.

"Quit playing possum. You need to go back to your room!"

"What's she doing in here in the first place?" the orderly asked. "I thought you had her on benzos."

"She is. And she shouldn't be out wandering around on the dose she's at. But this one is always having paradoxical reactions. We should just start giving her the opposite of whatever the books say." She shook Renata harder. Renata's body just flopped around, her head lolling as if her neck were made of spaghetti. "Renata! Get up! Wake up!"

Renata still didn't respond. The nurse started to pinch her, leaving a trail of angry red welts up Renata's arm. The big nurse growled impatiently when Renata still didn't wake.

"Why don't I just take her?" the orderly suggested.

"I suppose." She looked around. "Where's the wheelchair?"

The orderly shrugged. "I don't need it. She's probably eighty pounds sopping wet."

The nurse stepped back out of the way, and the orderly bent over and picked Renata up off of the bed. He held her cradled in his arms like a toddler, with no apparent effort.

"I got her. No trouble."

He and the nurse left again. Gabriel turned his attention to the Asian nurse who had brought his dinner. "Will she be okay?"

"We'll keep an eye on her. She's a tough one, that girl."

"Is she... crazy? All those things she talks about?"

"By most people's definitions," she admitted. "You can't believe the things that she says."

"But some of them... they make sense."

"She's not stupid. But she is... paranoid. Don't you worry about what she says." The nurse's lips pressed tightly together as she looked at him. "And keep in mind that she could be... dangerous. She's very charming, comes across all sweetness and roses... but she can be violent."

"Violent?"

"She doesn't think the same way you and I do. She's not just here for a med adjustment."

Gabriel teetered between believing that there could be something dark behind Renata's sunny attitude, and the suspicion that the nurses just didn't want him getting too close to her. He found himself wondering about conspiracies, like Renata.

Gabriel considered the nurse, wondering if she would tell him anything else. "Why am I here?"

She smiled reassuringly. "For evaluation."

"What kind of evaluation? I'm not crazy. Mentally ill. I just have mito. Renata says lots of kids with mito come through here."

She pushed the rolling table over Gabriel's lap. "Sometimes we need to sort out what is real and what is imagined. Or what a parent might have caused, intentionally or unintentionally."

"You think my mom made me sick? But it's not her. I have a disease."

"We'll get everything straightened out. That's why you're here. We're good at what we do. You're being taken care of."

"What if I want to see my mom? Is she allowed to come see me?"

She took the cover off of his plate. "What do we have today? Roast and mashed potatoes, and carrots and peas. Mmm. I'm not off shift for another hour and my stomach is growling."

"Do the mashed potatoes have milk in them?" Gabriel picked up the fork and poked at them dubiously.

"I would guess so, yes."

"But what about my allergies?"

She raised her brows. "They shouldn't have anything you're allergic to in them."

"But dairy…"

"Gabriel." She put her hand on his arm, stopping him. Her hand was warm and her dark eyes were calm and reassuring. "You need to trust us. We're not going to do anything to hurt you. We'll sort out your problems, and we'll work with your social worker, and everything will be okay." She patted him. "All right?"

Gabriel swallowed. The mention of his social worker did not calm him. He didn't even know who that was. How could she look after his best interests if she didn't know anything about him?

The nurse rearranged a lock of Gabriel's tightly curled hair. "I promise. It will all work out."

CHAPTER FOUR

THE NEXT DAY, RENATA skipped in cheerfully as if nothing had happened. She was every inch her old self. Gabriel smiled.

"Feeling better?"

"Man, did I sleep! Maybe I should come in here and sleep with you all the time. I don't know when the last time was that I really slept."

"Good."

"So what about you? You feeling any better? You're not so groggy lately."

Gabriel thought about it. His head wasn't hurting like it had been, now that his blood sugar was more stable. And his legs had felt better since the night that Renata had massaged them. He even felt like he might be able to get up and walk around the room for a few minutes. It would feel good to be upright.

"Yeah, little better," he agreed.

"Good. Sucks when they dope you out like that. It takes weeks to feel like you're wearing your own head sometimes."

"How often have they...?"

Renata made a puffing noise with her lips. "I don't know! I've been in and out of here since I was a toddler. You know things are bad when you gotta admit your preschooler to psych."

Was it really true or was it one of her stories? Who would put a toddler in a place like that?

"You remember anything else?" Renata asked. "About coming here, I mean? When they came and got you?"

Gabriel frowned and shook his head. It was strange to have those blanks. He was pretty sure it hadn't been anything so

39

dramatic as Renata had made it out to be. He had been sick. Keisha had brought him to the hospital. They said that he needed a different kind of evaluation this time. They didn't allow visitors during the program. Not anyone.

Nothing so dramatic as a kidnapping.

They heard squeaky wheels going down the hall and a clatter of wire baskets.

"Mail call," Renata advised.

Gabriel hadn't received any mail in previous days. He'd heard the wheels before, but hadn't known what it was. It sounded different from the lunch carts, but he hadn't been able to figure out what it was. No one was sending him any mail. He wondered if he were even allowed to get mail. Wouldn't Keisha have sent him something, if she could?

A candy-striper poked her head in the door. "I knew I'd find you here!" she told Renata. She came the rest of the way over and handed Renata an envelope. "Enjoy!"

She left again and continued down the hallway. Renata looked down at the card, and then measured the distance to the garbage can, aiming a throw at it. "Think I can make it?"

"You're not going to open it?" Gabriel demanded.

"No. It's a card." She shrugged uncaringly.

"Get well card?"

"Birthday card."

"When's your birthday?"

"Yesterday. I turned fourteen."

"Yesterday? Happy birthday!"

"Thanks."

"Why aren't you going to open it? Don't you want to see who it's from? If there's a good joke? Or money?"

"It's from my mom. I don't want to see it."

"Oh." Gabriel looked at the envelope. He didn't know what to say. "Can I have the stamp?"

She handed it to him. "You collect?"

"Yeah. I haven't seen this one before."

He didn't know if he should tear the corner with the stamp off and discard the rest of the envelope with the card unopened, or if there were some other action that would be more appropriate. He looked down at it, and then up to Renata's face.

"Why don't you want to read your mom's card?"

Renata's dark eyes glittered as she looked back at him. "My mom's not like yours. She's in prison, and I don't want to have anything to do with her."

"Oh. I didn't know; I'm sorry."

"That's okay. You couldn't know."

"Do you want to talk about it? What happened?"

"She went to prison for resisting the police when they came to take me away."

"Really?" Gabriel blinked, thinking about that. "So why don't you want to see her? I thought maybe she went to prison for drugs or something like that, and you were ashamed. But if she went there because of trying to protect you... why wouldn't you want to see what she had to say? She must love you."

"She was trying to kill me," Renata said. She looked around the room as if worried that someone might overhear her. "Would you want to see your mom if she was trying to kill you?"

Gabriel bit his lip. Another story. Another crazy claim. This was obviously a paranoid delusion. There was no way that Renata's mother really was trying to kill her. Parents didn't kill their children. Well, sometimes they did, but it was usually in anger or despair, not planned or plotted.

"You don't believe me," Renata observed. She folded her hands and looked down at them. "It's not my imagination. It's the truth."

"Why was she trying to kill you?"

"Why should I tell you, when you don't believe me? Do you think she would be in prison if I was just making it up?"

Gabriel looked down at the envelope. The return address in the corner was not recognizable as a residential address. It looked like a post office box. That could easily be either a house or the prison. There was no way to know.

"You don't have to tell me if you don't want to," he said.

She looked at him. After a moment of silence, she took the envelope back from him. She tore off the corner with the stamp on it and handed it back to him. She looked down at the corner of the card that she could see, then sailed it into the garbage can.

"Think about the kind of life she had trying to take care of me. How would you like to take care of a crazy kid? Not just a sick kid, like you. But a kid who couldn't love you back. A kid who can't sleep, can't eat, doesn't behave like other kids…"

"That sounds awful."

"You'd want to kill me too."

"It sounds awful for both of you," Gabriel clarified. "Not just for her."

"Yeah, well, I've never known any other kind of life."

Gabriel nodded. "Just like we don't know what it's like to live with the same cellular energy level as a normal person. We can only imagine what it must be like."

She clasped his hand.

"How would you like to get out of that bed for a while?" Nurse Kelly suggested as she pushed a wheelchair into the room. Nurse Kelly was a pretty blond, with a young face that made her look like she wasn't much older than Gabriel. He didn't have a crush on her, exactly, but he liked her best of all the nurses.

"Yeah, sure," he agreed. "Where am I going?"

"Just to the common room. Nowhere special. Except when you've been cooped up in your room as long as you have, everywhere is special, right?"

Gabriel nodded in agreement.

She pushed the wheelchair up to the bed. "How are your sea legs today?"

"I can get up." Gabriel swung his feet to the floor, and stood for a moment, his muscles shaky. He wished he could show off by walking briskly across the room, but he felt as weak as a newborn. Without any bravado, he slid himself into the wheelchair. The vinyl was ice cold. His gown offered no protection. "Yikes!" Gabriel grabbed the blanket from his bed before Nurse Kelly could wheel him away. She wrapped him up and tucked it around him.

"How's that?"

"Better. Thanks."

She wheeled him out of the hospital room, and for the first time, Gabriel saw the halls of the ward. It was very quiet, and there were closed doors at the ends of the hall that Gabriel assumed were locked for security, to keep wandering patients like Renata in and unwanted visitors out. There was an old man walking down the hall holding onto his IV pole for support. It gave Gabriel a bit of a start. He had thought that it was a kids' unit, a ward full of mito kids, from Renata's description. Nurse Kelly maneuvered him down the hall, around the slowly moving old man and pieces of equipment that looked like medieval torture devices.

In a room at the end of the hall, there was a TV blaring, sunlight beaming in through a big window, and a few other patients working on puzzles, playing cards, or watching the TV with blank expressions. Gabriel looked around anxiously, uncomfortable being around all of the strangers who could be crazy and dangerous. His heart beat rapidly and his breathing sped up.

"Here you go!" Nurse Kelly announced. "What do you want to do? Where do you want me to put you?"

Gabriel swallowed, looking around uneasily. The room was so big and bright after being confined to his own room for so long. He had an inexplicable urge just to go back to his room and climb back into bed.

"I thought Renata would be here."

"If I see her, I'll send her this way. You want to do a puzzle?"

"No!" Gabriel put his hands on the wheels to stop her from pushing the wheelchair toward a middle-aged woman with messy orange curls. "No... just... I'll watch TV."

"You should socialize," she told him.

But Gabriel shook his head. "No... not yet... just TV."

She obligingly steered him toward the TV. Even though there were other patients nearby watching the daytime drivel, none of them bothered to look at him or tried to talk to him. Gabriel looked over his shoulder at Nurse Kelly. "You'll see if you can find Renata?"

"I'll take a quick look, but I have other things to get back to."

Gabriel nodded his understanding.

It wasn't until a couple of hours later that Renata put in an appearance. She sat down on a nearby couch.

"So they let you out today! How's it feel to get out of your cave?"

Gabriel looked around and shrugged. "Okay."

"Why don't you come over here?" She patted the couch next to her. "It's a lot more comfortable than those chairs."

His bottom *was* getting sore from sitting in the wheelchair. Gabriel felt bad for people who had to sit in them all day, every day. He slid his feet off of the supports and braced his hand on the arms to stand. The wheelchair shimmied back.

"Set your brakes," Renata warned, moving closer to help him. "You'll end up on the floor."

His face hot, Gabriel engaged the wheel brakes. "I thought the nurse had."

"She should have. But sometimes they don't."

Renata watched Gabriel push himself to his feet and shuffle over a couple of steps to get to the couch. He leaned on the back of the couch and lowered himself carefully into it, proud not to have fallen or made a fool of himself. Renata gave him a shoulder hug when he settled and pulled his blanket around him. "Not bad, Gabe. A few more days and you'll be running all over the place."

Gabriel laughed. "Running isn't exactly my thing."

"Oh well, maybe shuffling."

Gabriel laughed, agreeing. It would be nice to be able to get around a bit.

Renata was looking around the common room, her eyes narrow, moving her head back and forth like a robin listening to a worm under the grass.

"What's wrong?"

She looked at him, momentarily distracted from her survey of the room. "I don't like being in here. I don't like them monitoring me."

"Oh." Gabriel sucked in his cheeks, wondering how he should react to her paranoia. Humor her? Ignore it and act as if it were perfectly normal? He didn't think that he should argue with her. Nurse Kelly said that Renata could get violent, and he didn't want to trigger an angry reaction.

"I don't need a tinfoil hat," Renata snapped at him. "Don't act like I'm crazy. Use your eyes." She pointed to the corners of the room, up by the ceiling, and Gabriel saw that there were, in fact, surveillance cameras monitoring the room.

"Oh, yeah... but I think they're just making sure... you know, no one gets violent or anything."

"They're always watching. Monitoring."

"I guess."

"They watch you right from the time you're born." Renata chewed on her thumbnail, eyes moving back and forth restlessly. "You know that? They start tracking you right when you're a baby. Hospitals starting files on you, home health nurses going right into people's homes, weighing and measuring and having a snoop around. Saw a news article the other day about DCF taking away a family's newborn twins. You wanna know why?"

Gabriel glanced around the common room for signs of a newspaper. Did they let the patients have access to news of the outside? Paranoid ones like Renata?

"Because they had a home birth," Renata told him. "Not a thing medically wrong with the babies. But they had them at home, and they wouldn't go to the hospital where the babies might catch something. So a home health care nurse went to their house to weigh and measure them and reported them for medical neglect. She said it was because they had lost weight. Babies always lose weight the first few days they are breastfeeding. So they took them away from where they were safe and sheltered and had their mom's antibodies from breastfeeding, and put them in a filthy home full of other kids. A cesspool of pathogens. They can't afford to let people live without all the monitoring."

Gabriel shifted away from Renata slightly. Her voice was getting louder. Some of the other patients were starting to look at her sideways, pretending that they weren't.

"Maybe there was something else wrong that you don't know about," Gabriel suggested. "You don't get the whole story from the newspaper. Just one side. They sensationalize."

"Didn't you say *you* were homeschooled?" Renata demanded.

"Uh... yeah...?"

"Big red flag for social workers. High risk for child abuse and neglect. Gotta be something wrong with people who don't think that the government is better at educating their kids. And you know what else happens when you homeschool? Less money. What happens to all that money that the school and state get for teaching you? It all goes away."

"They should be happy they don't have to spend money on me."

"Not the way it works. It doesn't cost them any more to educate thirty-one kids than it does to educate thirty. Right? But they lose all that money."

Gabriel glanced around to see if there were any nurses or orderlies close by. There was one orderly over by the puzzles talking to the red-haired woman, but he wasn't paying any attention to what was going on with Renata.

"Money for one kid can't make that much difference either," he suggested.

"Yeah? When's the last time you heard a school say that they had all the funding that they needed, thank you very much? Oh yeah, all our programs are funded and we have all the resources we need." She snorted.

Gabriel gave a wide shrug with his hands. "Okay."

"They don't like you getting away from the school monitoring you all the time. Homeschoolers, cults, preppers, they all try to get away from government monitoring, and *they* don't like that." Her voice was rising. "They'll watch for the first chance they can get to take you away."

"Vega," the orderly called from across the room, looking up from the puzzle lady. "Chill, all right? Tone it down."

Renata looked over at him and swore nastily. Gabriel inched away from her uncomfortably.

"You want me to take you down?" the orderly challenged. "Because I will!"

"Don't," Gabriel whispered to Renata. "Let's just watch TV."

"That's how they get to you," Renata warned. "That's how they get inside your head. It's all propaganda, Gabe; that's how they control you."

"It's just a soap."

"Down with Big Brother!" Renata shouted. She pumped her fist in the air. "Down with the establishment!"

"I told you to shut up!" the orderly growled, walking closer.

Renata swore at him again. "Down the Man! Down the dictatorship!"

"Shut up and watch your show."

Other orderlies and nurses were coming into the room, attracted by the shouting. Renata leapt to her feet, bobbing like a prize fighter. "Death to the Nazis!" she screamed.

"I've had enough of you!" The orderly grabbed at her, wrestling for a safe hold.

Renata fought back against him. She didn't do too badly for an eighty-pound girl with a faulty energy system, but she really didn't stand a chance against the big man. He pinned her to him, arms wrapped around her.

"Settle down or you're getting jabbed," the orderly threatened.

"Can't sedate her," one of the nurses advised. "Seymour said 'no' after what happened last time."

Renata smiled triumphantly at the orderly, struggling to get out of his grip.

"Wipe that smirk off your face!"

Renata spat, saliva hitting the orderly directly under the eye. He squeezed her furiously, face getting bright red. Looking at the nurse, he spoke between gritted teeth. "What are we supposed to do with her, then? Warm her up?"

"Renata," the nurse spoke to her in a firm, soothing tone. "Why don't you tell me what it is that's agitating you? Let's work this out instead of getting upset."

Renata swore and spat at her, but the nurse was standing too far away for the spittle to hit her.

"Let's try isolation," the nurse sighed. "If that doesn't calm her down, then we'll have to jacket her."

The orderly started to force Renata out of the room. She fought back against him wildly. He tightened his grip around her body, and there was an audible snap. Everybody watching froze. Renata stopped fighting, her face draining of color.

"What the hell was that?" the nurse demanded.

"Dammit… you broke my rib!" Renata wheezed. Now that she had stopped fighting, she sagged in his arms, looking as weak as a kitten. The flush had faded from the orderly's face, and he looked down at her with a pinched expression.

"Put her down. Here," the nurse motioned to Gabriel's vacated wheelchair.

The orderly deposited Renata into the wheelchair. Gabriel half-expected Renata to jump back up and start fighting again, but she just melted there, head lolling back, breathing labored. The nurse bent over her. She moved Renata carefully, listening to her chest and back with a stethoscope.

"Collapsed a lung," she advised. "Better get her down to Emerge." She took off her stethoscope, looking at the orderly. "You're going to have to stay with her. I don't want another escape. And they have to call up here before giving her so much as an aspirin."

He nodded and released the wheel brakes, pushing Renata quickly out of the room.

Gabriel looked at the nurse, aware that his eyes were wide with shock over what had just happened.

"Don't tell me *you're* going to cause trouble now," the nurse growled.

Gabriel shook his head, looking away. His eyes grew hot with tears. He was embarrassed by his reaction. He wasn't the one who had gotten hurt. They had told him repeatedly that Renata was unstable. It was no surprise to anyone but him. He blinked, trying to keep his emotions under control.

"Can I go back to my room?"

"Anytime you want," she snapped.

He glanced over where his wheelchair had been parked, but she didn't clue in. She walked away from him, her mind already on other things. Gabriel looked around for another wheelchair or someone to help him, but no one offered. He stayed on the couch, stranded, watching the stupid daytime programming and thinking about what Renata had said.

"Gabriel. Someone here to see you."

Gabriel just about got whiplash turning around to greet his visitor.

But it wasn't his mother. It was a woman that he didn't know. She gave him a faint smile.

"Hi, Gabriel. Nice to see you awake this time. Why don't we go somewhere that we can talk?"

"Who are you?"

She held out her long, narrow fingers with perfectly manicured nails toward him. "Carol Scott," she introduced herself. "DCF."

Gabriel had been putting his hand out to shake hers, but when he heard DCF he froze, and eventually he dropped his hand into his lap without shaking hers after all. Gabriel didn't say anything, completely at a loss.

Mrs. Scott lowered her hand. "Why don't we go back to your room?" she suggested.

"I can't."

She raised her brows. "Why not?"

"I can't walk that far."

He couldn't walk more than a step or two, but he didn't want to say that. He didn't want to sound like a cripple. He was limited in his ability to get around, but he wasn't a cripple. He hated it when the kids he had gone to school with called him that.

"Well, how did you get here?" she asked, bemused.

"I had a wheelchair. But... someone took it." Gabriel looked around as if one might have been brought into the room without him noticing, but no such luck. He did see a boy at the puzzle table behind him that hadn't been there before. Maybe ten or eleven with a tousled mop of blond hair. Gabriel stared, wondering where he had come from and what his story was. Was he another mito kid? Another kidnappee? Gabriel shook his head, grunting to himself. There were no kidnappees. He wasn't a kidnappee. That was just Renata's paranoia.

"I guess I'll see if I can find you one," Mrs. Scott said reluctantly. "Unless you think you could make it...?"

Gabriel shook his head.

She sighed and went back out of the common room. Gabriel could hear her inquiring of someone in the hallway.

In a few minutes, she was back again, pushing a worn, scratched-up chair. She shrugged at him. "It may not be pretty, but I think it will do the trick." Then she stood there, waiting for Gabriel to jump up and get into it.

"You gotta move it over here," Gabriel explained. "And put the brakes on."

She repositioned it and waited. Gabriel moved like an old man, pushing himself up onto his feet, shuffling in a quarter circle, and then lowering himself shakily into the seat, worried that he was going to overbalance one way or the other and fall down in front of her. He landed in the seat too quickly and bit the tip of his tongue. Gabriel swallowed a complaint and breathed out, tucking his blanket back around him. At least he was getting away from the mind-numbingly boring television programming. He'd had no idea that feminine leak protection and diet aids were such a big industry.

"Why can't you get around?" Carol Scott asked. She waited for him to propel the wheelchair. Gabriel sat there silently, refusing to ask for her help. Eventually, she took the handles and wheeled him back toward his room. "You were able to walk last time I saw you," she pointed out. "At your house, I mean."

Gabriel turned his head slightly to look at her. He didn't remember meeting her before, but obviously he had, during the time that was still missing from his memory. Renata said that he would be able to remember eventually, but he wasn't so sure.

"They took away my braces," Gabriel said. "And my meds. And they aren't giving me the right food and vitamins and herbs. So… I can't."

"Maybe you need to try a little harder. Don't let your… problem… get the better of you."

"Why don't you starve all of your cells?" Gabriel growled. "Then you can talk to me about how easy it is."

She didn't argue the point, but pushed him the rest of the way to his room. Gabriel was relieved to see his name on the plate beside the door and to enter the familiar dimness of his cave. She pushed the wheelchair up beside the bed.

"Here?"

Gabriel put the brakes on and stood up, eyeing the bed. It was a lot higher than he remembered. He couldn't just slide into it like his bed at home. He stood up as tall as he could, and held onto the side rail. With a little tip-toe boost, he got a corner of his bottom onto the mattress, but then he was stuck.

"Can you… help me?"

He tried to slide farther onto the bed, or to roll onto it, or to lift his weight with his arms. Mrs. Scott tried to lift his legs on, and pushed his hip, and tugged on his arms, and eventually Gabriel managed to slither up onto the high bed. He lay still, breathing hard.

"Whew."

"Well, that was interesting. Maybe next time we'd better get a nurse to help."

Gabriel just breathed. The social worker pushed the wheelchair away and didn't tuck it into the corner. She pulled the visitor chair closer to the bed, but not close enough to touch him. He wondered how Renata was doing, down in the emergency room.

"So, it's high time you and I had a chance to talk," Mrs. Scott said, settling herself into the chair and folding her hands in her lap.

"Are you going to tell me why I'm here?"

"I think that's already been explained to you. We need to re-evaluate. Get you into the program that treats your disease in the best way possible. We want to give you the best quality of life that we can. Get you healthy."

"I'm sicker here. I was doing good with my mom. I'd put on weight."

"Well, it's a matter of opinion whether you were doing better with your mom. And I'm sure that once they get your meds and diet straightened around here, and get you on the right protocol at the mito clinic, you're going to be doing much better." She gave him a bright, reassuring smile. Gabriel wondered if she ever wore hats. She looked like she should be wearing some kind of wide-brimmed, cheerful sun hat. Not sitting bareheaded in the dismal hospital room.

"I was doing better with my mom," Gabriel repeated. "Lots better. You saw, I can't even walk."

"I saw that you chose not to walk," she countered. "I don't know what you're capable of."

"I want to go back to my mom and my house. I hate it here."

"It's understandable that you're having a difficult time. It's a hard transition to make, and you don't understand it. But can you trust me for just a little while? I promise that we'll get everything straightened out."

"Where is my mom?"

"I assume she's at home."

"You didn't put her in jail?"

She raised her penciled eyebrows in surprise. "Why would I put her in jail? I don't think that your mother was being intentionally abusive, Gabriel. I didn't want to have to remove you... But I just don't think that your mom is qualified to take care of all of your special needs. Not when she won't follow the protocols that the doctors give her."

"She took care of me since I was born! She knows more about what works for me than any doctor. The weight clinic wasn't helping; I was losing weight there. Until Mom started figuring out what we needed to change."

"Your mother isn't qualified to make changes to your treatment. I'm sorry, but that's just a fact. She needs to follow what the doctors tell her."

Gabriel shook his head, frustrated. "When am I going home? What if she followed the program and I got worse? You think that's better?"

"I hear your frustration," she assured him. "But if you are getting worse, then the doctors will make adjustments to your treatment. Not your mom. I'm... I'm really sorry that I had to take you out of the home. I think that your mom is a good parent. She just didn't realize what damage she could do by changing the protocol. I think that if she'll agree to keep you at the mito clinic and follow the program, we might be able to get you back home again." She gave him a bright smile. "I sure hope so, anyway. I'm sure that you miss her."

"You can't just take kids away from their families for no reason."

"No. I can't. So you know that I had a reason. It's not something that we just do on a whim. I wouldn't take you out if DCF didn't truly believe that it was the best thing for you."

"You're wrong! I want to go to the court and to tell the judge that you were wrong. And the doctors. I want to be with my mom."

"I'm sure you do. We're working with the court, and they're making the best possible decisions for you."

"When is my mom going to be able to come see me?"

Mrs. Scott hesitated. "I'm not sure of that. I would like to keep her involved, but the doctors want to wait until you are more stable. It's better if we can just focus on your health, and not have her disrupting your treatment."

"But I want to see her." Gabriel rubbed at his eyes, trying not to cry in front of her. His throat was hot and tight. "I need my mom. I need to see my mom again."

"Gabriel. I'm truly sorry. But it's for your own good—"

Gabriel's body went rigid. He felt all his muscles clench up. His eyes rolled up; then he started convulsing, vibrating and bouncing the bed, making it bang into the wall as his body writhed uncontrollably. He couldn't see Carol Scott, but could hear her, swearing and panicky. She pressed the nurse's call button, then unable to wait for them, ran out into the hallway and called for help.

"I need a doctor! He's having a seizure! Someone needs to come here and help! Please!"

There was a rush of approaching feet and voices.

"It's all right," one of the nurses reassured. "It will pass in a minute or two. There's no need to panic."

Mrs. Scott was swearing, clearly distressed. "We were just talking, and he was getting upset—is it my fault for upsetting him? Did I do this?"

"Nothing that you did could cause a seizure. It will be over in a minute. He's completely safe in the bed."

Gradually, Gabriel's body stopped shaking, and he lay there blinking at them, sweat soaking his hospital gown and sheets. The nurse took his pulse.

"Feeling okay?" she asked him.

"I want my mom," Gabriel told her.

She looked at the social worker. They both shook their heads. Gabriel closed his eyes.

"What caused the seizure?" Mrs. Scott questioned.

"I don't think it was a seizure," the nurse said.

Gabriel opened his eyes, scowling at her. "It *was* a seizure," he argued. "You took me off of my meds. That's why."

"Doesn't look like a seizure," she repeated. "I think you're used to getting your own way when you throw a fit. Probably scares the bejeebers out of your mom and you get whatever you want. But that's not going to work here. We're onto you."

"It *was* a seizure!" Gabriel shouted, furious that she would doubt him. How could she think that it wasn't a seizure? She had seen him convulsing. They had all seen him convulsing. That was what happened when they took him off of his meds for no reason. They shouldn't go messing with his meds. Here they were, talking about how what his mother had done had been dangerous, and yet they could just pull him off of everything that the doctors had prescribed to keep him healthy. He hated being sick, and he hated being in hospital. He just wanted to be at home with his mother where he was safe and looked after properly.

"I think it's time for you to go," the nurse told the social worker. "Gabriel needs to have a rest."

When Gabriel opened his mouth to argue with her, she squeezed her eyebrows together. "Do you want me to give you a sedative? Is that what you need to calm down?"

Gabriel didn't want to be knocked out again. He didn't want to forget anything else. He shook his head. "No."

"Then I think it's time that you took a nap, don't you?"

He looked at the social worker and back at the nurse again. The other nurses were already retreating, going back to their duties.

Carol Scott nodded. "I think you're right. I'd better go. My being here is just making Gabriel more upset. I'll come back in a few days, Gabriel. Hopefully, then you'll be feeling better. Okay?"

He didn't answer her. She gave him a perfect smile, and he stared at her red lips, wondering how long it took to get them painted perfectly in such a bright, glossy color. Did she put it on in the car like his mother did, at a stop light, without even looking in the mirror? Or like he'd seen models do on TV, with a tiny paintbrush, painstakingly outlining in one color and filling in with another. They looked fake, like plastic Barbie lips.

The social worker left the room, never even having opened her shiny briefcase. The nurse looked Gabriel over one more time. "Too much excitement for you today. I don't think you were ready for it yet."

Gabriel remembered suddenly about what had happened to Renata. He had forgotten about her for a few minutes, arguing with Mrs. Scott about Keisha. "Is Renata okay? Have you heard?"

"She'll be okay. These things happen sometimes. Patients with chronic illness can have brittle bones. She takes nutritional supplements, but they aren't always adequate. They'll fix her up downstairs. She'll probably be terrorizing us again tomorrow." She smiled, tucking Gabriel's blankets around him. "You like her, huh?"

"Well, yeah..." Gabriel didn't want her thinking that he was having any romantic or inappropriate thoughts about her, which he wasn't. "She's the only one my age around here, so..."

She nodded. "It's nice that the two of you can keep each other company. Just be careful..."

"I know. She's paranoid," Gabriel parroted. "You can't believe anything she says."

"That's exactly right. She should be back tomorrow, I would think."

CHAPTER FIVE

It was a couple more days before Renata was back. She was wheeled in while Gabriel was making his way down the hallway, on his own feet, using the handrail and an IV stand for support. He couldn't understand why they wouldn't give him his leg braces and a pair of crutches so that he could get around better. But he was proud of himself for being able to make it more than a couple of steps down the hallway.

"Hey Gabe," Renata greeted, giving him an encouraging thumbs-up. "Looking good!"

He smiled at her and held onto the rail tightly while he looked her over. She was paler than usual, and there was some kind of drain coming out from under her gown that made him feel queasy. She sat in the wheelchair holding herself upright with her arms like she was afraid that it would hurt, or she would fall out of the chair if she let go. She had an oxygen feed into her nose, and an IV hooked onto a pole fixed to the chair. He wondered if she should really be back in psych already. They could probably give her better care downstairs in ICU. She didn't look ready to be moved.

"You back already?"

"I was causing too much ruckus downstairs." Her voice was softer than usual, and she didn't elaborate. The orderly pushed her down the hall and to her room.

Gabriel continued to work his way down the railing until he reached her room. By that time, she was already settled in bed; the wheelchair pushed into the corner. Renata turned her head to watch him as Gabriel stopped in the doorway, trying to figure out how to make it across the room to her bedside. It was only a few steps, but there was no handrail and he was already exhausted. Renata smiled.

Holding onto the IV pole for support, Gabriel shuffled into the room and made it to the chair. He didn't try to pull it over, just slid into the seat. His head spun, and he sat there catching his breath.

Neither of them spoke for a long time. Eventually, Gabriel felt well enough to take a look around, particularly at Renata's roommate. Gabriel was still alone in his room, so he was surprised to see that Renata's roommate was the mop-headed young boy from the common room.

"This is Skyler," Renata said, not shining any light on the mystery. "Sky, this is Gabriel."

Skyler looked over at Gabriel. He had dark circles around his eyes. He nodded and said hi. Gabriel looked back over at Renata. "Mito?"

She nodded. "Yeah, surprise, surprise, huh?"

Gabriel cut a glance toward the young boy and spoke in a low voice that the hoped only Renata could hear.

"I don't get it. Is he…?"

"I'm a boy," Skyler said firmly.

Gabriel wasn't sure whether he had heard the whispered question, or just interpreted the look on Gabriel's face. He felt hot and rubbed his forehead nervously. "Oh, okay… I didn't think they mixed genders. I thought they'd put you in with me… I don't have a roommate."

"I'm trans," Skyler said. "I was assigned as female at birth. They won't acknowledge my chosen gender here." He shook his head. "Stupid!"

"Oh." Gabriel looked at Renata to get her take on this. Her eyes were closed, and he wasn't sure if she was asleep or just resting. "I didn't know."

"That's why I told you. It's confusing for people sometimes."

"Yeah." Gabriel bit his tongue to keep from apologizing again, not sure what to say.

"Just think of him as a boy," Renata advised, without opening her eyes. "So… you're walking, huh?"

"Sort of," Gabriel agreed. "If you can call it that."

"You're on your feet. That's good. Any excitement while I was gone?"

"You're the one who brings all the excitement. It's quiet when you're gone."

She smiled. "Yeah."

"How are you doing? The orderly really broke your rib?"

"Uh-huh."

"That must have hurt."

"Still does. And they don't want to give me anything for it. No opiates for Renata." She shook her head sadly.

"Really? Ow. You must be mad at him for hurting you like that."

Renata opened her eyes and turned to look at Gabriel. "It's okay. Last year, I broke two of his ribs, so I guess we're even."

"You broke his ribs?" Gabriel repeated in disbelief. "How?"

"I *might* have hit him with an IV pole." She paused. "It's not my fault. I was on a break."

"A break?"

"Psychotic break. I wasn't in control."

"They messed up your meds?"

"No. I just went off. That happens sometimes. Something stops working."

Gabriel thought about it. "That must be scary."

"Life is scary. If you're paying attention."

"Yeah." He didn't want to get her going about conspiracies again, especially if she'd already been 'making a ruckus' downstairs. He tried to steer her to a safe topic. "So… what are you going to do when you go home? Play on the rugby team?"

Renata snorted and laughed, and for a minute, he was afraid that she was choking, not getting enough air. Renata took a couple of long breaths, pressing her hand to her chest. She shook her head.

"Yeah… no rugby. I do okay in school, other than phys ed. But they excuse me from that. I like to read. Write long, rambling essays for English LA. What about you? What do you like?"

"Science. Math. I'm not that great at writing. And I'd rather watch a good movie than read a book."

"Boys."

"What can I say? At least I'm not illiterate."

"How long have you been homeschooling?"

"Just over a year. School… just got to be too much. Getting up early. Carrying books. Up and down stairs. There wasn't any elevator. I'd make it to class late and then fall asleep."

"Don't learn much when you're sleeping. Do you miss it? You'll be back in public school when you go to your foster family. Are you going to like seeing other people again?"

"I still see other people… It was nice having friends to talk to during the day… but you couldn't *really* talk until lunch or after school anyway. And I can still do that now."

"Huh. It would be weird, your mom teaching you at home. I don't think I'd like it."

"I mostly did online. I liked it… And we did some stuff with other homeschoolers. I don't know if I can manage to make it around at public school again."

"Maybe they'll accommodate." Renata sighed. "Though Dr. De Klerk sort of pushes a 'treat them like everyone else and they'll be more normal' agenda. I don't like pretending to be normal… I don't *do* normal."

Gabriel laughed.

Gabriel could hear voices outside his room. A piece of an argument that had progressed down the hallway and he was just able to hear now.

"…granola-crunching, pot-smoking deadbeats! Some people should never be allowed to be parents. There should be some kind of system in place to evaluate people before they're allowed to have children. Foster and adoptive families have to be screened, why not natural parents? Filter out the dangerous ones before they're allowed to do any damage." The woman's voice was harsh and passionate. She sounded like a woman who had smoked or lectured for a lot of years, her voice getting husky with overuse.

There was an answering laugh. "A program like that would certainly make our lives interesting. I'm not sure you can ever weed out the bad ones. Especially not before the children are even born."

"Why wait? We can tell which ones are going to be problems. You can see the red flags. I have parents who walk into my office, and I know, without any question, that they are going to be a problem. I can't bear seeing children being abused and neglected. I won't stand by while their parents put them through hell."

"Nobody is suggesting you do. Just that… you need to be careful. Some like this one," there was a pause, and Gabriel imagined the second party gesturing toward one of the rooms. "Are a lot harder to prove in court."

"If you need more evidence or experts, you just call me."

"That's what I told the investigator."

"Good."

Gabriel looked up as a woman in a lab coat stepped in his doorway. She was tall, with curly black shoulder-length hair. She seemed vaguely familiar, but he couldn't remember having met her before. She stood in the doorway looking at Gabriel for a moment, then strode in. She smiled briskly, eyes devoid of emotion.

"Hello, Gabriel. How are we feeling today?"

"Not that great."

She looked down at a clipboard and flipped through the pages as if she'd never seen them before. "We're going to try adding back in a couple of your meds. That should help. Looks like you're losing weight again. We really can't have that." She raised her eyes above the level of the clipboard and looked at him like he was intentionally losing weight. "Are you eating everything they're giving you? Getting some moderate exercise?"

Gabriel fumbled for words. "Um… no…"

"No?" She wrote something down and frowned at him. She had a lot of fine lines around her mouth and eyes that pointed downward. "Why not?"

"They give me food I'm allergic to. And not enough snacks. And… I can't exercise. I can hardly get out of bed, or walk."

She scribbled a note. "Why can't you get around? You were walking last time I saw you."

"I… don't remember you."

She studied him again, putting on a pair of glasses that hung on a chain around her neck. After staring at him for a minute, she took them off again. "I'm Dr. Margot Seymour. I saw you the last time you came through the weight clinic. I'm the supervising doctor there, so I'm familiar with your case."

Gabriel had been at the weight clinic for at least six months and could not remember seeing her before. He had always met with Nurse Birch and the other nurses and administrators there, and had never met with the doctor. If she was familiar with his case, why was she asking him questions that she should have known the answers to?

"I have hypotonia in my legs," Gabriel told her. "But they took my braces away. I can't walk without them."

She raised her eyebrows. "Not at all?"

"Well… a little. But it's hard, and it hurts."

"Uh-huh." She wrote down another note. "I want you to work on that. Get some muscle built up. The best treatment for hypertonic muscles is physical therapy. Do you have a physical or occupational therapist?"

"Yeah. Doctor Michaels."

"Has he given you some exercises to do?"

Gabriel nodded reluctantly. He knew what the next question would be.

"Are you doing them?"

"They hurt my legs," Gabriel said uncomfortably. "I try, but…"

"How hard are you trying? When is the last time you did any of the exercises he assigned you?"

Gabriel bit his lip. "Before… when I was at home."

"You need to keep it up here. Were you doing them every day at home?"

"No."

"You need to follow your doctors' instructions if you're going to feel better, don't you Gabriel? I want you to follow all of the instructions that you're given. Not just the ones that are easy. I want you doing your PT every day."

Gabriel nodded, a lump in his throat. She didn't know how hard the exercises were for him, and they had never seemed to make any difference. Keisha had given up on forcing Gabriel to do them; it was such a fight every day.

"Good. Building muscle will help your energy. And your weight. We want to do everything we can to optimize your health, don't we?"

Gabriel nodded again. "Yeah."

"Good boy. And you make sure you're eating enough. Any nausea? Vomiting?"

"Some nausea… it helps if I eat more often, but they don't give me snacks here."

She flipped back a page or two, skimming over the various notes on his chart. "Your blood sugar has been more stable. But still not great. Hospitals aren't well-equipped to manage snacks between meals. But there should be a fridge that you have access to, with juice, yogurt, some things like that. Ask the nursing staff. Be careful of sugars and processed foods. High-protein snacks are best."

"All they have is juice and applesauce."

"Ask about it. I'll make a note." She wrote something on the clipboard and drew a circle around it. "Now, do you have any questions for me?"

"When am I going home?"

"Do you have any *medical* questions for me?"

"I shouldn't be here," Gabriel insisted. "I don't have any psychiatric problems. I want to go home to my mom." He stared at the lines around her mouth. "I want to know why you sent me here," he concluded bullishly.

Her mouth pursed like she'd eaten something sour. "You're here so that we can sort out which of your symptoms are physical, and which ones are caused by something else. We can only do that in a controlled environment. Once we finish the evaluation, you'll be able to be moved to a less restrictive environment while we treat you through the mitochondrial disorder clinic."

"I'm not crazy. And my mom didn't do anything wrong. I want to go home. You can't make me go to the mito clinic."

"Like I told your mother," Dr. Seymour said slowly and deliberately, "I can and I will. Parents cannot stop doctors from determining the proper course of treatment for their children. If they're going to be an obstacle to proper treatment, they're going to be removed."

He had a sudden vision of his mother's stricken expression when Dr. Seymour told her that. "You can't do that!"

"I can. I already have."

"I want my mom!" Gabriel's voice rose in his frustration and anger.

"If I have my way, you will never see your mom again."

Gabriel's jaw hung open. He stared at her in disbelief. Her words were spoken quietly and calmly, but he could hear the animosity behind them. She wasn't just mouthing words. She wasn't like Mrs. Scott, reassuring Gabriel that they would find the truth, and it would all work out in the end. She had already made a decision and acted on it. In her mind, Keisha was the worst kind of abusive parent, and she intended to keep Keisha away from her son permanently.

Neither of them moved or said a word for a long time. Eventually, Dr. Seymour's eyes dropped to the clipboard again. "You're making good progress, Gabriel. I hope to have you out of here and to a qualified foster family shortly. You remember what I said about eating and doing your therapy. The more diligent you are, the faster you will be able to recover your mobility and improve your quality of life." She touched his shoulder, her fingers light. "You take care of yourself, now. I want you to be well."

Gabriel nodded. He didn't know what else to do or say.

Renata hadn't come in to see Gabriel, so he decided to go see her. It took him a long time to make his way down the hallway, holding onto the handrail and the IV pole, to get a couple of doors down to her hospital room. But he was proud when he made it. He might not have a lot of independence, but he wasn't completely confined to his bed anymore. Renata turned her head as he dragged his feet into the room. She smiled.

"Hey, Gabe. I was just thinking of you. Can't quite make it out of bed yet."

Gabriel nodded. "Yeah. I figured you might be pretty sore."

She swore under her breath. "Oh, yeah. If anyone ever tells you broken ribs are fun, don't believe it."

Gabriel snickered. He looked over at the other bed and saw that it was empty. "Where's your friend?"

"I think he had therapy."

"So is he here because of...?" Gabriel trailed off and grimaced, embarrassed.

"Because of mito?" Renata questioned. "Yeah. He's got PDD, and they said they took him because his parents weren't handling his developmental delays properly, which was putting him in danger. You know, same old story. But the fact is, they're makin' too many waves, opening their mouths when they shouldn't, and *they* wanted to shut them up."

Gabriel wouldn't have believed it a couple of days ago, but he was finding himself gradually coming around to Renata's way of thinking. There was definitely something going on. Mito was a very rare, very difficult to diagnose disease, and for three of them to be in the same ward all at the same time—a psych ward, no less—seemed the height of improbability. Something was going on.

"What were his parents doing?" he asked. "What do you mean, making waves?"

Renata nodded toward the empty bed. "Sky has mitochondrial damage from a round of vaccinations," she said in a near-whisper.

Gabriel nodded. He'd heard of such things. One of the doctors said that Gabriel was probably born with mitochondrial disease, but that some things could trigger it or make it worse, and the doctors didn't know what they all were. Chemicals, viruses, vaccines, maybe even GMOs or other things in the food supply.

"Don't you get it?" Renata's eyes were wide. She readjusted the oxygen tube in her nose and scratched around it. "He has Pervasive Developmental Delays. Autism spectrum. From vaxes. The medical records show that he had an immune system collapse after getting nine jabs in one day. And that kicked his mito into overdrive. They have documented proof that his PDD showed up right after his vaccinations. Until then, he met all of his milestones. Language and social and everything. But right after, he had a high fever, meningoencephalitis, even stopped breathing. When he recovered… he wasn't the same."

"Yeah…?" Gabriel wasn't sure why she was making such a huge big deal out of the story.

"Well, you've heard the news, right? All the propaganda about how vaccinations don't cause autism? But in his case, they have proof that they *did*."

"But he was born with mito," Gabriel said. "I mean, probably. And that caused his PDD. Right? Anything could have triggered it."

Renata raised her hands and rolled her eyes. "All you need to know is, his parents started making noise about immunization injury causing his ASD, and he got taken away."

Gabriel nodded slowly. There *was* a pattern developing. He rubbed his temples, wondering if he was going crazy. Was he becoming paranoid like Renata? Seeing connections and conspiracies where there weren't any? It could just be coincidence. Three kids taken away from their families for three completely different reasons, just happening to end up in the same place.

"Vaccines are probably where mito came from in the first place," Renata said, her voice a hoarse whisper. "They've been tracking and experimenting on kids for decades, injecting them with different experimental drugs, keeping records on them. What better biological weapon is there than mito? Take away the enemy's energy, make it impossible for them to run or fight back. There's no bodies, just a passive populace." Her eyes were deep, black pools.

"That's..." he stopped himself before saying 'crazy.' "I don't know... You think they could keep something like that a secret? Experimenting on kids for that many years, that many people. It doesn't sound possible."

"People are more inclined to believe a big lie than a small one. Injecting the entire populace? You really think it's all about disease prevention? What government could pass up the opportunity to try out a few experiments while they were at it? And why the big push to vaccinate every single kid? They can take DNA samples, inject locator microchips—they can track every person in the country!"

"And if their parents refuse to vaccinate..." Gabriel started.

Renata nodded vigorously. "One more reason to take them away. Force vaccination, get them into compliant homes and get extra funding... Can you see how corrupt the whole system is? It's rotten to the core!"

Her face was getting flushed.

"Take it easy," Gabriel soothed, touching her arm. "You're getting out of breath."

She opened her mouth to object, then closed it and breathed through her nose for a few breaths, touching the oxygen feed.

"I'm okay."

"You don't want to make yourself sicker. You better keep cool."

She frowned, studying him through narrowed eyes.

CHAPTER SIX

RENATA WAS ASLEEP, SO Gabriel shuffled to the common room. He made it to the table where Skyler was working on a puzzle and fell into the other chair. Skyler didn't look at him. Gabriel looked down at the puzzle pieces and what Skyler had put together so far. They sat in silence for a while, just looking at the pieces. Gabriel reached for a piece with an orangey-red knob on it to try out.

"Don't touch," Skyler barked.

Gabriel froze, and looked over at him. "I'm just going to help. That piece there—"

"I'm doing this puzzle by myself. Don't help me."

"Oh…" Gabriel let his breath out. He really wanted to try the piece to see if it fit. But it was Skyler's puzzle and he had the right to say that he didn't want any help with it.

"Just that one?" he suggested. "Then I'll leave you alone. I didn't know that you didn't want any help."

"No."

Skyler picked up an all-black piece and fit it into place. Gabriel looked at the other all-black pieces, impressed that Skyler had been able to figure it out without trying more than one piece.

"I have good visual-spacial skills," the boy commented, without looking at Gabriel. "It makes me good at puzzles."

"Oh. Yeah. Good for you."

"You said that you like math and science. Renata likes English. I'm good at puzzles."

"I guess there's not much opportunity to do that at school."

"I have puzzles at home. I think about them while I'm at school, then put them together when I get home."

Gabriel tried to imagine that. "You put them together in your mind first? You have a photographic memory or something?"

"Yeah. Good visual spatial memory. I'm good at puzzles."

"Cool."

He watched Skyler in silence for a few minutes. It was more interesting than the TV, which was happily turned down too quiet to hear.

"So they're putting you into foster care," Skyler commented, still looking down at the puzzle.

"Well… I guess. When they decide they're finished with me here. I don't know how long that will be."

"Friday."

"What?" Gabriel demanded.

"They're discharging you and taking you to your foster family on Friday."

"How would you know that?"

"It's written in the planner."

"What planner?"

"At the nursing station. They keep a calendar, so all the nurses and doctors know what's happening."

"And you saw it?"

Skyler nodded. He fit another black piece into place, beside the last one.

"And it said I'm going to be discharged on Friday?"

"Yeah. Your social worker is Carol Scott. She's coming to pick you up. And your foster family's name is Foegel." He fit two more pieces into the puzzle in quick succession. "Do you think that's a variant of Vogel, the German word for bird?"

"How would I know that? I've never met them before."

"You should ask when you meet them. Maybe they have a family story about it."

"Maybe," Gabriel agreed faintly. He wished that Renata was awake. He really needed to talk to her now. He was going to be leaving on Friday. He'd thought that she would leave before he

70

did. He didn't think that they were done with him yet. He was starting to feel better as they added more of his meds back in, but he still wasn't quite up to par. He wanted to talk to Renata about going back into foster care.

"Are you scared?" Skyler asked.

Skyler looked up at Gabriel for the first time. He was so young. Gabriel had forgotten how baby-faced Skyler was. He couldn't be more than ten, but he spoke like he was a grown-up. More mature than a lot of grown-ups sounded.

"You look scared," Skyler observed.

"There's nothing to be scared of," Gabriel said with bravado. "It's just another family. They've been vetted by the state and everything. They'll be good."

"Renata said that children are five times more likely to die in foster homes than in their own families. I looked it up. It's true."

Gabriel swallowed.

"And they're three times more likely to be physically abused. What are you going to do if you're abused?"

"Aren't *you* in foster care?" Gabriel challenged, a band tightening around his chest, making his pounding heart feel squeezed.

"When I get out of here. Not yet."

"Aren't you scared?"

Skyler touched one puzzle piece, frowning. Then another. He rotated a third around one hundred and eighty degrees.

"Sky?" Gabriel prompted.

Skyler pushed himself violently back from the table and stood up. "This stupid puzzle is missing pieces!" he shouted. He reached out to swipe it off of the table, but couldn't bring himself to do it. He tried a second time, then threw his chair down on the floor with a crash. "It can't be finished!"

Gabriel put his hands up defensively, in case Skyler started throwing things at him.

"Time to take a break, Scarlett," Nurse Kelly said, walking over to them. "What else would you like to do?"

Gabriel looked at the boy. "Scarlett?"

"My name is Skyler," he insisted, and he his shook his finger at Nurse Kelly. "You know it's Skyler!"

"All right, Skyler. Time for a break, either way. So what do you want to do? Shall we see what's on TV? Play some cards? Maybe Gabriel would play a card game with you." She cocked an eyebrow at him. "Why don't the two of you do something together?"

"They're all missing cards," Skyler complained. "You can't play solitaire if you're missing cards."

"No, and that's not a two-person game. But you could play War."

Skyler looked at Gabriel. "You don't want to play, do you?"

"Um, sure. Why not?"

They both looked at Nurse Kelly. Smiling, she nodded and moved away from them.

"Do you really want to?" Skyler asked when she was out of earshot.

"Do you?"

Skyler looked torn. He looked at the offending puzzle. "I guess. Nothing else to do."

They moved over to the next table with a boxed deck of cards and sat down. Gabriel lowered himself carefully into the plastic chair and looked around.

"So…" he got the deck out of the box and cut it, then started shuffling it. There were a couple of cards from another deck, with differently colored backs, and he pulled them out and set them to the side. "Do you know anything about the foster family that you're going to?"

"Not yet."

"Have you ever been in foster care before?"

"No." Skyler's brows drew down in a scowl. "And yes, I'm scared about it."

Gabriel started to deal the cards between them.

"I called my mom," Skyler offered.

"You called her?" Gabriel leaned closer to the younger boy. "When? They let you call her?"

72

"Hung around at the nurse's station until they were all busy with other things. Then I used their phone. I only got a few minutes," his voice was flat. "But at least I got to talk to her. When I get to a foster home, I'm going to call her all the time."

Gabriel hadn't thought about doing that. He straightened his pile of cards and picked them up. "What did she say? What did the nurses do when they caught you?"

"She said she missed me. And that they were trying to get me back." Skyler and Gabriel each played a card, and Gabriel's ten beat Skyler's seven. Gabriel scooped both up and put them on the bottom of his pile. "I told her not to forget to feed the cat."

They played another card and this time Skyler won.

"They put me in the quiet room."

"What's the quiet room?" Gabriel asked him.

"It's just a room. An empty room."

"Was it bad?"

"It was boring."

"How long did they put you in there?"

"Four hours and twenty-three minutes."

They continued to play war.

"That's a long time just to sit in a room by yourself."

"It was boring," Skyler repeated.

Later on, Gabriel hung around the nursing station himself, watching for the nurses to be distracted by other jobs. But it seemed like one of them was always at the computer by the phone. He couldn't stand there all day. He couldn't stand for a long time. His legs started shaking after a couple of minutes.

"Do you need help getting back to your room?" Nurse Lee asked Gabriel with a smile.

Gabriel shifted his feet, holding onto the handrail. "My OT said I need to stand longer," he said.

"Okay. Good for you. Let me know if you need any help."

Gabriel smiled and nodded. Ten minutes ticked past. Gabriel staggered over to a wheelchair and sat down. He rested, and sat there watching the nurses. Sitting down seemed to make him invisible to the nurses. They bustled here and there, in and out of hospital rooms, answering phone calls and calling back and forth to each other.

Gabriel almost missed his opportunity; he got so interested in watching what was going on. Then he realized that the desk was empty. He hurried as fast as his uncooperative body would let him.

He hung over the desk, looking at the complex phone. He wondered if he had to press a button before dialing, or whether he could just dial straight out. Gabriel picked up the receiver, and the line one button lit up. He quickly tapped in Keisha's cell phone number. After a series of clicks, he heard the ring tone.

He wondered where she was. At home? At the grocery store? Meeting with a lawyer about what to do to get Gabriel back? Was her ringer turned on, or was it on vibrate? She always missed it when it was on vibrate.

"Hello?"

"Mom?" Gabriel's voice broke, shifting upward in pitch.

"Gabriel? Gabriel, sweetie, are you okay? Where are you?"

"I'm still at the hospital, but they're moving me soon—"

Suddenly she was gone. Gabriel looked down at the phone in confusion and saw the finger that had just pressed the line button, cutting off the call.

"No! Why did you do that?" Gabriel shouted. He had heard his mother's voice. He had been in a conversation with her. He was like a hostage, being allowed to speak just long enough to provide proof of life, and then being cut off, dragged back away from the phone and tied up again. Gabriel hit the desktop with his fist. "No! That was my mom! I have to talk to her!"

The nurse pulled him away from the desk and took the receiver out of his hand. She hung it up. Tears were leaking from Gabriel's eyes. He wasn't crying, but his throat was tight and hot, and the tears escaped his burning eyes.

"It's not fair! Why can't I even talk to her? What's wrong with that?"

"You need to go back to your room now. You behave, and I won't report this."

"I want my mom!"

Nurse Lee's eyes were sad, but her mouth was set. "You're a big boy, Gabriel. You're almost a man. You need to be strong. Now come on. Back to your room."

She held his elbow firmly and stepped toward his hospital room. Gabriel's knees buckled, and he didn't even try to stop himself from falling.

"Gabriel!" Lee's voice was worried and angry at the same time. She tried to catch him, but he was too big for the short Asian woman.

Lying on the floor, Gabriel curled up, holding his arms over his face. He wasn't crying. He wasn't going to cry in front of all the nurses. His face was wet, and he tried to rub the moisture away with his hands to keep them from seeing.

He was only vaguely aware of his undignified position, rolled up like that on the floor with his gown gaping open. Nurse Lee was calling for help, and it wasn't long before there was a knot of nurses around Gabriel, telling him to get up and pulling and prodding him. Gabriel groaned, wishing them all away.

"No, no. Just leave me alone!"

"Move out of the way," a gruff voice ordered.

The group of nurses quieted and moved back from Gabriel. Large hands closed around both of his arms, and he was hauled unceremoniously to his feet. Gabriel refused to take his weight, but the man simply dragged him back to his room and slung him onto the bed.

"What do you want done with him?" It was the orderly who had broken Renata's ribs. Andre, Gabriel had heard some of the other patients call him. As in 'Andre the Giant.' Gabriel didn't know his real name.

There was a sigh from Nurse Lee, who had followed them into the room. "I think you may as well just leave him there. Are you going to stay put, Gabriel? Or are you going to cause more trouble?"

"I just wanted to talk to my mom," Gabriel whined.

"Grow up, Mr. Tate. It's time to stop being a baby and behave like a mature young man. Grow up. Understand?"

Gabriel nodded, wiping his tear-streaked face. "Okay."

"You can stay in your bed, or you can sit in the quiet room, where there is no bed, and no chair, and no blankets. What's your choice?"

"I'll stay here."

"Your word?"

"Yeah."

"Tell me you promise to stay here."

"I promise," Gabriel snuffled.

CHAPTER SEVEN

H E AND RENATA HAD talked for a long time about getting out of the ward. Sooner or later, they would both be released to foster families. Gabriel sooner than Renata. But Renata whispered to him about escaping. Making a run for it instead of waiting until they were sent off to their foster families. Gabriel had listened to her various suggestions, wondering whether escape was really possible.

"I've done it before," Renata said. "It's not easy, but it's possible. And it's good if you've got somewhere to go. I didn't have anyone on the outside. Nowhere to go."

"Where did you go?" Gabriel prompted, curious.

"Just around," she said with a shrug. "Once you're out, you need to find some clothes. Too visible once you get out of the hospital, if you're still in blues."

Gabriel gazed at the window. "What floor are we on?"

"Seven. Too far to jump."

He laughed. "I'm not thinking of jumping! I'm not trying to kill myself."

"Probably wouldn't kill you. Just cripple you. Then you'd be worse off than this."

Gabriel knew his way around better on the lower floors. He'd had lots of hospital stays, so he knew where things were. If he could get down to the third floor, he knew places to hide. Where to get snacks. Where the children's wards were where he might find clothes in rooms while the kids watched TV in the common area. That would be the best bet. Then he could go home to Keisha. They could find a place for him to hide if the police or social workers came looking for him. Get everything all arranged so that no one could find him. And he could go back to his old life again.

"How did you get out?"

"Which time?" Renata asked.

"How many times have you escaped?"

"Umm..." she rolled her eyes up toward the ceiling, thinking back. "I think... six. You can do it if you watch for opportunities. Doctors aren't as careful making sure that doors lock behind them as the nurses are. There are all kinds of carts and bins that are pushed in and out of here. Laundry, lunch, gurneys, other equipment. Just keep your eyes open."

"I don't have very long."

"You can always run away from your foster family. They won't have security as good as here. Locks and alarms on the doors, maybe. But no orderlies."

"So you think I should wait? Run away from the foster family?"

Renata considered, chewing on her lip. "Foegels... I haven't been there before. There's only so many families that take kids with major medical needs. Sometimes they move you out of the city, if they think you might run or cause trouble or if there's no one who can take a medical case right now. That makes it a lot harder to run. You can't just hop a bus with a sob story like you can inside the city."

Gabriel's stomach gurgled grumpily at the suggestion of moving farther away from his mother. "I could just call her to come and get me from there," he suggested.

"No way. They'll tap her phone. Put a GPS tracker on her car. She tries to take you out of the foster home, and she's going to go straight to prison. I don't think you want that, do you?"

Gabriel shook his head. Renata might be happy about her mother being in prison, but the last thing he wanted was for Keisha to be thrown in jail. Eventually, the court system would prove that Gabriel had been taken away without cause, and they would let him go home again. But that couldn't happen if Keisha was in prison.

"She can't be part of it," Renata declared. "You've got to do it on your own."

"Would they move me out of the city? When I'm supposed to be going to the mito clinic? Don't they have to keep me here?"

"If it's a family that already knows the protocol, then you've only got to go to the clinic once every week or two. So they can be a couple hours' drive away and still keep you in the program."

Gabriel watched for his opportunity. He couldn't wait for the courts to straighten everything out. He wasn't going to wait for them to put him into a new home, farther away from his mother, where he might be abused or even killed. He kept running through the stats that Renata and Skyler had quoted. Foster care was not safe. He'd be out of the frying pan and into the fire.

No one paid any attention to him while he was sitting in a wheelchair. Somehow people ceased to see him. He became a part of the furniture. So Gabriel sat and watched, occasionally wheeling himself a few feet down the hallway, hanging around the various entrance and exit doors and stairways to see where the best chances for escape would be.

"You can't run," Renata had reminded him. "So don't try. Be stealthy. Just watch and wait."

He was near one of the stairway doors when an orderly came up from a lower floor and strode into the ward, leaving the pneumatic door to swing shut behind him. Gabriel slipped his foot off of the wheelchair foot platform and jammed it into the closing door. The door stopped. Gabriel watched the orderly to see if he would notice that the door hadn't clicked shut behind him. But the man just kept going, his mind obviously on something else. Gabriel waited there for a few long seconds, watching the man walk around the corner and out of sight. There were nurses and patients coming and going, but no one looked at Gabriel. No one noticed him with his foot in the door.

Trying to time his movements for when no one was looking his direction, Gabriel stood up, and as gracefully as possible, pushed through the door into the stairwell and let it click quietly shut.

He was out of the ward.

His heart was beating so hard and fast that he couldn't catch his breath. He tried to calm himself down, but was so anxious that someone would look through the narrow security glass and see him standing there that he couldn't force himself to relax. Slow, deep breathing did nothing for him.

Gabriel turned to dash down the stairs. It wasn't until that point that he had to confront the reality of his physical limitations. Stairs? He was just going to run down the stairs to another floor in order to escape and blend in? He was still barely able to walk down the hallway with the handrail and IV pole. That was an accomplishment for him. How was he going to get down the stairs?

Gabriel grabbed the railing and forced himself to put his foot down the first step. He just about overbalance and pitched headfirst down the flight. Gabriel gripped the rail tightly, trying to keep himself upright, battling vertigo as he looked down, and down, and down each flight of stairs. How had he thought that he could just walk right out?

Gabriel's legs were shaking. He sank down to sit on the top step. Was that it? He wasn't even going to be able to get down one stair. Once sitting, he felt a bit stronger. The hypotonia was worst in his legs. Those big muscles that were supposed to take all his weight. His trunk and arms were not as weak.

He used his arms to boost himself down to sit on the next stair. Going down still meant supporting his weight mostly on his arms for a few seconds, but he was working with gravity by going down instead of up, and he could rest for a few seconds between each stair. Lifting himself down one stair at a time, Gabriel worked his way down the first flight of stairs. He started to grin to himself. Maybe he could do it. Maybe he could still escape. They wouldn't be looking for him until supper time, and then no one would know where to look. Who was even going to remember him sitting in the wheelchair near the stairway? They wouldn't know that he was gone until it was too late.

Two flights of stairs meant one floor. Gabriel saw the doorway to the sixth floor. He wasn't sure what units were on the sixth floor; he'd never stayed there. But when he saw that the sixth-floor door also had a security swipe panel, he felt suddenly queasy.

He had assumed that only the locked wards like psych would have doors that needed security passes to get through. Was the sixth floor also a locked ward? Maybe a ward for dangerous offenders? Or were *all* of the stairway doors inaccessible without a security card?

Gabriel's heart pounded, and he rested his head on the wall, closing his eyes. He was not going to pass out. He was going to stay alert and focused and figure it out.

The door at the ground floor had to be able to be opened without a card, in case of fire. Hopefully, the doors below the fifth floor would not have security panels, and he could escape into the hospital and find a change of clothes. But if they were locked, the bottom door still had to open. Gabriel continued to bum his way down the stairs, one step at a time. His arms ached. They shook every time he put weight on them. How was he going to make it farther than the fifth floor if he had to? Could he make it all the way to the bottom?

He wasn't even sure what he was going to do if the fifth-floor door was accessible. What ward did it open into? It wouldn't help him much if it were maternity. He'd stick out like a sore thumb. And he'd have to walk or find a wheelchair. Probably both. 'Watch for your opportunity' hadn't been the best escape plan.

Gabriel heard a door open somewhere below him and footsteps started to mount the stairs. Somehow he hadn't thought about anyone else using the stairs while he was on them. He thought that it would be quiet. No one would use them. But the only way he had gotten into the stairwell was because someone had used them. People obviously didn't rely solely on the elevators. Particularly the hospital staff. Gabriel tried to hurry.

There was no telling how far away the intruder was. Or how high up he would come. Gabriel had to get to the fifth-floor door and get through it before anyone could see him. It would be obvious, with his gown and bracelet, that he was somewhere he wasn't supposed to be.

He scraped his elbow on the edge of one of the concrete stairs and bit back a cry. It was nothing. A little scrape. Though at a hospital, even a little scrape could end up getting infected with an antibiotic-resistant staph, or worse. Gabriel had suffered through hospital infections before, and it wasn't pleasant. Keisha always did everything she could to get him out of the hospital as quickly as possible, before he could pick up an infection or some other bug from another patient or a doctor who hadn't washed his hands properly.

Gabriel wiped off the dirt and then spit on his hand to wipe his elbow, which he then wiped with the gown. That was the best first aid he could do under the circumstances. He continued on, the intruder's steadily climbing footsteps getting closer and closer. Gabriel prayed that he would take another door, exiting the stairway, but he could hear every time the man walked through a flat landing and then started climbing up the next flight of stairs. Gabriel was frantic. He was going to be discovered. He finally made it to the fifth-floor landing and looked at the door. A security swipe pad with a red light glared at him.

Gabriel swore. The footsteps were now really close. There was no way to run or hide. He pulled himself to his feet, holding shakily to the handrail. Standing up was less suspicious than sitting on the stairs. If he smiled and said good morning in a confident way, like he was supposed to be there, then maybe the man would go on, not even registering his presence. Act like he was supposed to be there, and people would believe it. That was what they said on TV thrillers.

A man wearing a doctor's lab jacket came around the corner and continued to mount the stairs at a steady pace. Gabriel wasn't exactly sure how far the man had climbed, but it seemed like about three flights, and he wasn't even breathing hard. What

Gabriel wouldn't give for an energy system like that. The doctor's eyes went over Gabriel curiously. Gabriel tried to look like he wasn't hanging onto the rail for dear life and forced a pleasant smile.

"Morning!"

"Good morning." The doctor's pace was slowing. He stopped a few stairs below Gabriel. "Are you all right?"

"Oh, yeah, fine." Gabriel's legs were shaking like jelly. He was sure that the doctor could see, considering they weren't even covered by the blue hospital gown.

"Where did you come from?" The doctor looked up the stairs and at the closed fifth-floor door.

"I didn't know it would lock," Gabriel said. "I thought it was okay to use the stairs. It's…" Gabriel was short of breath despite himself. "It's good exercise, right? You should always take the stairs when you can."

"Sure," the doctor agreed with a friendly smile. He motioned to the locked door. "Do you want me to let you out?"

Gabriel continued to smile. "Yeah. That would be great."

The doctor swiped his security card, and the light turned green. Gabriel staggered from the handrail to the doorknob for support. He turned it. As he opened the door, the doctor's hand closed around Gabriel's arm. Gabriel was too weak to try to twist away from him. The friendly doctor rotated Gabriel's hospital bracelet to look at the details on it.

"Psychiatric," he observed. "I think you're on the wrong floor."

Gabriel just looked at him. The doctor walked him through the door, but it became quickly obvious that Gabriel couldn't go far under his own power, and the doctor grabbed a wheelchair from the unit they had walked into, which turned out to be nephrology. Gabriel expected the doctor to call security, but he looked at his watch and shrugged.

"I guess I'll take you back up. Faster than waiting for someone to come pick you up."

Gabriel didn't say anything. The doctor didn't make small talk, but wheeled him to the nearest elevator and headed up to the seventh floor, where he was required to swipe his card again to get off of the elevator. It caused quite a stir when he pushed Gabriel back to the nursing station. Gabriel hid his face behind his hands.

"I brought you an escapee," the doctor said cheerfully.

"Gabriel!"

"Where did you find him?"

"In the stairway, a couple of floors down."

The staff turned to look at the stairway door, which was now securely closed. One of the orderlies walked over and tested to make sure that it couldn't be opened again.

"Well, thank you, doctor," Nurse Barrett said, approaching and taking the wheelchair from him. "We'll take it from here."

"Keep an eye on that one!"

"Oh, we will."

Gabriel swallowed. Barrett pushed him back to his room, and without a word, she helped him to stand up and to get into bed. Once he was lying down, she checked his pulse and his temperature. Gabriel was soaked in sweat from the effort of his escape, but she didn't change him out of the damp gown; she just threw another blanket over him.

"I don't understand why you would do something stupid like that," Barrett said, putting the blood pressure cuff around his arm and starting to pump it up. "You're getting out of here in a couple of days, why the sudden effort to escape?"

Gabriel waited while she released the valve and listened with her stethoscope.

"I just... want to go home."

He was surprised when she pulled out a blood sugar monitor. He lay still while she lanced his finger and checked his glucose.

"You're crashing," she observed. "Why would you do something like that?"

"I want to see my mom. They're going to take me somewhere else. Maybe out of the city."

She shook her head. "If you are going to escape, you're going to need some help. You can't even walk out of here under your own power."

Gabriel grimaced and nodded.

"Stay put. I'll rustle you up something to eat."

"Thanks."

When she returned a few minutes later, she had a cheese string and a yogurt cup. Gabriel looked at the proffered snacks and then her face. "No dairy. I can't eat that."

"You need a snack. This is what we've got."

"I can't eat those."

"What about the yogurt? It's predigested. It's not dairy anymore."

"No," Gabriel shook his head. "I can't!"

"Honestly!" She rolled her eyes and stalked back out.

Gabriel didn't know if that meant that she was going to look for another snack, or that he was screwed. He pulled the blankets around him. He was starting to shiver in spite of the extra blanket, the hospital gown clammy against his skin.

He was beginning to think that Nurse Barrett had given up and was just going to let him crash, and then Nurse Lee came in.

"Sugar for you!" she announced. She put an applesauce cup and plastic spoon down on his rolling table and also pulled out a needle and vial. "Which arm?"

Gabriel pulled his left out from under the covers and held it out for her. Lee tapped his arm along the vein and didn't bother with a tourniquet. She filled the needle and expertly slid it into his vein, hitting the bulls-eye the first time. Gabriel watched as she pushed the plunger in.

"There you go. That should help. Now eat. It's a couple of hours until dinner and this is all I could find."

"Thanks."

She nodded and put a bandage on the injection site. Gabriel suddenly remembered his scraped elbow and held up his arm to show it to her.

"Can you clean that too?"

She held his arm still and took a closer look. "What did you do that for?"

He gave her an embarrassed smile. "I was injured in my daring escape attempt."

Lee laughed. She got some alcohol wipes out of the side table drawer and cleaned the graze.

Gabriel gasped at the burn. "Oh! Ow! Oh, that hurts."

"That'll teach you not to go running away. Now, nap time. You eat your applesauce and stay in bed, or I'm going to get the doctor's permission to sedate you. Then you can sleep until Friday."

It was the first day that Renata was able to be up and around. Gabriel didn't know where she got all her energy. Most people with a punctured lung would have been happy to stay in bed for a few days. But maybe it was because she was used to functioning with so little cellular energy, a little thing like traumatic injury couldn't slow her down. She pushed a wheelchair into Gabriel's room. Her oxygen tank was on the seat of the wheelchair and her IV hung on a pole attached to the back of the chair, and she was pushing it instead of sitting in it. She had a lot more stamina than Gabriel did. But then, from what he could tell, she was actually in psych for psychological issues, instead of for the amorphous 'evaluation' that Gabriel was there for, which seemed to mean taking him off of all of his meds to see how sick it would make him, and then putting him back on all of them, all for no particular reason.

"Ding, ding, trolley coming through," Renata announced, in a mock-British accent.

"Hi!"

"Hi yourself. So, you enjoy your freedom yesterday?"

"No, not much."

"Yeah." Renata removed the oxygen canister from her wheelchair and sat herself down. "Getting out of the ward is one thing. Getting out of the hospital isn't such a simple thing."

"Why didn't you mention that you can't get back out of the stairwell without a security card?" Gabriel demanded.

"I dunno. You didn't ask. I figured you knew."

"I didn't. Thought I'd be home free once I got out."

"Nope. You gotta make sure you've got a swipe card too. Nurses leave them lying around all the time."

"Well, I guess that's it for my brilliant escape plans. I'm not going to get out again between now and when the social worker comes."

"Yeah." Renata reached for Gabriel's table, which had been pushed to the side. "Hey. They left your chart here."

Usually, the ubiquitous clipboard was carried in and out of the room by the nurse or doctor and kept at the nursing station between visits. This time, there had been a ruckus in the hallway, with an old man yelling and cursing. The nurse had left to see what was going on and had not returned.

Renata picked up the chart and started flipping through it.

"Hey, you can't look at that," Gabriel objected. "That's private!"

"Well, you have a look, then. Usually, they won't let you see it."

She held it out to him. Gabriel hesitated. But why not? It was his chart; he had a right to see his own information. He took it from Renata, glancing at the door to make sure that no one was watching. He scanned the front page, but it was boring, mostly just vital signs and a few squiggles that he wasn't sure of. He thought they might be shorthand for medications and dosages. He flipped back through the stack of papers, reading a few words in cramped handwriting wherever it was legible. Then he skipped straight to the back. The earliest records, from when he was first admitted. He looked over the chaotic, disorganized notes in several different hands.

"Munchhausen by Proxy?" he read aloud.

"Yeah, that makes sense," Renata said. "Means they suspect your mom of trying to make you sick, to get attention and sympathy. It's an easy way to get any medically fragile kid away from his parents."

"Why would they think she was trying to make me sick?"

"They don't. Not really. But that's what they tell the social worker and the judge. Yes, this kid is dangerously ill, and we think that most or all the symptoms are being caused by the mother poisoning him. So he must be taken away immediately, for his own safety. Easy to keep mom out of the picture, too, because they need to have you by yourself to evaluate which symptoms are real and which ones are being caused by something she's doing."

"That's crazy!"

"Hence the psych ward," Renata laughed.

"No, I mean, it's crazy that anyone would think that."

"Think about it. Mito kids have a lot of bizarre, seemingly unrelated symptoms. There is no 'usual' course, they're all different, and it can affect every system in the body." She straightened up taller, trying to see what else was on the clipboard. "The other thing that they'll say is that it's psychosomatic. Does it say that?"

"Psychosomatic?" Gabriel searched the page. "Why would it say that? If she was poisoning me, then it wouldn't be psychosomatic."

"Why not? She could be making you sick by giving you something, but she could be making you more sick by suggesting things too. The body does what you tell it to."

"She doesn't do that! She'd never do that!"

"It could be very subtle," Renata said. "You wouldn't even realize she was doing it."

"My mom is not trying to make me sick!"

Renata shrugged. "Maybe not," she agreed cheerfully. "But could you *prove* it?"

Gabriel opened his mouth to argue, then closed it again. How could he prove that someone wasn't telling him he was sicker than he was? It wasn't like testing for arsenic. How could doctors even tell if a symptom was psychosomatic? And if it was, how could they tell where the thought came from? They couldn't trace people's thoughts.

He looked back down at the clipboard and skimmed through the words and phrases that he could read. "My mom isn't making me sick. They think because she changed my diet and supplements that she's making me sick? I was sick before that. She was helping me to feel better."

"Munchhausen works every time. Kids with Munchhausen by Proxy parents get better and sicker all the time. Drives the doctors crazy, because they can't sort out what's going on. Every time the kid starts to get better, his health takes another nose dive. You fit the pattern, right? You get better, you get worse, you get new symptoms. You go to the hospital; you get better. You go home, you get sick and have to come back again..."

Gabriel shook his head. "No..."

She reached to take the clipboard from him, but Gabriel pulled it back. He didn't want to share his private information with her. Renata leaned back again. She scratched at the bandaging under her gown, wincing and shifting her position.

"They've got her. She's never going to be able to get you back. She wouldn't put you in the mito clinic. She wouldn't follow the protocol at the weight clinic. Your health keeps getting better and worse. Classic Munchhausen by Proxy, and that means they can never give you back to her."

Gabriel pressed the button to call a nurse. Renata looked at him, frowning. Gabriel rested the clipboard in his lap and put his head back, closing his eyes.

"Are you okay? You sick?"

Gabriel didn't answer. One of the nurses came in after a few minutes. "You called? What do you need?"

Gabriel opened his eyes. "I want to go to sleep. I want to be alone."

The nurse looked at Gabriel, then at Renata. She picked the clipboard up from Gabriel's lap. "Let's go, Miss Vega."

Renata didn't make a move, staring at Gabriel.

"I'm tired," Gabriel repeated.

The nurse grasped the handles on Renata's wheelchair and turned her around. Renata didn't say good-bye.

CHAPTER EIGHT

H E FELT LIKE HE should be excited to leave the psych ward, but Gabriel just felt bad about it. He didn't want to go to a foster family that he had never met before. He was worried about all of the things that could happen to him there. Not only would he not have his mother to take care of him, but all of the doctors and nurses would be gone too. How could a family that he had never met before, without any medical training, be expected to take care of him properly?

He hated the psych ward, but he was surprised to realize that it had become sort of a cocoon for him during the time that he had been there. He didn't like it, and he wanted Keisha, but at least he felt safe and protected. If something really bad happened, they would be able to look after him. Getting ready to leave the hospital, he had stomach cramps and a sort of vertigo, like he was going to fall off the edge of a cliff.

Gabriel waited all morning for Renata to come visit him and say good-bye, but she didn't. He felt a little like he needed to apologize for kicking her out the previous day, but he was also outraged about the things that she had said. Now that he wasn't going to have to listen to her craziness anymore, he felt bad about leaving her behind.

Breakfast came and went. Lunch came and went. No one seemed to know what time he was being moved. Gabriel was on edge the whole time, his whole body tense with waiting.

Finally, he heard high heels clicking down the hallway. No nurse would ever wear heels to work. And visitors, the few that came to the psych ward, were usually casually dressed, in walking shoes or sneakers. The high heels approached his doorway and then stopped, Mrs. Scott framed in the opening.

"Well, Gabriel, are you ready to get out of here?"

It was weird wearing street clothes again. They felt scratchy and tight and uncomfortable. But they also felt more… secure and protective. Gabriel ran his finger down a seam of the jeans.

"I'm ready."

"Let's go, then."

She waited while Gabriel turned, sliding his feet off the side of the bed, and got to his feet. He wasn't sure how they were expecting him to be able to walk all the way by himself. But there was a nurse behind Carol Scott, shooing her out of the way and pushing a wheelchair in.

"I don't think he needs that, does he?" the social worker asked.

"It's routine for discharges, especially if they have any kind of mobility challenges. We wouldn't want Mr. Tate tripping and injuring himself on the way out."

Gabriel sat down when she positioned the chair behind him. At least he wouldn't have to embarrass himself by collapsing on the way to the car.

"But he doesn't need it after he leaves here," Carol said. "He can get around on his own."

"He'll get tired fast," the nurse said as if Gabriel wasn't even there. "He can walk around if he puts his mind to it, and he'll continue to get more stamina now that he's on the proper medications, but he's still going to tire quickly."

Carol nodded. "Good. The house isn't wheelchair user accessible."

Gabriel swallowed as the nurse pushed him out of the hospital room. Was it not wheelchair user accessible because there were a couple of steps up to the front door? Or was there a whole flight of stairs? Maybe even an apartment, with three flights of stairs to get to it. But Mrs. Scott had said 'house.' So it probably wasn't an apartment. And most apartments had elevators.

Goosebumps prickled on Gabriel's arms when the nurse swiped her security card and pushed him into the elevator. He was getting out! Despite his fear of the unknown, he was overtaken by feelings of relief and excitement over finally getting free of the secure ward. He turned his head to look at the nurse behind him.

"Will you tell Renata I said good-bye?" he asked, suddenly regretting that he hadn't made the journey down the hall to tell her himself. He should have put his annoyance aside and just done the right thing. Friends didn't treat each other like that.

The nurse nodded and smiled. "I'll tell her."

"Good. Thanks."

"You made some friends at the hospital?" Carol asked. She was wearing a brilliant yellow blazer and skirt. Keisha would have liked it. Would have looked good in it. Social workers usually wore tweeds, plaids, and muted colors. Gabriel had never met one who was so flashy.

"A couple," he said. He looked away from her, watching the floor lights count down slowly. "Other kids with mito."

"Mito?" she repeated. "Oh, your disease. Interesting."

"It's a rare disorder." Gabriel looked back at her again to see her reaction. "Why do you think they would take us all away and put us in psych?"

She didn't look at him. "I'm sure I don't know," she murmured. "They had their reasons. It's a small world, isn't it?"

Gabriel frowned, trying to figure out how 'small world' explained anything.

They got down to the main floor, and the nurse pushed Gabriel right out the big front doors. "Where are you parked?"

"I'm just here, in the loading zone." Mrs. Scott gestured to her car. Not a station wagon. Gabriel knew stamps better than cars, but even he could appreciate the sleek lines of the aqua blue car sitting there with its blinkers on.

The nurse applied the brakes, and Mrs. Scott unlocked and opened the car door for Gabriel. Gabriel only had to take one step and turn around to get into it.

"Bye, Gabriel," the nurse said with a smile. "You take care of yourself, okay? Be well."

Gabriel nodded. There was a lump in his throat, but he wasn't sure why. He was happy to be leaving. No more monitoring, no more security, no more arguing over meals and snacks and meds. It would be better for him. Back on almost exactly the same chemical cocktail he'd been on before being apprehended, he would get his strength back, so that he could live a normal life. As normal as he could, at a foster home. There was no reason to be sad about leaving the hospital, or sentimental over a few kind words from a nurse on his departure.

He pulled the door shut.

"Are you excited?" Carol Scott asked, after pulling out into traffic.

"Not excited... I'm glad to be out of the hospital..." he hesitated about how much to say to her. "I'm... kind of nervous."

"Of course you are. Anyone would be. Don't feel badly about that. But everything is going to be okay." She flashed him a bright white smile. "You're going to like the Foegels, and they are going to take good care of you. They are an experienced foster family, and they are used to kids with medical needs."

Renata had been right about that part.

"Do they know about mito? Are they in the city?"

"Oh, yes. They're familiar with mito and have taken care of kids at the clinic before. They're a little ways away, but close enough to get you back here for check-ups and treatments."

Two more checkmarks. Considering how many times the nurses had told Gabriel not to believe anything that Renata said, she certainly seemed to be right a lot.

"Are all the kids at the mito clinic in foster care?"

A small line formed between Carol's brows as she navigated through the traffic. She made a clicking noise with her tongue, and her mouth made a few different shapes before she answered him. "Of course they're not all in foster care. There are lots of kids at the clinic. I have no way of knowing *how many* are in custody."

"But you've taken mito kids away before, to get them into the program?"

"That's not the way it works. Most parents want their kids in the program. Why wouldn't they? They want their kids to be as healthy as possible. DFS never removes a child just to put them into a voluntary program. That would be… unethical."

She looked unhappy, her pretty lipsticked mouth forming a frown. She tapped her nails on the steering wheel. After a few minutes of silence, she turned the radio on and found a light rock station. If the foster home was 'a ways away,' they were going to have to either get used to the silence or find something to talk about.

"The mito clinic…" Gabriel started, "…is it an experimental program? I mean… there's not an established protocol for mito… it's all individualized."

"It's not experimental… I wouldn't use that word. They are at the forefront of research… they have grants to run drug trials that are vital for kids with mitochondrial disorder to live a normal life…"

Gabriel wondered how she could consider that *not* experimental.

"These drugs have been *proven* to be very helpful for patients with mitochondrial disease," Carol explained. "Life altering."

That sounded exciting and for a split-second, Gabriel wondered what it would be like to live a life without physical limitations. What if he had all the energy he needed to get through the day, doing whatever he liked? What if he didn't have to rest so much, watch what he ate, and to budget out his limited energy for daily living tasks? What if he could run and play, maybe even be on a sports team?

Gabriel tried to pull his mind away from these thoughts. It was never going to happen that way. He had to live with his broken mitochondria his entire life, however long that was. "If they're proven, then why are they still doing trials? Why aren't they on the market?"

This answer seemed to come to Mrs. Scott more easily. "The regulating authorities require vigorous drug testing. Drugs can remain in trials like this for years before the government approves them. Which means that the only way to get them is for you to participate in the trials."

That sounded reasonable. Even if they found a cure for mito, heart disease, or cancer; even if it blew everyone away with its effectiveness in the initial drug trials, they wouldn't be able to put it on the market right away. They would still have to test it out to make sure it didn't cause horrible side effects for some people. To make sure that there weren't negative long-term effects, or didn't actually make the disease more resistant, stronger the next time it came around.

"I get it," he said.

Carol gave a smile of relief, turning toward him for an instant to express her approval before facing forward and concentrating on the traffic again. "Won't it be great?" she asked him. "Wouldn't you like to live like a normal kid, without all these issues?"

"If it works," Gabriel said cautiously. "It might not work for everyone."

Gabriel kept an eye on the dashboard clock. It took about an hour and a half to get to the Foegels' house in one of the outlying small towns. 'Bedroom communities,' Keisha always called these suburbs. It always made Gabriel feel kind of weird about them, like the bedroom and what happened in it was the focus of these homes. They weren't places to work, or eat, or entertain. Just bedrooms.

But the house that Mrs. Scott pulled up to was definitely not all bedroom. It was a big house with faux-brick siding. It looked like it had started out as a rectangular bungalow, but had been added onto and renovated four or five times, with rooms and wings jutting out in various directions that didn't quite match the original homestead. The sidewalk was long and sloped upward, and the front door was just one step up, not a whole flight like Gabriel had worried. As Gabriel got out of the car, a woman opened the front door and called out hello to them.

She was a medium-sized brunette with mid-length hair that curved around her face. A white woman. Gabriel hadn't even thought about race when he was wondering what kind of home he would be put into, but he realized now that he had pictured a black family. Father a bit round, mother petite like Keisha, but strong and good-humored. Maybe one or two little kids of their own, and one of those side rooms would be Gabriel's. But the mother did not fit the vague picture in his head. Probably nothing else would either.

Gabriel made his way up the sidewalk. There was no handrail to hold onto. Gabriel had been working on walking, but he always had something to steady him and take his weight when his legs got tired. Walking up the sidewalk was like running a marathon after training for a 5K. Or he imagined it was, having never run either a marathon or a 5K. Or even a one hundred meter.

Carol walked behind him, and Gabriel could feel her impatience at his slow progress. She didn't say anything, but she was standing too close behind him, dogging his heels. When Gabriel was about halfway up the walk, the foster mom walked down to meet him.

"Is there anything I can do to help, Gabriel? Do you need…" she looked around helplessly for inspiration. "I could bring a chair for you to rest on for a few minutes… or we could sit on the lawn here together and have a little snack or something. Like a picnic."

Gabriel tried to laugh, but it was an effort to do anything on top of walking. "Don't know if I could get back up."

"Oh." She measured him with her eyes, but she could see that even though Gabriel was skinny, he was taller than she was, and even together, she and Mrs. Scott might not be able to get him back on his feet.

"Maybe if that chair's not too heavy, I could lean on it… use it like a walker…" Gabriel suggested.

She nodded and went back into the house. Gabriel struggled to keep moving. His legs were vibrating with fatigue. Mrs. Foegel was quick, rushing back out of the house with a kitchen chair. Not a heavy wooden one, but one with tubular aluminum legs that made it lightweight. She put it down in front of Gabriel, and he leaned on it, taking a deep breath.

The longer he took, the more tired he was going to get, so Gabriel moved forward as quickly as he was able, shuffling the chair forward, leaning his weight on it, and dragging his feet another step each, then repeating the arduous process. By the time he got to the end of the sidewalk, he was huffing and puffing, drenched in sweat, with black spots pulsing in front of his eyes. He couldn't get the chair up that last step, and he couldn't raise his feet high enough even with the chair to lean on. He used the chair to lower himself to the sidewalk and crawled over the last step and over the doorstep into the house.

For a few seconds, he just lay on the floor, exhausted. He'd hoped not to embarrass himself, but to appear as strong as a normal kid. He'd failed miserably at that. Gabriel pushed himself back up to a sitting position and leaned against the wall.

"Are you okay?" asked Mrs. Foegel. "Can I get you a drink? Help you up?"

"A drink," Gabriel agreed between breaths. "Not milk."

"Oh, okay."

She disappeared down the hall. Gabriel didn't look at Carol Scott, acutely aware that she was standing there staring down at him.

"I need my braces," Gabriel told her. "And crutches. And sometimes a wheelchair."

"The doctor said you didn't need those things. You just need to believe in yourself and build up the muscles with exercise."

"Yeah," Gabriel sneered. "I just got this way by being lazy."

Mrs. Foegel returned with a glass of orange juice. Gabriel took a long sip.

"Nobody thinks you're lazy," Mrs. Foegel said. "We can see how difficult that was for you. I will talk to the doctor about what we can do for your mobility issues."

Gabriel drained the glass. He looked around. He was at the edge of the living room or family room. With the last of his energy, he crawled over to the couch and climbed onto it.

"Gabriel… Gabriel, it's time to wake up…"

Gabriel opened his eyes and blinked, trying to clear the stickiness and figure out where he was. He looked around the unfamiliar room, and into the unfamiliar face. White face, brunette hair curving around it. Mrs. Foegel. Gabriel rubbed his eyes. He was curled up in a ball on the couch, with a thick, fuzzy blanket tucked around him. He didn't remember the blanket.

"Hi," he greeted.

"Hi." Mrs. Foegel gave him a genuine, warm smile. "Have a nice nap?"

"Yeah."

"Good. It's time for supper. Do you think you can join us?"

Gabriel straightened and stretched. He rubbed his cramped legs for a minute and nodded. He used the couch for support and managed to make it to his feet.

"Bravo," Mrs. Foegel applauded. "Why don't you lean on me? It's not far."

Gabriel was hesitant to touch a stranger, much less lean on her for support. But she had offered, and the only other option was to lean on the walls. He ended up doing both, holding onto his new foster mother and leaning on the wall so that he was supported on both sides. They walked toward other voices, and Gabriel saw the other members of the family as they entered the dining room. Mrs. Foegel helped him into a chair. Gabriel hunched over, resting his body.

Mr. Foegel looked older than Mrs. Foegel. He was a tall man, graying, with glasses and the beginning of a double chin, even though he didn't have a big belly. He was talking to a little black boy with tight black curls, maybe four or five years old. There was a baby carrier on the end of the table, containing a fat blond infant with Coke-bottle glasses that made her look bug-eyed. And a skinny girl of about eight, also blond, her hair stringy, whose unfocused gaze made Gabriel wonder if she was blind.

"This is Gabriel," Mrs. Foegel introduced. "Gabriel, we didn't get a chance to talk before you zonked out. I'm Heather. This is Matt," she motioned to her husband. "Josiah, Luce, and baby Alex."

Gabriel nodded. "Hi."

"Welcome to our home, Gabriel," Matt Foegel said cheerfully. "We're glad to have you!"

Gabriel didn't know what to say. He certainly wasn't happy to be there. "Is your name German?" he asked, remembering Skyler's comment at the hospital. "Um—for bird?"

"That's very smart of you. Yes, it is! Now how did you figure that out? Do you know any German?"

"No, just a friend. He mentioned it."

"Well, you're right. It's a variant of Vogel, that's the German spelling, but I guess they pronounce Vs as Fs. So that's how it was translated when they emigrated."

Gabriel nodded politely. Mrs. Foegel was passing the supper dishes around, though Gabriel was the only child dishing up for himself. Mrs. Foegel put a few bits of food on Luce's plate, and Mr. Foegel put food on Josiah's plate, carefully ensuring that nothing touched. The baby was making gurgling noises, and after the serving dishes had all been passed around, Heather Foegel got out a bottle of formula and connected the tube on the end with a tube that she pulled out from inside baby Alex's sleeper. She set the bottle down, made sure it was flowing properly and turned her attention to her own plate.

"Oh, I hope this doesn't gross you out," she said, seeing Gabriel's gaze on the baby's feeding apparatus. "She has a gastric tube for feeding. Some people would think it wasn't appropriate to do at the table with everyone else…"

Gabriel blinked. "Why wouldn't you feed her at the table?"

She made a little shrug, smiling.

"My friend at the hospital had one of those. I never saw her use it, but she showed it to me."

"That's unusual for a teenager. But sometimes there are certain conditions, or if a child never learns to eat properly after having had one…"

"Yeah. She had mito, like me. But I can eat. Most things." He looked down at the meat and vegetables he had put on his plate. "Did they tell you that I have allergies? And I have to have snacks to keep my blood sugar stable? They hospital had trouble with giving me stuff I could eat."

"They gave me some guidelines. But you'd better give me more details later, so I don't poison you."

Gabriel nodded and began to eat. He watched the smaller children. The little girl paid no attention to anyone, but he saw that he was wrong about her being blind. She could definitely see the food on her plate. She picked at the food and held it close in front of her eyes before eating anything. Josiah, the boy, chattered away, eating copious amounts and making Mr. and Mrs. Foegel laugh.

"So why don't you tell me about your family, Gabriel?" Heather suggested. "Are you an only child?"

"Yes. My dad is overseas, mostly. We don't see him much. So it's really just me and my mom."

"I bet you're close."

Gabriel stared down at his food, not letting himself think about how much he missed her.

"We'll try to get some visitations set up," Heather assured him. "You should at least be able to have supervised visits with her. Now that you're out of the hospital and ready to live your life."

Gabriel thought of a hundred things to say. But anything that he said would just bring the tears. Or anger; and Heather didn't deserve that. She had been kind and understanding with him so far. She said that she would try to get him visitation, so it wouldn't do for him to be whining to her about how he had so far been denied any visits by the hospital or DFS. She obviously knew that much already.

"My mom—" Josiah piped up. "My mom is visiting me next weekend. I get to go to McDonalds!"

Gabriel wasn't sure whether Josiah was more excited about his mother or McDonalds. "That's very nice."

"That's tomorrow, Josiah," Matt told the little boy.

"Tomorrow? I get to see her tomorrow?" He bounced in his seat, wreathed in smiles. "Oh, boy! I get to see her tomorrow!"

They all laughed at his excitement.

Gabriel could hardly wait until he could say the same.

After dinner, Matt took Gabriel to his bedroom, which Gabriel was relieved to find was on the main floor and not down in the basement. He glanced around the blue room, feeling suddenly queasy. It was obvious which bed was empty and which one was taken. But it was also obvious from the posters and the items jumbled on the top of the dresser that the other occupant of the room was not a five-year-old boy. Gabriel looked at Matt, feeling a frown creasing his forehead.

"Your roommate is Collin," Matt offered. "He wasn't around for dinner tonight because he had an away game."

"What does he play?" Gabriel sat down on the neatly-made bed, looking at the ominous posters on the other side of the room.

"Football. He's quite good. He won't be back until late. Depending on what time you head to bed, you might not see him until morning."

Gabriel had had enough run-ins with football players and other jocks when he went to school. Now he was stuck in the same room as one of them. But surely DFS and the Foegels wouldn't have put a skinny, defenseless, medically fragile teen together with a bully who was known to be abusive? Not all football players were like the jerks who had teased and bullied Gabriel in the past. That was just a stereotype.

"I know you had a nap before supper," Matt said, studying Gabriel's face. "But you're still looking pretty wiped out. Do you want to have a rest? Early bedtime? Is there something else you need?"

Gabriel looked around the room. "I think I'll just lay down for a while. Maybe find a book or watch TV or something later...?"

"Sure. Now, clothes..." Matt frowned. "Heather can give you a hand later. We try to keep a few things on hand, in different sizes, for when we get new kids who might not have anything. Sometimes they arrive with nothing more than a nightgown, or t-shirt and boxers. I'm not sure what we've got. You're taller than I expected, but you're thin. Any of Collin's things will just swim on you. But Heather is in charge of clothes. She'll see what we've got for tonight and can pick up a few things tomorrow."

"Okay." The segue hadn't done much more than reinforce to Gabriel how much bigger than he his roommate was.

"All right. Give a shout if you need anything," Matt said and walked back out of the room.

He had thought that he would wake up after an hour or so and find a book like he had told Matt, but the next time Gabriel woke up, the room was completely dark. He could tell from his sluggishness that he had been asleep for a long time.

There were voices and banging down the hallway, and then a large figure filled the doorway and flipped the light switch on. Gabriel covered his eyes, blinded. He squinted through the cracks between his fingers.

"Don't forget that the new boy is here today," Heather called from across the house. "Try not to wake him up."

The other boy put down his big bag of equipment with a crash and turned to look at Gabriel's bed. He swore.

"Sorry, man. I forgot."

He thumped over to the lamp on the dresser and turned it on, then turned off the bright overhead light. Gabriel pulled his hand away from his face. "Thanks."

"Yeah."

Collin began to shed his clothes. "I thought they said you were fifteen."

"Uh-huh." Gabriel rubbed his eyes. "I am."

"You're fifteen? Sheesh. Lightweight, are you?"

"I've been sick," Gabriel explained. It wasn't as if he'd been built before his stay at the hospital. But it wasn't lying to say that he'd been sick, and let Collin think what he liked about how hefty Gabriel might have been before his illness.

"Yeah, they mentioned that."

Collin stripped all the way down to his shorts. Leaving his clothes on the floor and not stopping to brush his teeth before bed, he pulled back the covers of his bed and climbed in. He reached over and turned the lamp off, plunging the room into darkness.

Gabriel closed his eyes, expecting to fall back asleep immediately. But instead, he lay there awake and restless, the smell of Collin's sweaty clothes and football equipment taking over the room. Collin's breathing was slow, rough, and regular. He'd obviously been spent by his game and travel. Gabriel tried to imagine what it would be like to have that kind of energy every day.

CHAPTER NINE

IT WAS EASIER TO forget about Renata's crazy conspiracy theories once Gabriel was out of the hospital and settling into the new foster home. Everything was so different from the two places that he had grown up—home with Keisha and at the hospital—that Gabriel was constantly exhausted by the mental stress. He was doing better getting around the house without help. He learned how far he could go at one time, and established resting places in each room, or on both sides of each room.

He pushed all of Renata's dire predictions and theories out of his mind and just tried to settle into the new life. Heather promised that she was working on getting him visitations with his mother, and Gabriel believed her. School was out of the question to begin with. Heather said that once he was onto the protocol at the mito clinic, he should have enough energy to attend school. Until then, she arranged for a school outreach program that brought tutors to the house twice a week, and he had reading and assignments to do in between.

"I couldn't homeschool myself," Heather declared. "Especially not advanced math. That would just kill me. I was never very good at school and have hardly cracked a book since."

She was a nice lady and seemed bright, so Gabriel was surprised to hear such a thing from her. Keisha had always been so vocal about lifelong learning and upgrading your skills, and insisted that Gabriel spend as much time as his health would allow on schoolwork and studies. She would stay up long after he was in bed, studying his textbooks so that she would be able to teach him or help him as he advanced through each subject. What she didn't know, she learned, and while sometimes Gabriel caught her mistakes and pointed them out, she was usually one step ahead of him.

"Math isn't bad," he told Heather. "I like it better than reading."

"Well, at least reading is something I do every day. I don't have anything to do with math if I can help it."

Gabriel shook his head and focused back on his reading assignment. He didn't have to like it, Keisha always said, he just had to buckle down and do it.

Heather answered the phone and was chattering away as she moved from room to room with the phone tucked into her shoulder and a laundry basket on her hip, picking up discarded clothing and toys that needed to go back to the children's rooms. Collin and the little kids were at school, so it was just Heather and Gabriel and baby Alex at home. Alex was sleeping or talking to herself in the crib. Gabriel immersed himself in his lesson.

"That was the clinic," Heather announced, coming back into the room. "We've got an appointment for you for Wednesday afternoon."

Gabriel looked up from his work and focused on her for a minute, replaying what she had just said in his mind to process it. He nodded.

"Okay."

"It will take us a couple of hours to drive in, so we'll need to leave right after lunch. Bring your books with you; you may as well get your work done in the car or in the waiting room instead of wasting your time and being bored."

"Okay."

Heather bent down to get Gabriel's attention and look him in the eye. She smiled widely. "Aren't you excited? These new drugs that they're using at the clinic are really making a difference. If I was you, I'd be super excited about having the chance to try them out."

Gabriel forced a smile. "Yeah. That would be good," he agreed.

He wasn't going to set his hopes on the drugs making a big difference in his case. They wouldn't work for everybody. And if it was a proper drug trial, then not everybody would be getting the new drug. Some people had to be in the control group and get a placebo. And with his luck, he'd get a placebo. And then not even get the placebo effect.

When they called it a 'clinic,' Gabriel had pictured the Lantern Clinic as a little, dark, research facility in the back room of some mall or professional building. Like the walk-in clinics in his neighborhood or the cheap vet clinic farther down the block. So he was stunned to see the Lantern Clinic when they pulled into the parking lot. It was a big, modern building with lots of glass, an atrium in the front with a working waterfall, a juice bar, coffee shop, and what looked like a spa for middle-aged women. Everything was sparkling new and impressive.

"Whoa," Gabriel said, looking around the lobby. "This is… just… wow!"

Heather nodded, laughing. "Not quite what you expected, hey? This place always blows me away."

"My mom could never have afforded to bring me here," Gabriel realized. He sat on a bench to get his energy back and Heather waited patiently.

"They pay for participation in the trials. You don't have to pay them; it's the other way around. They pay you to come here and be pampered like this."

Gabriel remembered the millions of dollars that Renata claimed the clinic got for arranging for patients to participate in the trials. After seeing the Lantern Clinic, he could see where she had gotten the idea. They certainly weren't hiding their wealth.

"How many kids are in the trials?"

"Somewhere around forty new kids per year. I think that's the number that was in the brochure. And they do long-term follow-up too; I'm not sure how long they monitor the patients. But forty active at any one time."

"I didn't think mito was that common."

"There's over a million people just in the valley. Mito occurs in something like one in eight thousand…" Heather trailed off, shrugging. "Well, it seems like there'd be enough."

Gabriel tried to calculate it in his head. "A hundred twenty-five," he said, frowning, "in every million."

"Something like that."

"Forty new per year?" Gabriel repeated. "Even if you took the population of the whole state, you'd run out in a few years. And it's only kids, right? How can they find enough kids for the trials?"

"I never stopped to think about it. But they come from all over, even out of state. As long as you can make it back here about once a month, it doesn't matter how far away you live…"

Gabriel shook his head. He got to his feet again, and they walked to the elevator, where there was another bench to rest on while they waited for the glass-walled elevator to make its leisurely way down to the atrium level to pick them up. The elevator took them up to the fifth floor. Gabriel looked at the list of doctors and departments on the wall.

"This place is huge!"

"Yes, it is. This way."

Heather led him to the waiting room for Dr. De Klerk. It wasn't like the little waiting rooms at the doctor's offices that he usually went to, with the chairs crammed right up against each other and mismatched children's toys in a jumble on the floor. It was open and spacious, with white moldings around the ceiling, comfy padded chairs, a series of children's playhouses with brightly painted walls, dark green plants with broad leaves, and another waterfall, a smaller one, that provided a tranquil background for the waiting patients and parents. Heather motioned to the chairs, and Gabriel sat down. She went to the receptionist desk to check Gabriel in. The receptionist pulled out a file that had already been made up.

"It looks like DFS, Dr. Seymour, and the hospital have provided us with everything that we need." The pretty receptionist looked across the room at Gabriel. "I think that we can probably handle Gabriel. You're welcome to go down and make use of the spa while we're working him up."

She handed Heather some kind of coupon. Heather looked down at it. She went over to Gabriel, looking uncertain. "I'll stay with you if you like, Gabriel…"

"No, you can go," he encouraged. "I'll be fine."

Heather looked down at baby Alex in the carrier. "Well then, come along Alex, it looks like we get a day at the spa." She smiled at Gabriel. "They've got my number, so you just have them call if you need anything. I'll be off getting my nails done."

They weighed and measured Gabriel, took his heart rate, blood pressure, blood sugar, and had him walk on a treadmill, which didn't work out too well. They ran every other test that Gabriel could think of, and some that he'd never even heard of. It was exhausting, but the nurses whisked him from one place to another in a wheelchair. They at least didn't act like the psych nurses had, like he was pretending or playing for attention. They just took it in stride.

After a few hours, Gabriel was delivered in his wheelchair to Dr. De Klerk's office. It was a luxurious dark-wood room, with shelves and shelves of hard-bound books. There was a big gold clock on the desk, with a glass base that allowed him to see all the complex clockworks inside. Gabriel stared at it, mesmerized.

Dr. De Klerk had silver hair, a narrow face, and a mouth that pointed downward with deep wrinkle lines. He was tall. He leaned back in his big leather chair looking through wire-frame glasses set low on his nose at the file that the nurse had handed to him. Dr. De Klerk didn't look like the evil super-villain that Renata had described. More like somebody's grumpy grandpa or the next-door neighbor who didn't like kids playing in the yard. Gabriel watched the whirling clock parts, waiting.

Eventually, Dr. De Klerk spoke. "Well, Mr. Tate, how would you like to feel better?"

Gabriel shrugged without looking at him.

"You don't want to?" De Klerk pressed.

"I don't know if anything will help."

"We have some very promising medical trials. We've seen some astounding results."

Gabriel didn't want to think about that. He didn't want to get his hopes up. He didn't want someone else's normal; just his own. He considered his answer carefully. This might be his only opportunity to drive his own fate.

"What if I promise to participate in your trials if you'll let me go home to my mom?"

De Klerk took off his reading glasses and looked at Gabriel. "That's an interesting proposition, Mr. Tate. But here's the thing. You can't make a contract with me. You're not of age. I don't need your agreement to participate in the program. I only need your guardian's and I've got that."

Gabriel swallowed. "If I went back to my mom, I'd be closer to you. And I wouldn't cause any trouble; I'd do everything you said."

"I am not the person who makes decisions on your custody. But your mother has unfortunately already proven that she can't follow the protocol that she is given. Her decision to tweak it and make unsupported changes has put your health in serious jeopardy. I could not, in good conscience, recommend her as your caregiver."

"I was getting better with her changes. I was putting on weight and feeling better. I had more energy..."

"Having more energy was an illusion. A placebo effect. Your tests tell a completely different story."

Gabriel's voice rose in anger. "I want to go back to my mom! It was not a placebo; I was doing lots better at home. She doesn't have Munchhausen by Proxy. My sickness isn't imagined, and neither were the improvements! You don't know what you're talking about!"

Dr. De Klerk pushed Gabriel's file away from him slightly. "Sounds like your mother isn't the only one who thinks she is more qualified than the doctors. Tell me, how long did you go to medical school?"

It was a rhetorical question and Gabriel had no answer or rebuttal.

"I have dedicated my life to helping kids like you, Gabriel. I know more about mito than any person on the planet. I have a more effective treatment than is offered anywhere else. Do you know I have a boy who is flown in from Germany every two weeks? Because his family understands that I have the only effective treatment in the world! Your internet research doesn't even begin to touch on what I know."

Gabriel watched the inner workings of the clock. Dr. De Klerk might have a huge ego, but what he said was compelling. Where else would Gabriel be able to get such expert care? The dirty little clinics and doctors' offices that he was used to couldn't compare to the huge, glassed-in Lantern Clinic. Most of the doctors he had dealt with over the years could barely even remember what a mitochondrion was, and Keisha had had to educate herself in order to be able to explain it to the doctors and get Gabriel adequate care. There was no comparison to De Klerk's facility and his knowledge and training.

"I'm sure you want to feel better," De Klerk said in a quieter voice. "All the kids who come through here are desperate to feel better. To be able to walk and run like typical kids. To be able to go to school and study and play like their friends. I can help you with that. And there's no cost to your family. We will give you everything you need to be successful."

Gabriel nodded.

"Good. I want you to sign this form." De Klerk opened a drawer and drew out a single-page form. He slid it across the table and put a fat, shiny pen on top of it.

"I thought you said I can't sign a contract," Gabriel reminded him.

"This isn't legally binding. This is a personal agreement, between you and me, that you will follow your treatment plan. I realize that it would not hold up in court. But you will be morally bound. You know that a man keeps his promises. And no matter what happens, you will know that you signed this. That you made a promise to me."

Gabriel looked down at the paper entitled 'Patient's Bill of Rights.' It didn't seem to be so much what his rights as a patient were, but the patient promising to follow the protocol and do what he was told. He chewed on the inside of his cheek, frowning. Dr. De Klerk sat there waiting silently.

Gabriel wondered where Heather was. She said that he could call her. Maybe she was even back in the waiting room now, expecting him to be done soon. If Keisha had seen that 'Bill of Rights,' she would have been furious. There was no way that she would have signed it or allowed him to sign it. With his stomach knotted with anxiety, Gabriel pushed it back across the desk, shaking his head.

Dr. De Klerk didn't react. Gabriel expected him to explode. Or if he didn't explode, to get purple with rage. But he just looked across the desk at Gabriel, face expressionless. "So, I see where we stand," he said, picking up the paper and putting it back in the desk drawer. He pulled out another paper, this one printed on green paper. He put it in front of Gabriel. "Here is the protocol that you will be following for the next two weeks. You will be taking these three medications," he pointed with his pen to three lines of letters and numbers, "in addition to the meds that you are on now. Two tablets of each, three times a day. If you find that they are making you nauseated, don't take them on an empty stomach. You will need to keep a log." He pulled a yellow paper from his drawer. There was a ruled table with columns for date, time of day, energy level, symptoms, and so on. "On rising, mid-afternoon, and bedtime every day. Mrs. Foegel can call the inquiry line if she has any concerns."

Gabriel nodded.

"I'm very excited about this treatment program, Gabriel, and I hope you are too. I understand that you've been through a lot of disappointments, a lot of meds and treatments that just haven't worked for you. So you're skeptical. But I think the next time I see you; you'll have a different attitude."

"I hope so."

Dr. De Klerk pushed a button on his desk. Hardly a second passed, and his door was opened by a nurse. Gabriel picked up the green and yellow papers.

"We are done for the day. You can take Mr. Tate back out to Mrs. Foegel," De Klerk said.

The nurse wheeled Gabriel back out of the opulent office. They went through a couple of corridors to reach the glass elevator.

"Long day?" the nurse asked, as Gabriel smothered a yawn.

He nodded. "Yeah, and a couple more hours to get home."

"Maybe you can sleep in the car."

"I probably will."

They made their way back to the waiting room where Gabriel had separated from Heather. She was back ahead of him, flipping through a women's magazine. She looked cheerful and refreshed, her hair and nails done. Gabriel wished that Keisha had brought him to the mito clinic. He would have liked to see her pampered at the end of a long day instead of tired out and irritable. It wasn't easy for her, caring for Gabriel every day, teaching him, dragging him around to doctor's appointments or emergency rooms, doing hours of research on things that she could try to help him. Gabriel tended to go to sleep pretty early in the evening, but she usually looked tired and worn by that time, and he knew that she stayed up hours after he was asleep, researching and cleaning. He knew that she stayed up late, because often when he would awaken with leg cramps or sick, she hadn't yet been to bed, even in the small hours of the morning.

"All ready?" Heather asked with a smile.

"Yeah." Gabriel stood up from the wheelchair and waited for a moment to get his land legs, as Keisha was fond of saying. He stretched his neck and blinked, trying to push away the fatigue. "Do we need to stop somewhere for prescriptions?"

"I've already got everything." She held up a small bag with the clinic's logo on it. "Let's go."

They made their way back to the elevator and back down to the lobby. Mrs. Foegel looked at her watch in the elevator. "It's getting to be time for you to eat. Shall we stop at McDonalds on the way out of town?"

Gabriel's appetite was not what it should be, since leaving Keisha. The thought of burgers or chicken nuggets made him queasy. "Why don't we go here?" He leaned on the glass wall for support and pointed at the juice bar as they descended. "Do they have anything to eat?"

"Well, we could go see what they have. It's on our way and might save some time."

In the lobby, Gabriel sat on the bench outside the elevator. "I'll just wait here while you take a look," he suggested.

She looked at him for a minute, then nodded. "I'm going to leave the carrier here." She put the occupied baby carrier on the floor beside Gabriel. "What do you want?"

Gabriel shrugged. "Just a sandwich or pasta or something."

While she went over to the juice bar, Gabriel leaned forward with his elbows on his knees, looking at baby Alex. She babbled and moved around, but he wasn't sure how much she could see through those big, thick lenses. He stuck a finger into her hand, and she grasped it tightly.

Heather was a few minutes and came back with a wrap and some sort of chocolate square. "I'm not sure what it will be like," she said. "It's raw food cuisine, so I don't even know what everything is made of. But it looked all right. If you don't like it, we'll stop somewhere else on the way home."

"Sure." Gabriel took the food. Heather took the baby, and they headed back to the car. Gabriel unwrapped his food while Heather got Alex settled in the back seat, and then they were on their way.

Heather looked over at Gabriel after he'd taken a couple of bites of the wrap. "Well, how is it?"

"A bit dry. But it's okay."

"Good. How did things go with Dr. De Klerk? Did he explain everything to you?"

Gabriel looked away from her, pretending to be interested in something outside the window. "Yeah. He explained everything."

Gabriel woke up with his face against the car window and a crick in his neck. He opened his eyes and straightened up, wiping a trail of drool from the side of his face. He used his sleeve to mop it all up. The back car door slammed, and he saw Heather taking the baby carrier up the front walk to the house.

His wrap was still in his lap, only half-eaten and drying out even more. It didn't look appetizing at all. And the chocolate square was on the floor somewhere. He moved his feet looking for it, trying not to step on it and make a big mess.

After Heather had put Alex in the house, she came back to the car. She opened Gabriel's door and smiled. "Have a nice nap?"

Gabriel cleared his throat. "Yeah, sure," he agreed, rubbing his eyes.

She offered him a hand out of the car and Gabriel accepted. He started up the sidewalk with her at his side. Not touching, just close by to help him if he needed it. About halfway up the walk, he needed to rub his legs and then to steady himself on her shoulder as he pressed onward. By the time they got to the house, he was leaning on her pretty heavily, but she didn't complain. At least he didn't have to crawl over the last step and into the house. He leaned against the house and managed to get in on his own two feet.

Heather was looking at her watch as he settled into the couch to rest up again. The baby was starting to fuss in the other room. "They said to give these to you around seven, so I guess it's time for your first dose. Do you want some milk—some juice?"

"Just water."

"You need to get more calories in you if we're going to get your energy up. Those little mitochondria need to be fed!"

Gabriel rolled his eyes. "Okay. Juice."

"Okay. Wait just a minute. Here, take this." She handed him the bag of pills. While she was getting the juice, Gabriel took the three bottles out of the bag. The bottles were marked with the letters and numbers that were on the protocol sheet. Two of each, he remembered. He expected all of the pills to be white and nondescript like generic painkillers, but one bottle held pink pills, one blue, and one yellow. A nice balanced approach. Gabriel took out two of each and was ready when Heather returned with the juice. He downed them all in one handful, chased with a few gulps of the juice.

"Okay? Need any more?" Heather questioned when he handed the cup back to her.

"No. I'm good."

They both looked at each other for a minute. Gabriel couldn't help feeling a little stir of excitement over having taken the first dose of the pills. Dr. De Klerk hadn't given him any indication of how long it might take before he started noticing any changes. A few hours? A few days? A few weeks? It might be months before the pills reached full efficacy. No one had bothered to say.

Heather raised her eyebrows and gave a crooked little grin. "Now, I guess we wait!" She put a light, slim hand on his shoulder. "I hope it helps."

"Yeah. Me too."

The answer was, not even an hour. In about twenty minutes, Gabriel was way past 'possible nausea' and hanging over the toilet regurgitating the raw wrap from the juice bar. He was thankful that he hadn't had a burger and fries, although the bits would probably have been softer and not hurt as much if they got caught in his nasal passages.

"The inserts say you should take them with food if they cause nausea," Matt said, standing in the bathroom doorway reading the information from the clinic.

"This is more than nausea!" Gabriel pointed out.

"Well… yes… How are you holding out there, bud?"

Gabriel groaned, resting his head on the toilet seat. His body felt like a wet rag. Damp, and limp, and cold.

"Sorry… if you think you're done, I'll help you back to your room. You can have a bucket, in case it starts again."

Gabriel considered. There was nothing left in his stomach, so he hoped that the retching would stop, and he wouldn't be dry heaving and throwing up mucousy strings of acidic yellow bile for the rest of the night. It would feel better if he could lie down on his bed instead of sitting on the cold tile. And his head was steadying a little.

"Yeah. I think so."

"Okay." Matt put the papers on a knick-knack table in the hallway and returned to the bathroom. He gave Gabriel a hand up. Gabriel leaned heavily on his arm, and Matt walked him slowly to the bed. Gabriel stretched out with a sigh.

"You'll get a bucket?" he reminded.

"You bet. Be right back."

Gabriel closed his eyes and waited for sleep to come. Matt was shaking him awake what seemed like only seconds later. Gabriel opened his eyes, blinking and trying to figure out why Matt would wake him up. Matt was looking at his face intently.

"You'd better sit up for a few minutes," he said. "Your nose is bleeding."

Gabriel pushed himself up to sitting and held the tissue that Matt handed him up to his face. It came away stained with blood.

"Pinch and hold tight. It should stop in a couple of minutes. You probably just ruptured a membrane throwing up."

Gabriel held the tissue pinched over his nose, leaning on his other hand for support. He really wanted just to lie down and go back to sleep. Heather stood in the door of the bedroom, watching with worried eyes.

"Oh, poor Gabriel. I hope you feel better soon. If you're going to sleep now, we'd better fill out this log before you do."

"Okay."

She read the questions to him and transcribed his answers. "Side effects vomiting and nosebleed—anything else?"

"Nuh."

"Okay. I'll give the clinic a call in the morning before you take another dose. See if there's something we can do to keep you from getting sick. Or if there's one of the pills that you should stop taking."

Gabriel nodded. He pulled the tissue away from his nose and waited to see if it was going to drip more. He could feel a clot in his nose like a giant booger and wanted to blow it out, but didn't dare in case it would start bleeding again. He dabbed at his nose gently. "Think id stopped."

Matt scrutinized his face and nodded. "Looks like it. Maybe lay on your side so that it doesn't drain down your throat if there is any more bleeding. We'll check on you again before going to bed."

Gabriel lowered himself back to the bed and lay on his side.

Matt patted him on the shoulder. "Bucket's beside you if you need it. Holler if there's anything else."

Gabriel awoke when Collin went to bed. The light went on and Collin swore. "I keep forgetting about you." He turned on the lamp and turned off the overhead light. He began to undress for bed. "Sheesh, you stink. You oughtta take a shower or brush your teeth or something. Phew. Uggh."

"Sorry," Gabriel murmured. He didn't get up to go clean himself up. If he had to put up with Collin's football stink, Collin could put up with his sickness. Gabriel didn't have the energy to wash up.

Collin kicked the bed, making Gabriel jump wildly. "I'm talking to you," Collin growled. "Are you listening?"

"I said sorry. I'm sick."

Collin kicked the bed again. Gabriel put his arm up over his face to protect himself. But Collin wasn't hitting him, just the bed. Collin grunted and went back to undressing. He climbed into bed and turned off the lamp. Gabriel lay in the dark, his heart still thumping hard in his chest.

CHAPTER TEN

W HEN GABRIEL GOT UP and made his way to the kitchen for some breakfast, he figured that Heather would tell him that he didn't have to take one of the pills anymore. But she laid them beside his plate: pink, blue, and yellow. And she got out his other pills. Gabriel eyed the rainbow pills while he ate a piece of toast.

"I have to take them all?"

"The clinic said that your body would adjust. Make sure you have enough to eat, and at least two glasses of water, and you should do better this time."

Gabriel ate the piece of toast and had a glass of water. His stomach was protesting about being too full. He couldn't get another glass or piece of toast down. Reluctantly, he picked up the pills and swallowed them.

"Okay?" Heather questioned. "You don't want anything else?"

"No."

Collin had already gone to school for an early football practice, and Luce sat across the table from Gabriel playing with some cereal and cut-up fruit on her plate. Gabriel had tuned out Josiah's chatter, but looked at him now, focusing on what he was saying.

"Are you going to school today?" Josiah asked. "Do you have a day off again? When are you going to school?"

"I don't know," Gabriel told him. "I'm doing school at home right now. I'll go to school… when I'm feeling better."

"When will you feel better? I don't like being sick. When I was sick at my mom's house, they had to call an 'bulance. Have you ever been in an 'bulance?"

Gabriel nodded. He put his hand over his stomach, which was starting to gurgle and writhe. "Yes, a couple times."

"Were you scared? I was scared. I thought I was going to fall off the bed," Josiah declared.

Gabriel smiled at him. "They didn't strap you down?"

"No, an' I thought I was gonna fall off!" Josiah reiterated.

"Yeah," Gabriel agreed. He stood up, leaning on the table.

Heather caught his eye. "You okay?"

Gabriel shook his head. He took a couple of steps to get to the wall for extra support and moved his feet as quickly as he could, pushing his lips together and willing his stomach not to revolt before he could get to the bathroom. He was hardly aware of covering the distance that would normally have taken him several minutes.

Between heaves, he could hear Heather trying to keep Josiah distracted and out of the way. The curious boy obviously wanted to come and watch the fun. After she got him on his bus, she came to see how Gabriel was managing.

"Settling down again?"

Gabriel wiped his mouth. "Don't know how they're going to do any good if I can't keep them down."

"Well, the clinic said just to keep trying. Try to eat a little bit more next time."

"Eating more just means I'm going to throw up more."

"I know it can't be much fun for you, but let's keep it up for a while. They know what they're doing, and they said that your body would adjust."

Gabriel shook his head and sat back against the wall, closing his eyes.

"I have good news for you," Heather offered.

"What, another pill to add to the cocktail?"

"No, something that you wanted."

There was only one thing that Gabriel wanted. He opened his eyes again and looked at Heather. Her eyes were dancing, and her mouth curled up in a smile.

"My mom?" Gabriel gasped.

She nodded.

Gabriel sat up. Leaning on the wall, he forced himself to his feet, so that he was looking down at Mrs. Foegel instead of up at her. "When? When do I get to see her?"

"This afternoon. Mrs. Scott will be taking you to a neutral meeting place to see her. It will be a supervised visit."

"I don't care. I just want to see her."

The meeting with Keisha had luckily been scheduled long enough after Gabriel's lunchtime meds that his stomach had settled down again so he could travel. But his gut was tied in knots with anxiety and excitement over seeing her again. He sat on the couch looking out the window, waiting for Carol Scott's little aqua blue sports car to pull up. Heather walked by once or twice while he waited and smiled knowingly at him. She kept busy and out of the way with housework and taking care of Alex. Luce was home too, as her school apparently had the day off, but she didn't pay any attention to Gabriel or anyone else. She drifted from one activity to another like a ghost, as if there were no one else in the house. Heather redirected her once or twice, but Luce was quiet and didn't seem to get into much trouble.

The car pulled up, and Gabriel pushed himself off of the couch to his feet. He already had on his shoes and jacket. "She's here. I'm going."

"Okay, see you later," Heather called back.

Gabriel was careful not to trip on the steps going out the door and shuffled down the sidewalk as fast as his shaky legs would let him. He leaned on the car for a moment before opening the door, steadying himself and trying to catch his breath again. He opened the door and got into the car, trying not to show how excited he was to the social worker.

"How are you doing today, Gabriel?" she asked, pulling out into the street just as he pulled his door closed.

"Umm… well, okay right now."

"Oh? What's wrong?"

"The new pills from the clinic make me sick. But I'm okay for now."

"Oh, well that's annoying, isn't it? What did the doctor say?"

"They said just keep taking them; my body will adjust."

"Good." She turned the radio down a bit, so they didn't have to raise their voices over it. "Are you excited to see your mom?"

"Yes!"

She smiled. "I thought you would be. Mrs. Foegel's really been pushing to get you visitation. I hope she hasn't stepped on any toes getting it set up."

"Stepped on toes? Whose toes?"

Mrs. Scott shook her head. "Foster parents just have to be careful. They aren't in charge. Foster parents who get red-flagged for being difficult… well…"

"With DFS? Or who?"

She waved a hand at him, indicating to drop it. "I shouldn't have said anything to you. Forget about it. The Foegels are a good home. I just wouldn't want them to end up in any difficulties. Maybe you can back off a little on the demands to see your mom so that she'll back off of us."

Gabriel looked out the window, biting his lip. It didn't matter much to him if the Foegels got themselves in trouble with DFS. He wasn't about to tell Heather that he didn't care about seeing his mother anymore. And she would know better even if he tried to tell her that.

"Okay, Gabriel?" Carol persisted. "Would you do that? Tell her to just ease up a bit?"

"Yeah. Sure."

"Good."

They were quiet for the rest of the drive, and Carol turned up the radio again to minimize the silence between them. Gabriel wasn't sure where they were meeting, and didn't know his way around that part of town very well, so he had no idea how close or far away they were. When Carol pulled the car into a parking lot, he sat up straight and looked around, trying to see where they were meeting or if he could see Keisha or her car. Carol pulled into a handicap space close to the big professional building. Gabriel opened the door and started toward the building ahead of her. He was slow, so it didn't take her long to catch up and take the lead. Gabriel could see the DFS logo on the outside of one of the doors and headed for it.

He stumbled over the slight ridge of the doorframe and looked around the reception area. Keisha was sitting in one of the chairs, a magazine open on her lap, but her eyes on the door. She jumped to her feet and ran to Gabriel.

He pulled her into his arms and held her tightly, tears running down his face. "Mom, I missed you so much! I wanted you to come see me so bad!"

Keisha's words were jumbled together between his. "I wanted to come—Are you okay?—Have they treated you all right?"

Gabriel pressed his face into her hair, breathing in her sweet scent and holding her as close as he possibly could. "Mom. Oh, Mom, don't ever go. Don't ever let go."

"I know, sweetie. I never wanted them to take you. I would have stopped them if I could." She looked over at Carol Scott, who had entered the reception area and was watching them with a sad-looking smile. "Even the investigator knew I would never abuse you. She was crying when she took you, but she said she had to."

Carol didn't confirm or deny this. She looked away as if she was embarrassed about the whole thing. "Let's grab a meeting room for you guys. This wasn't meant to be a lobby meeting."

Keisha held tightly to Gabriel, but they separated enough to walk, following Mrs. Scott through a security door with an electronic lock, down a short hall to a little meeting room. There were a table and three mismatched tubular chairs, a worn rust-colored couch on the wall, and a toy bin with ratty looking plushies and Duplo building blocks.

Keisha looked at the table and chairs and decided against them. She motioned to the couch, and she and Gabriel settled into it, cuddled close together. Keisha held Gabriel's hand, weaving their fingers together.

"How are you, baby? Are you okay?" She touched his cheek.

"You're not to talk about his health," Carol Scott said.

They both looked at her.

"I'm not allowed to ask how he is?"

"No," Carol said flatly.

They looked at each other.

"I'm so sorry this happened to you," Keisha said finally. "I never knew… it never occurred to me that they could take you away for disagreeing with a doctor."

Gabriel nodded.

"You're not allowed to talk about the investigation or apprehension," Carol intoned.

There was so much that Gabriel wanted to talk to Keisha about. The hospital, what had happened before that he couldn't remember. The clinic. The side effects of the drugs. But he couldn't talk about any of it. He cast around for something to say. Something to ask.

"Are you… okay?" he asked her.

"I'm perfectly fine," Keisha said, rubbing Gabriel's shoulder and back. "And your dad is good. Everything is fine for us. Other than…" she trailed off and looked at Carol.

"I made a friend at the hospital," Gabriel blurted. "She has mito too."

They both glanced at Carol, but she didn't say anything.

"What's her name?" Keisha asked. "Tell me about her."

"Renata. She was nice and visited me a lot. She had trouble, though, that was why she was in… that unit."

"Renata. That's a pretty name. What kind of trouble did she have?"

"I don't know all of it… but she had paranoia, so she thought there were a lot of plots and conspiracies going on."

Keisha nodded. "You liked her? Was she your age?"

"She just turned fourteen, while we were there. But she's really, really smart. She knew a lot of stuff."

"How sad, to have your birthday in hospital. You had one... I think you were six. Do you remember it? You were in ICU."

Gabriel thought back. He shook his head. "No... I don't remember that. Did we celebrate at the hospital?"

"No, I just waited until you were home and we had a party then. It doesn't make any difference to a six-year-old. You didn't know which day was your birthday without being told."

"I guess not," Gabriel agreed. "Especially in the hospital... it's easy to lose track of what day it is."

"So did Renata celebrate at the hospital? Did her parents come? It's a bit different for a fourteen-year-old. They know the day."

"No." Gabriel tightened his grip on Keisha and looked at her face. "She said—I don't know if this is really true—she said that when the police came to take her from her mom... that her mom fought back against them, and they sent her to prison for resisting arrest. So she couldn't come, just sent a card."

They both looked at Carol again. The social worker looked uncomfortable and started scratching at some unidentifiable spill or mark on the table with a manicured fingernail. But she didn't stop them.

"That's awful, sweetie. Do you think she was telling the truth?"

"I know she believed it. But she thought a lot of weird things, so I don't know what's true or not. She said that her mom was trying to kill her and I don't believe that part."

"Why would her mother try to kill her? I agree, that part has to be her paranoia."

"She said it was because she is so badly-behaved and hard to care for. She can't even eat; she's tube fed."

"Considering how hard it is to get food into *you* and keep your weight up, that sounds easy. Just hook you up like the car at the gas station, instead of nagging over every snack and meal..."

Gabriel giggled at the mental image of being filled up at a gas station with a pump that dispensed formula instead of gas. "My foster family has a baby that's tube fed. But you have to be careful about infection and everything too. Around her incision." He had seen the care that Heather had to take to ensure that everything was kept clean and sanitary.

"What's your foster family like?"

"No discussion about Gabriel's foster family," Carol Scott warned, without looking up from the table.

Keisha and Gabriel looked at each other in frustration. Gabriel fell back to discussing Renata, since she seemed to be one of the only allowed topics. "Renata gets around better than me, mostly. But then one of the orderlies broke her rib. It punctured her lung, so she was laid up."

Keisha made a pained face. "Oh, that poor girl! How did he break her rib? Were they abusive to the patients?"

There was a warning look from Carol, but no comment.

"He was trying to hold her still. She was acting crazy, being disruptive and they were going to take her to the quiet room. But he held her too tight. The nurse says she probably has brittle bones because of her mito or feeding problems."

"Poor girl," Keisha repeated. "So sad, to be taken away from her parents, her mother in prison, all by herself in that place... to be hurt and sick and not have anyone to hold her hand or look after her..."

Gabriel nodded, a lump in his throat. He scratched his neck. He knew that Keisha wasn't just talking about Renata. She was talking about him too.

"She thought that her mom was trying to kill her, so she was okay with being there alone. But a normal person... someone who wasn't paranoid like that... would be sad and lonely."

"And her mother must be frantic, not able to contact her or find out how she's doing... if she's sick or doing okay..."

"I guess... even if she was really hard to care for, and didn't behave... her mom would still miss her and want to go see her."

Keisha squeezed Gabriel's hand. "Yes, baby. No matter what. She couldn't stop loving her own daughter, no matter how bad things were."

For a few minutes, they were silent, both too emotional to continue the conversation. Keisha patted Gabriel's face, then something in her expression changed.

"What?" Gabriel asked, confused.

She touched his collar, moving it to the side and frowning. "What's wrong with your skin? You have a rash."

Gabriel looked down. He pulled his shirt away from his body and looked down the neck hole at his chest. Sure enough, there was a bumpy red rash. It wasn't easy to see on his dark skin, but it was definitely rashy.

"There's no discussion about his health," Carol reminded.

"It must be from the new meds," Gabriel said, rubbing the itchy red bumps with his fingertips, but not scratching them. "The clinic just started me on these experimental drugs..."

"Gabriel," Carol Scott said in a firm warning voice.

Gabriel looked at her, then looked back at Keisha.

Keisha gave him a protective hug. "How can I not talk to my baby about the way he feels? Look at that rash! Do you see it? It needs to be treated. And he needs to be taken off of anything experimental. I can't believe that they are allowed to experiment on foster kids. They are so vulnerable, and no one—"

"This visit is over," Carol snapped, standing up. "Gabriel, say good-bye. It's time to go."

Gabriel tightened his grip on Keisha's hand. "No... please..."

Keisha's expression oscillated between anger and anxiety. "No. I won't say that. Please, don't take him away yet. Let us visit."

Mrs. Scott shook her head. She motioned for Gabriel to exit the room ahead of her. Gabriel looked at Keisha, agonized. Ten minutes was hardly long enough to say hello to his mother, certainly not long enough for the first visit in a month. Keisha looked stricken. She hugged Gabriel.

"You'd better go, baby. We don't want them to block the next visit."

Gabriel nodded, sniffling and trying not to let the hot tears escape his eyes. "I'll see you... next week?"

"I don't know. As soon as we can. I'm sorry. I'm so sorry."

"It's okay." Gabriel clung to her.

"Let's go, Gabriel," Mrs. Scott insisted.

Gabriel released Keisha reluctantly. She held his hand for another instant, giving it one last squeeze. Gabriel tried to swallow the lump in his throat and turned away from her to exit the room first. His knees were shaking. His whole body was weak and shuddery. He didn't look back at Keisha, or he wouldn't be able to go on. When they got to the front door of the office, Carol took him by the arm. Gabriel was angry at her presuming that she could touch him, but he needed the support, so he tried to swallow the anger welling up in him over the injustice and invasion of DFS into his life. He said nothing and Keisha didn't either.

It was a good thing that she had parked so close. Carol helped him into the car and shut the door. Gabriel leaned against the inside of the door and closed his eyes, forcing himself to breathe evenly and not let the sobs take over. It wasn't fair. After the days and weeks of being separated from his mother, he should have been able to have a nice long visit, to get all caught up on what happened that he couldn't remember, and what she was doing to fight to get him back, and to let her know what was happening with him. The brief visitation left him feeling even more lonely and desolate than before.

Carol Scott got into the driver's seat beside him. He didn't look at her. "I'm sorry, Gabriel. I have to enforce the rules that DFS has dictated. Your mom is no longer in charge of your medical care. Her even talking to you about your health could have a detrimental effect."

He said nothing. Even if he wasn't struggling to hold it all together, he didn't know what he would have said. It was all so wrong.

"I know you don't understand that. But even if you don't, you and your mom still have to follow the rules for a visit. You—" she foundered for words. "You just do!"

Gabriel didn't open his eyes or turn his head. He scratched his itchy neck and chest, digging his nails in. It hurt, but it felt good to hurt on the outside.

CHAPTER ELEVEN

MRS. FOEGEL FINISHED UP the daily log while Gabriel lay in bed, again wrung out and exhausted. "I don't think you threw up as much tonight. That's an improvement."

Gabriel's stomach felt like he would never be able to keep down another bite. Even though it was empty now, it hurt, aching like it was being stretched like a balloon, nearly at breaking point. He rubbed it tenderly.

"The Benadryl seems to have taken the rash down," Heather went on. Her positive outlook was not improving Gabriel's mood. He still felt just as crappy. He had thrown up less because he had hardly been able to choke anything down. Benadryl had improved the rash, but they still wanted him to keep taking the meds in spite of the allergic reaction, and he knew that the Benadryl was going to make him feel hung over in the morning. It always did. It would sap his energy for days, and he couldn't afford to be any weaker.

"Night," Gabriel told Heather, closing his eyes and turning away from her.

Heather stood there for a minute before turning the light off and heading out the door.

Gabriel had been restless for a long time before he finally woke up. He had been dreaming, tossing and turning, and sweating into his sheets. When he managed to pull himself from unconsciousness, he sat up, reaching for his legs. The muscles were pulled taut with excruciating pain, like the worst charlie horse ever in every muscle of his legs.

131

He rubbed them, groaning aloud. Was it another side effect of the drugs? Or just his screwed-up body deciding to add variety to his existence by replacing hypotonia with hypertonia for a change? Gabriel dug his thumbs in, trying to rub the cramps away, but the muscles tightened further under his touch, making him cry out in pain.

"What the hell—?"

The lamp went on and Collin squinted across the room at him. For once, he'd remembered not to turn the overhead light on and had gone to bed without waking Gabriel up. Gabriel was disoriented, unsure what time of night or morning it was.

"What's the matter with you?" Collin demanded.

"Got leg cramps," Gabriel forced out, barely able to speak.

"Leg cramps?" Collin repeated. "Go back to sleep!"

"No! It hurts. It hurts!"

"Quit being such a baby!"

Gabriel cried out again, gripping his legs, his breath coming in gasps. Everything around him got blurry, and for a minute everything whirled, and he thought Collin would get his wish and Gabriel would just pass out. But the vertigo passed, and everything was sharp and crystal clear. Gabriel swore, determined that Collin should understand that these were no ordinary muscle cramps. "Get them! Help me!"

Collin didn't move, looking at him. Gabriel half-expected that he would just turn off the lamp and go back to sleep again.

"Please!"

Collin blew out an exasperated breath and climbed out of bed. He left the room, and Gabriel could hear him walking down the hall and waking the Foegels up. Heather was the first one to come into the room. "What is it, Gabriel? What's wrong?"

"My legs! Feel them!" Gabriel continued to try to rub the cramps away.

Heather touched Gabriel's rigid calf tentatively. She looked at his face, her brows drawing down. "What's going on? You just woke up with them cramped like this?" She rubbed his calf, trying to soothe him.

"It hurts! You need to get me something for the pain. Take me to the hospital! Please!"

Heather bit her lip. "I'm not supposed to give you any painkillers. They specifically said…"

Gabriel started to sob. "Please…"

"Why don't we try some heat?" Matt suggested from the doorway. "Heating pads, hot towels, see if that will relieve the cramps."

"Take me to the hospital," Gabriel begged.

"Let's try some heat," Heather agreed.

"I guess I'll be sleeping on the couch," Collin growled. He pulled the top blanket and his pillow off of his bed. Heather turned her head to watch him stalk out.

Gabriel lay back down, crying. Hopeless. He could hear Matt running water and getting things out of the hallway linen closet. Heather continued to rub Gabriel's legs gently, but her touch was light and had little effect.

"Hang in there, Gabe. It'll be okay. It will pass. Muscle cramps don't usually last long."

In a few minutes, Matt returned with heating pads and crawled around Gabriel to reach the plug-in behind his bed. He laid them over Gabriel's legs and turned them on. "Get those started warming. I'll have hot towels in a few minutes."

It seemed like hours passed while Gabriel tried to 'hang in there' as the Foegels massaged his muscles and applied heat, trying to keep him comfortable. Eventually, the pain started to ease, and Gabriel was so exhausted from fighting the pain, from the muscles demanding all of his energy, that he fell into a troubled sleep.

Though he wanted to sleep late, tired from the long, restless night, Gabriel wasn't able to get back to sleep. His head was thick, pounding with pain, and his rash was starting to itch again. His legs, hypotonic once more, felt like something dead. He felt anxious about getting them moving and making sure that they would still work.

Gabriel managed to get out of bed and down the hall to the kitchen.

"Up already?" Heather observed, turning around from the coffee maker to watch him sit down at the table. "I thought that you would sleep in." Her hair was a little mussed, and she was still in her bathrobe. Luce was sitting at the table playing with her food. Collin was working on a huge bowl of oatmeal and didn't look at Gabriel as he sat down. No sign of the baby or Josiah, though Gabriel had heard Josiah's voice earlier as he had tried to make his body go back to sleep.

"Couldn't sleep in. Can you get me a Benadryl?"

"Still got that rash? Let me have a look."

Gabriel didn't move. Heather came over with a fresh mug of coffee and moved Gabriel's collar around to have a look at the rash. "I think it's better today."

Gabriel grunted, not agreeing or disagreeing.

She got him a Benadryl and put it in front of him. "What can I get you for breakfast?"

"Nothing."

"You have to have a good breakfast before you take your pills."

"Then I throw up more!"

"They said that eating and drinking lots of water would help."

"It doesn't."

"We need to follow the protocol that the clinic has given us. And that includes eating before taking the pills."

Gabriel shook his head.

"Gabriel… you need to cooperate. If you don't eat, they'll just put you back in hospital again. They'll put you on a nasal gastric tube and feed you that way. You can't stop eating, and you can't go off the protocol."

Gabriel looked at her in disbelief.

"I'm sorry," Heather said, shaking her head. "I don't want it to go that far. So please eat breakfast. What can I get for you?"

Gabriel rested his head in his hand. "Toast."

"Okay, but that's not enough. A couple pieces, maybe some juice and some fruit…?"

"Toast," Gabriel repeated. "And I need a Tylenol."

She was already on her way back to the counter to put some bread in the toaster. She stopped and looked back at Gabriel. "I told you last night; we're not allowed to give you any painkillers."

"Why? Because of the protocol?"

"No… because of your medical history. Let's just leave it at that. I can get you ice for your head. Is it your head?"

"Never mind."

She didn't pursue it. After Heather had given Gabriel his breakfast and his pills, she ran her fingers through her mussy hair. "I'm going to go take a shower. Collin, will you please put Luce on the bus for me? It should be here in ten minutes. I have to take Josiah to school for an interview."

Collin grunted. Heather apparently took it as a 'yes' and headed back to the bathroom to get herself ready. Gabriel worked on his toast, having difficulty choking it down, knowing that it was just going to be coming back up after he took the experimental meds. He washed it down with as much water as he could.

Collin looked up after scraping his bowl clean. "Hope you had a good sleep," he sneered at Gabriel.

"Sorry for waking you up," Gabriel said, his voice low.

Collin got up from the table, leaving his dirty bowl behind, and walked around the table toward Luce. He punched Gabriel in the shoulder as he walked by, with such force that Gabriel nearly fell out of his chair. The bigger boy continued to walk by. He went over to Luce, who was still playing with her food, eating a bite only occasionally.

"Come on, Luce. Time for school now," he told her.

Luce paid him not even a flicker of attention. Collin grabbed her arm and pulled her roughly off of her chair. Luce made a squeal of protest and reached for the food remaining on her plate. Collin jerked her farther away from the table.

"Hey, take it easy," Gabriel protested. "You're a lot bigger than her."

Luce tried to free herself from Collin's grip, and when she couldn't pull away, tried to bite him. Collin released her arm and grabbed her hair, twisting and jerking it back. Luce flailed. Collin continued to drag her toward the door by the hair.

"Collin!" Gabriel protested, following a step or two.

Collin turned and looked at him. "You wanna be next? You don't weigh much more than she does."

Gabriel froze where he was, gulping. He looked toward the bathroom where the shower was running. Too late to get Heather.

"Keep your mouth shut," Collin warned. "I know where you sleep."

Collin let go of Luce at the door. She didn't move to get farther away from him. She didn't put on her coat or shoes or pick up her pink backpack.

"Get ready for the bus," Collin ordered.

Luce still didn't move. Collin reached over and pinched her arm, twisting the skin sharply. Luce cried out and pulled away. He pinched her again. "Get ready for the bus."

"Leave her alone!"

"You heard Heather tell me to get her on the bus. That's what I'm doing."

"Quit hurting her."

Collin looked at Gabriel and pinched Luce again, holding on until she howled. When Collin let go, she bent over and started to put on her shoes. "You see?" Collin pointed out. "She knows what she's supposed to be doing. You just have to persuade her. Get her attention."

Gabriel stood there watching as Luce put on her shoes, then her coat, and took her backpack from Collin when he held it out to her. Collin opened the door and held Luce's hand to walk her to the curb, where they waited for the yellow school bus. Gabriel could see them through the front window. Luce climbed onto the bus and it pulled out.

"How are you feeling?" Heather asked as she got Josiah ready for school.

"Okay," Gabriel said with a shrug.

She gave him a big smile. "You see? You are adjusting to the medications! That's good news. I bet you're relieved about that."

Gabriel nodded. But there was a tightness in his chest, and he knew why. He hadn't taken the pills. Since Heather wasn't around to make sure that he took them, he had simply washed them down the drain. He couldn't face another morning of throwing up, itching from the rash, nosebleeds, and the possibility of another night with unbearable leg cramps. He felt guilty for not taking them and for lying to Heather about it. He hadn't told her that he had taken them, but he knew it was still a lie, even if he said nothing. He had also found a bottle of Tylenol in the cabinet above the sink, and he took a couple of those.

"I'm going to go lie down…"

"Sure. Catch up on some of the sleep that you missed last night," Heather agreed. "I have to go to Josiah's school, so you'll have a couple of hours with the house to yourself. Enjoy it!"

"Okay. Thanks."

Gabriel went and lay down on his bed while Heather finished getting ready and left the house, calling out to him before she left the house to let him know that she was going. But he found himself lying in bed unable to find sleep. He wanted to go back to sleep, but his body and his brain wouldn't let him.

He had to get out of the research study. Gabriel had gotten out of taking the pills once, but he wasn't going to be able to keep pretending to take them. The Foegels would catch on before long. And he imagined that when they repeated the tests at the clinic, they would know that something was wrong too. They might even have some kind of radiation tag in the pills so that they would be able to tell the levels in his system.

Gabriel shook off the thoughts. That was crazy. It was like something that Renata would say. Radiation tags. He wondered briefly whether her paranoia was a side effect of her treatment at the clinic, or whether it was her mito. She had claimed to have been in psych very young, though. If that were true, then it wasn't the experimental meds.

With everyone gone, he had the house to himself. And that gave him his first opportunity to phone Keisha and talk to her without being monitored. As soon as he realized that, Gabriel got out of bed and went back to the kitchen. While he hadn't seen anyone use the landline in the kitchen, he had seen where the phone was. Gabriel sat at the writing desk and picked up the receiver. He started to dial Keisha's cell phone number, then stopped. He pressed the hang-up switch and released it, realizing that there was no dial tone. He pressed and released the switch several times. But it was no use; there was no tone.

Gabriel put down the phone and covered his face. He had only seen the Foegels use their individual cell phones, and they had both taken their phones with them. They didn't want him to be able to communicate with his mother. They'd left him without any means of communication, even if there were an emergency.

CHAPTER TWELVE

GABRIEL WAS STILL SITTING at the writing desk in the kitchen when Heather got home. She put down the baby carrier and looked at him, cocking her head to the side. "I thought I'd find you in bed. Feeling better?"

"Couldn't sleep."

"Oh… well, at least you've had some time to rest." She looked at her watch. "You need a snack?"

It had been a couple of hours since breakfast. Gabriel nodded. "Yeah, that would be good."

"What do you want? Granola bar?"

"Yeah." She was careful not to get bars that were full of dairy and sugar, but the higher protein ones, like athletes used.

Heather went into the kitchen and got him one. Gabriel started to unwrap it.

"How was school?" he asked politely.

"Oh, it went okay. They have concerns over Josiah's behavior. Like we didn't already know there were problems going into this. We did talk to them about him before he started attending. But somehow… it always comes as a surprise. Then they want to know how to manage him."

"He talks too much?" Gabriel guessed.

Heather chuckled. "Yes. Among other things."

Gabriel chewed on a bite of the granola bar, thinking. Heather got baby Alex out of her car carrier and took off her jacket. Alex looked like a big bug with her thick glasses.

"Who represents me?" Gabriel asked.

"Who represents you? How do you mean? I do, for things like school and doctor's appointments."

"What about in court?"

"In court then Mrs. Scott represents you. She's the one that is in charge of your welfare at that level."

"But she doesn't do what I want her to."

"Well, no, it's not like that. She tells the court what is going on, what would be best for you, and then they decide. So in some ways, the judge represents you too. Because he's listening to everyone and sorting out what is best for you."

Gabriel peeled back the wrapper farther. "But he's *not* listening to everyone. No one is listening to me."

"I know it's kind of hard to wrap your mind around. How everyone else could be deciding what happens to you. But we really do have your best interests in mind."

"Do I get a lawyer?"

Heather frowned. She put Alex belly-down on the floor. The baby tried to push up on her hands, but her head and body seemed to be too heavy for her. Gabriel felt sorry for her.

"No, you don't have a lawyer," Heather said slowly. "DFS has a lawyer and I assume that your mom has a lawyer. But not you personally. Sometimes the court appoints a guardian *ad litem*. But they haven't in your case."

"What if I want one?"

"What is it you're worried about, Gabriel?"

"I want to go back to my mom, and I want to get off of these stupid drugs. If I could explain to the judge, he'd understand everything…"

Heather patted Alex on the back. "I know it must suck to have everybody else deciding what's best for you, Gabriel. But they—we—do have your best interests in mind. Going back to your mom wouldn't necessarily be the best thing for you."

"You don't know my mom. You only know what they've told you."

"I suppose that's true. But I don't think you understand all the issues that your mother has had with your care, either."

They were just talking in circles. "I want to talk to the judge," Gabriel repeated. He tried to keep his voice steady and strong, to sound mature and grown up instead of like a little kid.

Heather scratched her temple. "I guess I can give Mrs. Scott a call, find out when the next time is that your case is coming up before the court. Let her know that you'd like to attend."

"Yeah. If I can just explain to the judge…"

Heather stood up. She ruffled Gabriel's hair as she walked by him. "Just… don't get your hopes up, Gabe. There are a lot of other factors for the judge to consider. Kids aren't taken away from their parents without due consideration. There were a lot of factors working against your mom."

At lunch, Gabriel was able to eat more than he had before, since his stomach didn't feel as sick, and he hoped that eating more would stave off the vomiting. He felt so guilty about skipping his morning pills that he went ahead and took his lunchtime ones. And forty-five minutes later, he was in the bathroom puking his big lunch back up again. Heather stood in the doorway between heaves, giving him a frown.

"I was really hoping after how well you did this morning that we were past this," she said. "Did you have enough to eat? What do you think is different?"

Gabriel rubbed the sore muscles of his stomach. "I didn't take them this morning."

"What?"

He felt better confessing it. "I just feel so bad when I take them; they make me so sick. I just… couldn't. I needed a break."

"You can't do that, Gabe. We need to keep the chemicals in your body at a consistent level. You can't skip doses."

Gabriel wasn't sure how much of the pills he could actually be absorbing when he was throwing up less than an hour later.

"It's like chemotherapy," Heather said. "Even though the side effects are bad, you have to keep taking it to get the good effects."

"It's not going to cure my mito," Gabriel pointed out, "and I'm not feeling any better."

"You may not be noticing it because it is so gradual. But I think you're managing a lot better than you were when you first got here. You can make it up and down the sidewalk. I see you walking around the house without having to lean on anything or take as many rests. Even this morning; you had the opportunity for more sleep, but your body didn't need it that much. Normally, you would have been conked out the minute your head hit the pillow."

Gabriel rested his head on his arm, propped on the toilet seat. Probably not the most hygienic place to be resting, but he didn't think he was done being sick yet.

"If I had my braces, I could walk better. Why won't they let me have braces?"

"They want you to build up the muscles in your legs, instead of letting them atrophy by having them immobilized all the time. And it is helping, don't you think?"

"No," Gabriel snapped. He closed his eyes, shutting her out.

Collin wasn't at the supper table, which Gabriel was relieved about. He sat picking at his dinner and tried to think of how to bring up Collin's behavior to the Foegels without putting himself at risk. As soon as they talked to him about it, Collin would know that Gabriel had squealed, and Gabriel had to room with the guy. There was no escaping.

"Gabriel…?"

He looked up at Heather, realizing suddenly that she had been talking to him, and he had completely zoned out thinking about Collin.

"Sorry… what?"

She shook her head, rolling her eyes at Matt. "I said I talked to Carol—Mrs. Scott—about your request to be in court the next time your case was heard."

"Oh! What did she say?"

"They're doing a review next Tuesday. It's just supposed to be a routine thing, filing updated reports and so on, but she figured if you wanted to be there, to see the judge and feel like you had a voice, there shouldn't be any issues."

"Tuesday? I can go on Tuesday?" Gabriel's heart pumped faster and harder. He couldn't believe that he was going to be able to get in to see the judge so quickly. He figured they would put him off for a couple of weeks at least. Maybe even a month. If he could talk to the judge on Tuesday, explain everything to him, maybe he could even be back with Keisha by the end of the week. He could go back to his old life. Like nothing had ever happened. "That's great!"

"Glad you're pleased. Now, Monday we're going to have to go to the clinic, so I need you to—"

"Monday? Why? It hasn't been two weeks!"

"No, but you're having such a difficult time with the meds that they want to see you again. Do an update, see if there's something that they need to tweak."

"I don't want to go back there so soon!"

"I thought you wanted them to do something to make you feel better," Matt said, putting down his fork and looking at Gabriel. "You should be happy that you don't have to wait for so long."

"Well, I... can't they just take me off of them? Or take me off of whichever one is causing the trouble? Why do I have to go back?" Gabriel was aware that he was whining, but he really didn't want another trip to the clinic to be poked and prodded, and to have Dr. De Klerk get after him for skipping a dose and being such a whiner about the whole thing.

"I'm sorry," Heather said, her voice firm. "They want to see you. It's not exactly how I planned to spend my day either, Gabe. But we have to put up with the inconvenience in order to find out what will work for you and make you feel better."

Gabriel swore under his breath, staring down at his nearly-full plate. He knew that he shouldn't. Heather was just doing what a foster mom should, even if it meant four hours of driving and an hour or two of waiting for him. That was a long time for her to take out of her day too. And she would have to arrange for afterschool care for Josiah and Luce, and Gabriel had an idea that it wasn't too easy to find people to take the two children.

He lifted his head to look at Heather again. "Do I have to see Dr. De Klerk? Or just the nurses?"

Heather's eyebrows went up. "I don't know. Does it make a difference?"

"I dunno."

"Gabe? Do you have a problem with Dr. De Klerk? He's a very busy man; I know he can come across a little gruff, sometimes… impatient…"

"Yeah. I guess that's it." Gabriel looked back down at his plate.

"Well, don't you worry about that. If you want, I'll stay with you, and I can act as a buffer. He can talk to me instead of you."

It was a tempting offer, but Gabriel thought that might be worse. De Klerk would think he was being a baby, and Heather would end up pressuring Gabriel instead of protecting him. She wasn't like Keisha. She didn't really care how he felt. Just whether they were cooperating with DFS and the clinic. She thought that whatever the clinic said was right.

"No. Thanks."

She looked at him for a minute and then shrugged. "Okay. So Monday to the clinic, and then Tuesday for your hearing."

Gabriel nodded. Hopefully, they would withdraw the meds that were making him sick on Monday, so that he only had a few more days to take them. It still felt like an eternity.

Gabriel was asleep when Collin came in to bed. Collin didn't turn the overhead light on, but turned on the lamp. He towered over Gabriel for a moment, looking down at him. Gabriel froze, sure that if he moved a muscle, Collin was going to smash him. Collin reached out a big hand and shoved Gabriel's shoulder, pushing him down into the mattress and letting it spring up again.

"You keep your mouth shut," he ordered. "I don't want your scrawny little butt making any trouble for me; you got it?"

Gabriel nodded, his heart thudding so hard in his chest that it made him cough.

"I can't hear you," Collin pressed.

"Yes," Gabriel said.

"Yes, what?"

"Yes, sir." Gabriel hoped that was what Collin was looking for.

Collin nodded. His eyes were narrow, glittering with the reflected light from the lamp. "All I want is to be left alone. I got another year in foster, maybe two if I'm lucky and can get an extension. That's how long I got to get picked up by a scout. After that, I'm on my ass in the cold, hard street. Flipping burgers or begging for money, with no place to live and no team to play for. I just want everyone to leave me alone, so I get my one chance to get on a team."

"Yes, sir."

"So you shut up and don't make any kind of trouble for me. Or I'm gonna be seriously pissed. If I'm gonna get in trouble anyway, I'm gonna mess you up to make it worth my while."

Collin gave Gabriel's shoulder one more shove, then turned away to get ready for bed. Gabriel watched him; his eyes squinted almost shut so that it would look like he was going back to sleep. He hadn't really looked at Collin's body before, embarrassed by the bigger boy's physique and lack of self-consciousness as he changed. This time, he did look, assessing him. Did Collin have what it took to become a professional football player? Or at least to be scouted by a college team and given a scholarship and paid-for dorm?

Collin's body was big and bulked up with muscle. He wasn't fat and sloppy like some of the football players that Gabriel had seen. His muscles were well-defined. Cut. Size and strength weren't all it took to make a good football player, but Collin moved with self-assured grace, his movements quick and economical. In the light from the lamp, Gabriel could see silvery marks on his back and arms. Scars. Collin had a big tattoo on one shoulder and an armband tattoo around the other arm, a geometric monochrome black pattern.

Collin didn't turn back around and look at Gabriel, but climbed into bed, reached over to turn off the lamp, and was quiet. Gabriel listened to his slow, steady breaths, waiting to fall back asleep.

Gabriel had been dreading going to the clinic and yet anticipating it at the same time. If he just knew that they were going to fix his meds, he would have been excited about it. But there was no way to know what they were going to do. Heather and Matt were patient and reassuring, telling Gabriel every time that he threw up that the clinic would get everything taken care of, and that the meds were helping. Pretty soon, he would be all better, able to do all the things that a normal kid could do. Somehow the toxic chemicals were going to change his metabolism so that he had all the energy he needed and none of the adverse effects of mito. Gabriel knew that wasn't going to happen. He had wished, prayed, and daydreamed about it many times. He knew it wasn't going to happen.

At the clinic, they read through his log and made him explain everything as if Heather hadn't already called the clinic to report Gabriel's problems on a daily basis. The nurse who took Gabriel's weight noted it down and shook her head.

"You have lost weight," she accused. As if he had somehow done it on purpose.

"Yeah. I keep throwing everything up when I take the pills."

"You need to eat and drink enough before you take them."

"And then I throw up more!" Gabriel insisted.

"Honestly," she shook her head and scribbled something else on his chart. Gabriel couldn't see what it was, but imagined it was something like 'patient is uncooperative' or 'patient refuses to follow instructions.' He closed his eyes and waited for directions about where to go and what test he was supposed to take next.

In the end, he didn't even see Dr. De Klerk, which was a huge relief. He was just shown into the final exam room, where a nurse or intern came in to give him his instructions. It was a young Asian man, who ran his fingers through his hair as he looked at the clipboard. He sat down on the rolling stool and didn't look at Gabriel as he went through the instructions.

"Okay. We've added an antiemetic to your protocol. That should keep you from throwing up and make a big difference to how much of the meds you can absorb. Hopefully, that will let you put on some weight again. We've switched you to a different antihistamine; Benadryl causes drowsiness in a lot of people, and we want you to be alert and energetic, don't we? I think the nosebleeds are probably just a result of throwing up and tearing those membranes. We'll just keep an eye on the leg cramps and see if they resolve themselves."

Gabriel scowled. "The muscle cramps are really bad!"

"I think they'll probably go away as your body gets more used to the medications. In the meantime, keep on with gentle heat and massage, that's the best thing for them."

"What about painkillers? Can't I have Tylenol or aspirin or something for the pain?"

The intern looked at Gabriel for the first time, glancing up from the clipboard. He flipped through a couple of pages of the clipboard, but Gabriel didn't see his eyes going back and forth. He wasn't actually reading anything.

"No painkillers allowed on your protocol at this time," the man said, and let the papers fall back into place on the clipboard. "Do you have any other questions?"

Gabriel sighed in exasperation and swallowed his anger and frustration with a big lump in his throat. "The protocol isn't helping. I want to just go back to what I was doing with my mom before."

"You haven't been on the protocol long enough to evaluate whether it's making a difference or not. Especially when you aren't able to absorb the full dose of medication. Give it some time. We'll see you back in... two weeks."

The intern stood up, and swept out of the room without so much as a wave or 'good-bye.' Gabriel sat there for a minute, wondering what he was supposed to do next. A nurse poked her head in the door.

"All done? Let me take you back to your mom," the young blond said, with a pretty smile that made Gabriel feel flushed. He looked down at the floor as he followed her out, pretending that he needed to watch his feet to make his way down the hall. A couple of twists took Gabriel out to the waiting room where Heather sat tapping on her phone.

She looked up at him and smiled. "All set, then?"

"Yeah. I got a couple of new prescriptions. Did they give them to you?"

"Got them. We'll stop at the pharmacy downstairs before we go. Do you want another wrap from down there?"

Gabriel shifted his weight. "No... maybe something else this time."

"What do you want?"

"Just... I dunno. Something from the gas station. Nuts or a granola bar or something."

"I have granola bars for emergencies in the car. Does that sound good?"

"Yeah. Sure." Gabriel wasn't too keen on the weird wraps from the juice bar. But he also wondered how long the 'emergency' granola bars had been sitting in the car. Just what constituted a granola bar emergency?

"Sounds good," Heather enthused.

They walked out to the elevator.

"So they're putting you on something for nausea," Heather observed. "That's good. I think that's the worst side effect. If you can get over that, you'll be much happier."

"Uh-huh..." Gabriel had to admit that being able to eat a meal without throwing up again sounded like heaven. He hadn't realized before what a blessing it was to actually be able to eat. He couldn't imagine how bulimic girls managed to make themselves throw up all the time. It was awful. "But they didn't give me anything for the muscle cramps."

"Maybe they'll go away on their own. If not, we'll just keep doing what we have been."

"That's not helping. They could at least give me painkillers or a muscle relaxant or something."

"Let's work on one thing at a time. This will help, and maybe by the next time we come back, the muscle cramps will be gone. And you'll be feeling a lot better, being able to eat."

Gabriel watched out the side of the glass elevator as it descended, keeping any other complaints to himself. He already knew whose side Heather was on. If she voiced any complaints or didn't follow the clinic's instructions to a T, they knew what would happen. DFS wouldn't have any problem taking him away from the Foegels just the same as they had from Keisha.

In spite of the antiemetic, Gabriel was feeling pretty queasy when they walked into the courthouse. He was beginning to regret his insistence that they let him appear before the judge. He was feeling small and inadequate. He didn't know what he was going to say to the judge if they decided to let him talk. He didn't want to see Carol Scott and her red manicured nails. He didn't want to hear the allegations about Keisha repeated. He didn't want to be there at all.

"Not much farther," Heather said, putting her hand on Gabriel's back as he slowed.

"I'm just... sorta nervous."

"You don't need to worry. You don't have to be eloquent. You don't even have to address the court if you don't want to. You're here, and that's a big thing. Just sit back and listen, and see what you think. You've never been to a court hearing before, right?"

Gabriel tugged at his collar and the tie around his neck. It was too tight, choking off his breathing. Heather had insisted that he couldn't appear in court in a t-shirt, or even in a nice polo or button-up shirt. It had to be a crisp white, long-sleeved, button-up shirt with a tie. Like he was going to a wedding or a funeral. Even at weddings and funerals, he'd been able to get out of wearing a white shirt and tie before. Unless the invitation said formal, and nobody he knew ever did formal.

"No, it's my first time," he choked out.

"It isn't anything to be scared of. It's formal, but nothing to worry about. No one is going to yell at you or criticize you. It's all for your welfare."

"Yeah. Okay."

They arrived at the correct courtroom. There was an electronic announcement board, and Gabriel's name was on the screen. It made him feel even more queasy. Heather rubbed his back gently and pointed him toward a bench to wait on. Gabriel sat down and massaged his shaky knees. He really wished that they would give him his braces back.

"You're doing a lot better at the walking," Heather offered. "You're getting around a lot better these days."

He had even noticed it at the clinic, where he hadn't needed a wheelchair to get around like he had the first day. And he had been able to walk down more than one corridor at a time. But he didn't want to think about that. He just wanted to get out of there.

"Gabriel!"

Keisha's voice ran through him like an electric shock. Gabriel sat bolt upright, his head whipping around to see her before he even had a conscious thought.

"Mom!"

"Oh, I'm so glad that you came!" Keisha rushed over to hug him. Gabriel stood up to hug her, but after a moment, she was pushing him back down to the bench. She sat beside him, winding her arm around behind his back to give him a squeeze.

Gabriel hadn't even thought about her being there. He had been so focused on getting a chance to talk to the judge and to tell his story that he hadn't thought that she and her lawyer might come to fight for his return as well. It was silly, thinking about it, that he hadn't.

"How are you?" Keisha whispered in Gabriel's ear.

Gabriel looked around for Carol Scott, but she wasn't present yet. "Mom… I didn't know you'd be here."

"Of course, I am! Sometimes they don't notify me of a hearing until a few hours before. But I'm here for every single one."

Gabriel felt warm and comforted by this. He hadn't been able to fight for himself, but she had been there. Every time.

Keisha stroked his face. "You're so thin, baby. It makes me so mad that I was getting some weight on you, and they went and did all this… you look like you'd blow away in a strong wind!"

"It's better now. The meds were making me throw everything up; but they've got me on something now to calm my stomach down."

"My poor baby. That must have been so awful. And I couldn't be there for you, to take care of you…" She shook her head, her eyes dark and full of pain. "I just can't forgive myself for letting this happen to you. If I had known a couple of months ago what I know now… I would have taken you to that damn clinic. It makes me so mad!"

"It's not your fault. I don't think you should have either. It wasn't just you. I still wouldn't go there, if I had any choice."

"Shh. You can't say that. Don't let anyone hear you talking like that." She glanced around at the gathering people. "We just have to go along with it."

The courtroom doors opened. A court clerk in a brown uniform looked around and announced: 'Gabriel Tate hearing.'

"That's us," Heather said, touching Gabriel on the shoulder.

He looked at her, and she laughed self-consciously.

"I guess you knew that," she giggled.

Gabriel and Keisha got up. They all went into the courtroom. The judge wasn't there yet; the room was empty. They went up to the front row of seats and sat down. Gabriel leaned his cheek on Keisha's tightly curled hair. He closed his eyes and inhaled the familiar scent. He'd almost forgotten what she smelled like, but it all came flooding back as they sat there. Everything about her brought back rushes of memory. The way she moved, the way she talked, her touch on his skin. And her smell.

"I love you, Mom," he whispered. "I'm so glad you're here."

"You too, baby."

Other people filed in behind them and sat down. Gabriel glanced back now and then but didn't recognize most of them. Were they just spectators? There to see how a hearing was run? He hadn't expected there to be any kind of audience. He thought it was rude to keep turning around and looking at people, so he stopped and just faced the front.

The clerk announced Judge Kenneth Dreyer's name, and everyone stood up. Gabriel hurried to get to his feet. The judge walked in and glanced over the courtroom. He sat down, and the clerk advised everybody to be seated. Gabriel sat back down again.

"Markus, nice to see you," Judge Dreyer commented. "I thought you'd be taking advantage of the good golf weather."

Gabriel turned around, his chest tight. Dr. Markus De Klerk was sitting a couple of rows behind him, looking just as proud and arrogant as ever.

"Can't ignore my civic duty," he said in a lazy drawl.

Dreyer nodded. He looked around at the other people filling the courtroom. "What is this?" he demanded. "I don't think I declared this an open courtroom, did I?" He glared at the court clerk.

"Do you want a closed hearing?" the clerk asked.

"Yes, closed," Dreyer snapped, looking down at the papers on his desk.

"Only those with a direct connection with the case will be allowed," the clerk advised. "Everyone else, please leave the courtroom."

There was the hum of low voices and feet shuffling as the spectators made their way out of the courtroom.

"Damn vultures," Dreyer muttered. "Everybody else here has a direct connection with the case? Who are you?" he demanded of Mrs. Foegel.

"I'm Gabriel's foster mother."

The judge considered this for a minute, then nodded. His eyes focused on Gabriel. "I assume that you are Mr. Gabriel Tate."

Gabriel nodded, swallowing. "Yes, your honor."

"The biological parent," Judge Dreyer observed, nodding at Keisha and making the title sound like a curse. "And her lawyer. The good doctor. Where is the social worker?"

"Here, your honor," Carol's voice rang out as she hurried up the aisle. "I'm sorry I was late. I... ran into some road bumps."

He glared at her for a minute. "You're lucky I don't hold you in contempt," he growled. "Leave time for unexpected delays when you are coming into my courtroom." He looked around the courtroom at the small group, then straightened his papers, tapping them into a neat pile. "This is a progress hearing on minor Gabriel Tate. Court is in session. We'll hear a report from the social worker."

Carol stood up, smoothed her skirt, and outlined Gabriel's status in a few sentences. He was out of the hospital and in foster care. He had attended at the mito clinic and was following the protocol. He had had a supervised visitation with his biological mother. Carol believed that he was doing well and was in the best place for him. She sat back down.

Dreyer nodded. "That all sounds satisfactory. Dr. De Klerk, did you have anything to report?"

"Gabriel has been following the mito protocol, with one exception..." De Klerk paused to let this sink in. Gabriel stared down at his hand. He hadn't realized that Heather had reported his failure to take one dose of his medication. "He is progressing satisfactorily in all areas."

Dreyer nodded and wrote something down.

"Your honor," Keisha's lawyer spoke up. "I believe that Gabriel has, in fact, lost more weight since he started the protocol."

Judge Dreyer's gaze shifted over to Dr. De Klerk for his response.

"Gabriel lost some weight initially," De Klerk confirmed. "But we made some changes to his treatment, and I believe we have it under control now. Gabriel was in the weight clinic previously. As we are all aware. But I'm sure we will see an improvement in a couple of weeks at his next evaluation."

Dreyer nodded. "That sounds reasonable." He looked around. "Anything else to report? Mrs.—ah—Foegel?"

Heather rose a few inches out of her seat, looking like she was curtsying. "No, your Honor. Gabriel is fitting in and working hard."

She landed back in her seat again.

Dreyer picked up his gavel. "Good. We will meet again—"

"Your honor," Keisha's lawyer protested. "The biological parent would like an opportunity to speak. Gabriel himself is in the courtroom today, and I think he would like to be heard. His input in these proceedings is very important—"

"The biological parent and the minor are not scheduled to speak."

"It's vital that the court hears all viewpoints—"

"We have heard from the biological parent before," Judge Dreyer growled. "Repeatedly, in fact. The court has been more than generous with its time with Mrs. Tate."

"What about Gabriel? This is the court's first opportunity to hear from his own mouth—"

"This court does not hear from children. We know that Mr. Tate has been influenced and indoctrinated by his mother for years. We are just going to hear Keisha Tate's words parroted back. And as I said, this court has indulged Mrs. Tate repeatedly in past hearings."

He rapped the gavel down.

"We are adjourned. Let's get another update in a month. If there is anything before that, please make an application to the court."

He stood up and walked back out through the small door at the back of the courtroom. Gabriel sat with his mouth hanging open in disbelief. "That's it? Is it over? He didn't even give me a chance!"

Keisha gave his hand a squeeze and looked at him with a helpless expression. "That's how it's been right from the start. At least he didn't throw me out this time."

"He threw you out?"

She nodded. "He hasn't been as 'indulgent' as he makes out. He doesn't want to hear from us." Keisha turned around and looked at Dr. De Klerk. "Only from his cronies."

Gabriel was afraid to turn and have Dr. De Klerk look at him. "Shouldn't there be some kind of rule about him hearing from a friend? Shouldn't he let a different judge hear it?"

"The rules are pretty narrow. He doesn't have to recuse himself unless they are in business together or something like that," the lawyer said, hearing them and leaning toward them.

Gabriel looked at the lawyer. "He's allowed to say that I can't speak when the whole hearing is about me?"

"I'm sorry, but... yes. He's not required to hear from you. Most courts would allow you to speak, and would take the wishes of a fifteen-year-old into account, but he doesn't have to. And he gave a reason; he didn't just deny you. There's nothing we can do about that."

"Can't we... appeal it? Go to his boss, or a higher court or something?"

The lawyer shrugged helplessly. "The judge is the highest authority in this case. There is a court of appeal, but for rulings. This wasn't a ruling, just a procedural question. And one with clear precedent."

Gabriel looked at the lawyer. He'd heard 'no' buried in the answer somewhere. He turned his head slightly toward Keisha. "Maybe you need a new lawyer."

"Mr. Holland has been very helpful, Gabriel. You haven't seen all that we're up against. Judge Dreyer is..."

"A prominent judge, with lots of political cachet," Holland murmured. "You have to be extremely careful of your step with a judge like that. There could be a lot of negative... repercussions."

"You don't want to be debriefed," Gabriel guessed.

Holland smiled. "If you mean disbarred; yes, you're right."

"Oh." Gabriel shrugged. "Right."

Keisha pulled Gabriel's head against her, cuddling him. "We'll beat them somehow, Gabriel. I'm not giving up. I'll get you back home."

Gabriel blinked and sniffled. He took a deep breath, giving her a hug back. "I know."

"Folks, if you would move along, please. We have another hearing coming up," the court clerk said, motioning that it was time to leave.

They all walked toward the door, Gabriel and Keisha still holding each other, even if it did make it more difficult to walk down the aisle without tripping.

"When is our next visitation?" Gabriel asked.

"I don't know yet." Keisha sighed. "They said that you need more time to settle in at your foster home without me stirring things up. So I'm trying to keep my distance, but still keep nudging them for a new date."

"Okay."

She rubbed his back. She glanced over at Heather, who was talking to Carol Scott a few feet away. "How is your foster family? Is it okay?"

"Pretty good," Gabriel said, thinking about Collin. "They try to make things easier. The hospital never helped me with anything. And they're better about my food allergies and snacks. But… it's not home."

"No, I know. Are they feeding you good? You've lost so much weight."

"Mostly at the hospital, and then throwing up with these drugs. But it's better now. I can eat again."

"Sit down here," Keisha ordered, motioning to the bench they had been sitting on earlier. She could feel his legs shaking as she held onto him. She touched his leg when he sat beside her. "You don't have your braces on. What did you do with them?"

"They took them away at the hospital." At the familiar tightening of her lips, Gabriel rushed to defuse her anger. "But I'm doing okay without them. My legs are getting stronger. Please... don't cause trouble over it."

"They can't take them away! Your hypotonia—you need them."

"Don't. Please."

She shook her head. "All right... but..."

"Just don't. They're not going to let me go back to you if they think you're going to interfere with the medical treatment."

"Okay. Okay, I hear you, Gabriel. I'll keep my mouth shut. But it makes me so mad!"

He didn't tell her about their removing him from all his meds at the hospital. He could just imagine how that would go over. She would be furious if she knew everything that they had done at the hospital.

"Gabriel, I'm sorry, but we have to go now," Heather hovered nearby, not wanting to interrupt the moment. "I have to be at Luce's school this afternoon."

Gabriel kissed Keisha's cheek. "I'll see you... soon."

"I love you, Gabriel... don't forget that."

CHAPTER THIRTEEN

F OR THE NEXT COUPLE of weeks, Gabriel tried to just keep his head down and not cause any trouble. If he fit in and didn't make any waves, then maybe DFS would be quicker to let him see Keisha again. It was easier to take his pills now that he wasn't throwing them up again an hour later. He still got nauseated, but he rarely threw up. The nosebleeds were also negligible and the new antihistamine cleared up the rash without making him hung over the next day.

The excruciating leg cramps still returned every few nights. Gabriel tried not to call for Matt and Heather unless the cramps were particularly bad, suffering through them in silence. He slept with electric blankets that he could turn on as soon as they started to cramp up.

It seemed like barely any time had passed before it was time to go back to the clinic for another update and round of testing. Gabriel picked at his toast, feeling queasy even though he hadn't taken his pills yet. They were all laid out beside his plate. With his usual meds, the protocol, and the additional anti-nausea and allergy pills, he was now taking a total of fifteen pills in the morning. It was a wonder he didn't rattle when he walked.

"Collin, would you take Luce to the bus?" Heather asked as she buzzed around the kitchen getting the lunches put into backpacks. "I don't know what Josiah is doing this morning; I've got to get him moving."

Gabriel looked up from his breakfast at Collin. "I'll do it," he offered.

Heather stopped her frantic packing. "Well, that's very nice. Thank you for volunteering, Gabriel. Are you sure you're okay to stand out there waiting?"

"Yeah. I can do it." Gabriel stood up and swallowed his pills in a couple of handfuls, washing them down well. He went around the table to where Luce sat, holding an apple slice up over her head, looking at it against the light. "Hey, Luce. It's time for the bus."

He pressed a couple more apple slices into her other hand and picked up her plate. "Come on, time to go to the door." He couldn't hold her hand because both were occupied, but he took her by the wrist and gave her a gentle tug.

Her eyes followed the plate in Gabriel's other hand, and she went with him like the proverbial donkey led by a carrot.

"Good girl," Gabriel murmured. "That's right."

He knew he had to do what he could to encourage her because he didn't have the strength to pull her or force her to do anything. It was pretty bad when he couldn't overpower a wiry eight-year-old girl, but Luce was powerful when she was upset. At the door, he put down the plate on the bench, and Luce followed and grabbed a cube of cheese.

"Shoes now, Luce."

Gabriel offered her shoes one at a time and she slid her feet into them without objection. Gabriel did up the velcro.

Heather strode to the door and put down Luce's backpack. "Thanks again, Gabriel. You're doing great. It's a big help."

Gabriel offered Luce her coat and she put her arms through the sleeves one at a time without looking at him. She held the cheese in front of her face, turning it around and around before nibbling the corner.

"You'll need to carry your backpack."

She picked it up and walked out and down the sidewalk when he opened the door. She seemed to be into the routine now and didn't need so much encouragement. She went to the end of the sidewalk and stood there, waiting. Gabriel followed a little behind, not quite as quick on his feet. When he stopped beside her, she slid her hand into his, not once looking at him or trying to say anything. He hadn't heard any clear words out of Luce yet. He'd heard her scream, grunt, and make random noises at the top of her voice, apparently getting a thrill just out of hearing herself. He'd heard her babble to herself while she played, or hum the theme songs of her favorite TV shows when she watched them. There had been a few times when he had seen her grab Heather's hand, and make noises to her, which Heather seemed reasonably adept at translating. But she had no way of telling the Foegels if someone was abusing her. She was completely vulnerable.

The yellow bus arrived a few minutes later. Luce stepped onto it and went directly to her usual seat. The bus driver gave a little wave at Gabriel, shut the doors, and pulled out. Gabriel headed back into the house. When he got to the door, Collin was lacing up his huge high-tops. Gabriel waited, not wanting to compete for the space.

Collin stood up. He pushed his face aggressively toward Gabriel's. "You like little girls?" he demanded. "You like it when they can't talk back? Huh? Is that it?"

Gabriel swallowed and licked his lips. "No," he said, mouth dry as cotton. "I just don't like seeing her get hurt."

"She's like an animal," Collin growled. "She doesn't feel pain the same way you do. Or maybe *you* don't either." He knocked Gabriel roughly back into the doorway. "Are you an animal too?"

Gabriel steadied himself on his feet. "I'm not bothering you," he pointed out. "If you just want to be left alone, then leave *me* alone."

Collin's mouth twisted sourly. He looked like he was going to push Gabriel again, then changed his mind. "Fine," he agreed. He swung his sports bag over his shoulder and walked out the door.

Gabriel let out a sigh of relief and shut the door. He sat down on the bench for a minute to rest his shaking legs. He could hear Heather arguing with a whiny Josiah down the hall. Still in the bedroom; it didn't sound like she had managed to get him to the breakfast table yet, and his bus would be there in another five minutes.

Gabriel went back to the kitchen, cleared away his unfinished breakfast, and put the dirty dishes into the dishwasher. Glancing through the cupboards, he put a juice box, a granola bar, and a string cheese on the counter next to Josiah's Superman lunch bag. Heather hurried in a minute later, dragging Josiah behind her. She had his backpack and reached for the lunch bag. She looked at the small pile of snacks on the counter, frowning, as she tucked the lunch bag into the backpack.

"For his breakfast," Gabriel explained. "I thought he could eat that on the bus."

"Good idea," Heather approved. "Thank you. Josiah, take these. Get your shoes on."

"Is that enough for him?" Gabriel checked.

"Yes, it will do just fine."

She picked up the backpack and hurried Josiah to the door to get ready. Josiah was just going out the door as the bus pulled up. Heather shut the door and came back to the kitchen, shaking her head. "It is a challenge some mornings, Gabriel!"

"Yeah," Gabriel agreed. "You have a lot of kids to look after."

"Five doesn't really seem like a lot. I grew up in a family with eight, and we've had more kids at a time than that before. But when you start to add special needs into the mix…" She took a deep breath. "Well, it's just great if everyone can pitch in. And you did that today." She went over and picked up Alex, who was starting to fuss. "You're so good with the little ones. Sometimes an 'only child' has a hard time relating when they get put in a family with foster siblings."

"I haven't lived in a home with other kids. But I've shared rooms at the hospital a lot. And played in children's wards."

"I hadn't thought about that."

"Sometimes you see the same kids over again, another time. The chronic ones. I like little ones better than ones my age or older, usually." Gabriel thought about the last hospital stay. "I got along good with Renata, though."

"You mentioned her. Well, I appreciate you volunteering to help today, and seeing a need without being told, too. You were very kind in the way you got Luce ready."

Gabriel looked at Heather's face, wondering if she knew how Collin treated Luce.

"I'm going to get Alex fed," Heather said, looking down at the baby and making faces at her. "Then we'll need to head out to the clinic."

Gabriel was worried about having to see Dr. De Klerk at the clinic again, and he hadn't even thought about any of the other medical professionals that he could run into there. When he walked into the nurse's office to be weighed and have his vitals recorded, he stopped dead. The nurse following behind him bumped into him, almost knocking him down.

She grabbed at him. "I'm sorry—I'm so sorry, I wasn't paying attention. Are you okay?" She hung onto Gabriel's elbow, rigid, like she expected him to fall right over.

Gabriel pulled away from her. "It's okay." He didn't want to go in, but there was nowhere else for him to go. The nurse who was waiting for him was Nurse Birch from the weight clinic. She looked just as shocked to see him as he was to see her. Her face drained of all color.

"Mr. Tate." She took the clipboard from the nurse behind Gabriel and looked down at it. "Well, let's work you up. Step onto the scale and we'll see how you're doing." Her voice was harsh, the words coming out too fast. Gabriel stepped up onto the scale and waited for the electronic readout to display his weight.

Nurse Birch read it aloud and wrote it onto Gabriel's chart. She flipped back to the previous update. "And that means that you have gained... wait—you've lost four pounds." Her brows drew down. "Why did you lose weight? You're not still throwing up, are you?"

"No."

"You are not getting enough calories. What has your appetite been like?"

"Not great. And I still get nauseated, so it's hard to eat much."

"Come sit down." She gestured to a chair. She took his pulse and then listened to his chest and back. She was scowling as she jotted figures down. "Put your arm in the cuff." They had a fancy automatic blood pressure device instead of the manual sphygmomanometer.

Gabriel put his arm in and waited as it cycled.

Birch looked at the final reading. "Hold still. Let's try that again."

Gabriel waited while she ran the machine through another cycle. He was careful not to move in case the machine was extra sensitive. Some of them were quite persnickety.

"It's pretty high," Birch said, her mouth turned down. She flipped back through the chart to look at the previous reading. "It wasn't that high last time. That is concerning. Are you feeling stressed?"

Gabriel coughed. "Uh… yeah."

She looked at his face. Gabriel turned away, hot and self-conscious. There were several long seconds of silence. Gabriel closed his eyes and rubbed his nose, waiting for her to continue with the tests or to send him to the next room.

"Why are you stressed?" Birch questioned.

Gabriel's stomach twisted. His pulse was pounding in his temples. He could hear the rushing in his ears. "It's nothing."

"Mr. Tate. You need to be honest with me. Whatever is going on is obviously affecting you physically. Without knowing what it is, we can't know how to address it."

Gabriel put his elbows on his knees, holding his hands over his eyes. He groaned.

"Gabriel."

Gabriel didn't look at her. "*You.* You reported my mom to DFS, didn't you?"

"What?" her voice rose several tones, shocked. "What makes you think that?" For a minute, Gabriel thought that he and Renata had been wrong. It hadn't been Nurse Birch who had reported him after all. "Those reports are confidential," she said. "Who told you I reported you?"

He squinted at her through his fingers. "Nobody. Just figured it out."

"Oh." She stared down at her clipboard. For a long time, she was silent. "I'm going to write down that it's situational hypertension. I recommend that someone else take another blood pressure reading before you leave today."

Gabriel nodded. "Okay."

She looked like she wanted to say something else to him. Her mouth kept pursing, her jaw muscles tensing, grinding her teeth.

"You were wrong. You shouldn't have reported her. My weight was going up," he said emphatically. "Since then, it's only gone down."

"It will stabilize," Birch said. "Now that you're not throwing up, we only need to get your calorie consumption higher."

"My mom had it working. The hospital couldn't even give me food I wasn't allergic to. My mom had me on supplements that were working. The stuff she was doing was helping."

Birch's eyes showed doubt. "It is dangerous to be adding herbs and other supplements that are unproven, especially with all the meds that you are on. It's irresponsible. They could be contraindicated. There isn't enough research into interactions."

"Look at me." Gabriel looked down at his bony arms and chest. "Does it look like I'm healthier taking these pills? Or the ones my mom had me on?"

She wrote something else down on his chart. "Down the hall to room four-twelve," she instructed. "You can find your way?"

Gabriel got up. She handed him the clipboard to take with him. Once out into the hallway, Gabriel looked down at it to see what she had written. He saw the word 'supplements.' It was circled, and there was a question mark next to it.

Gabriel looked with distaste at the glass next to his plate.

Heather saw him eyeing it. "You need to drink it, bud."

"I know I'm supposed to… but it's not officially part of the protocol, is it? I mean, the pills are the protocol. The formula is just a suggestion to help me put on weight."

"It is to help you put on weight," Heather agreed. "And you need to drink it."

"My mom would never let me drink something like that. It's not food; it's just straight chemicals."

"If you didn't have the nerve to be allergic to dairy, you could have a dairy-based formula," Heather said with a teasing smile.

"It tastes awful."

"You can add some chocolate syrup if you think that would help. Or you can drink it down as fast as you can without tasting it. It's all up to you. But you need to drink it."

"It's… chalky… sludgy."

"Sounds horrible," she said cheerfully. "Enjoy it. Do what you can to get enough calories other ways and maybe you won't have to take it any more after your next appointment."

"Urggh." Gabriel shuddered.

Heather left him to his meal. Gabriel took his pills and his sandwich. He took the cup of formula away from the table. "I'm going to sit outside," he called to Heather.

She answered something from down the hall. Gabriel stepped outside and sat down on the wrought iron bench in front of the house. He swirled the drink in the cup and took a small sip. It was wretched stuff. He couldn't do as Heather suggested and just gulp it down. He would gag and throw it up again. He could only get it down a bit at a time.

"You don't need to look so miserable about it."

Gabriel's head snapped up. Renata was standing halfway across the lawn from him.

"Renata! What are you doing here?" Gabriel stood up but didn't know whether he should shake her hand, or hug her, or something else.

Renata laughed. She walked the rest of the way across the lawn and gave him a brief hug. "How are you, Gabe?"

"I'm... I'm good. What about you? You're out of the hospital. Does that mean you're feeling better?"

"I'm doing great. Let's sit down." She motioned to the bench.

Gabriel sat back down again, and she sat next to him. She held his hand. Gabriel still had his formula in the other hand. He took another sip, grimacing at the taste and texture.

"That looks painful," Renata laughed. "Doesn't taste good?"

"Uggh."

"You should take it like I do!" she touched her stomach where the tube was.

"It'd almost be worth the surgery."

She laughed. She looked him over critically, the corners of her eyes crinkled. "You're looking a lot better. Walking around. You don't look half-dead anymore."

Gabriel shrugged. "I guess. Still not as good as I was before they took me away from my mom, though. And they put me on this stuff instead of the diet that was helping me to gain weight before."

She shook her head and stared at the glass. "What's in it? It could be some kind of poison. Experimental bioweapons. Viruses. Nanobots?"

"It's just a stupid soy supplement. Vitamins and minerals ground up in gritty soy milk and sweetened with corn syrup. To help me gain weight."

She considered. "I'd rather drink nanobots."

Gabriel studied Renata in turn. "How about you? You're feeling better? Your ribs and your... psych stuff?"

"They let me out. The ribs are still tender, but they're healing. Got the drain out. Lung's staying inflated."

"How did you end up here? Is your foster family close by?"

She looked at him sideways. "No. I just decided to look you up. See how my psych ward buddy was doing."

"So... what? You ran away?" Gabriel took another gulp of the formula.

"Why don't you just dump that?" Renata asked. She motioned to the little overgrown garden behind them. "Nobody would know."

"I have to do what they say. If I want to be able to go back to my mom—"

"Oh, Gabriel. You're away from me for a few weeks, and they already got you brainwashed again. You know they're not sending you back to your mom. Ever."

"She said if she knew it would get me taken away, she would have put me in the mito clinic. If I follow all of their instructions, and she says she'll keep me in the program…"

Renata raised an eyebrow at him. Gabriel cleared his throat and took another drink. If he didn't believe that there was some chance he could go back to Keisha, Gabriel didn't know if he could go on.

Heather came out the front door. "Oh… you have company!"

"Uh… yeah." Gabriel let go of her hand and looked at Renata. He didn't know what to say. He didn't want to cause any trouble for her. "This is Renata."

"Oh, your friend from the hospital."

"Yeah." Gabriel glanced over at Renata, sensing the smile before he saw it. "I might have mentioned you."

"Well, I would hope so!"

"I didn't know that the two of you were keeping in touch…"

Gabriel couldn't explain what he didn't understand himself, so he said nothing. Renata gave Heather a bland smile. "You can find anything on Google."

Frown lines appeared between Heather's eyebrows. She looked at Gabriel. "You finished your drink?"

He displayed the cup's contents to her. "Just about."

"Good. Don't you go pouring it out. My garden may need weeding, but it doesn't need a dietary supplement."

Renata giggled.

"Why don't you bring Renata in, and you guys can have a couple of cookies?"

Gabriel took a breath and drank the rest of the formula. "Cookies sound good."

"However we can get extra calories in you."

Gabriel and Renata got up and passed by Heather to enter the house. Gabriel led the way to the kitchen. He knew where to find the cookies. He put a couple each on a plate and sat down at the table with Renata. She looked at them.

"Those are homemade! Nobody makes homemade anymore!"

"They're really good," Gabriel informed her. "I helped make them."

"You?"

He nodded. He waited for her to help herself to one and then realized his mistake. "Oh... I forgot...!" Gabriel looked at Heather.

"Renata can't have cookies?" Heather asked. "Is it the sugar? What can you have, Renata?"

"Nothing by mouth," Renata said. "I have a tube."

"Oh. Yes, I think I remember Gabriel mentioning that. Well, I'd offer you some of Alex's formula, but you probably have a specific one that you're supposed to be taking."

"Yeah. What does Alex get?"

Heather told her the brand and variety, and Renata nodded. "Yeah. That would make me puke. It's all gotta be predigested and chemicals and stuff."

"Fun. You won't be staying long, then. You'll need to go home for another feeding."

Renata nodded, her eyes on Gabriel while he ate one of the cookies.

"Where are you living, Renata? Is your foster family in town here?"

"No. Closer to the valley," Renata said vaguely.

"I know most of the foster families around here who take kids with medical needs."

"Uh-huh." Renata didn't volunteer any information about her family at this broad hint. "So how old is Alex? What's wrong with him?"

"Her," Gabriel corrected. He looked at Heather to supply more information about Alex. He'd never asked her what was wrong with any of the other foster kids.

"Alex has something called Shaken Baby Syndrome," Heather explained. "She has neurological damage from one of her biological parents shaking her."

Renata nodded. Gabriel could tell by her expression that she had a theory on this, but she kept her mouth shut and just smiled politely.

"I'll... leave you kids to talk. Your tutor is going to be here in about an hour, Gabriel."

"Okay. Thanks."

They waited for her to leave again. Gabriel looked back at Renata. "Okay. Let's hear it."

"What?"

"Shaken Baby Syndrome."

She grinned. "You already know what I think. It's bull. There wasn't any such thing until social workers needed another reason to take babies away from their bio parents. So they made something up."

"But Alex is damaged. You can see that looking at her. It isn't made up."

"Neither is your mito, but that doesn't mean they can't make up Munchhausen by Proxy to take you away from her, does it? A baby is sick and you say she was shaken, so you can take her away, get more money by putting her in foster care."

They went back out to the bench in front of the house. Gabriel shook his head. "If they say she was shaken, they would have to be able to prove it..."

"Just like they had to prove that your mom was poisoning you? Or she was neglecting your medical care? Or was she putting things into your head to make you think that you had symptoms that you didn't? They just throw everything that might pass in the charges. The judge takes one look at all the medical double-talk, and a kid with obvious medical problems, and say remove her. Get her out of there before the parents kill her."

"They must have done something. I've seen Alex."

Renata laughed. "You'd make a great judge. You don't know anything about what happened. Preemie baby has a brain bleed, must be Shaken Baby Syndrome. Floppy baby with neurological problems? Must be Shaken Baby Syndrome. Petechial bleeding? Shaken Baby Syndrome. Neck damage? Broken ribs? It's all Shaken Baby."

"How can they do that?"

"Do you think they actually do experiments to see what kind of injuries shaking a baby will produce?"

"Well... no."

"So how do they know?"

"Because some people really do shake their babies."

"Do they? Have you seen people do it? Like the social workers say you have to do to produce these injuries?" Renata demonstrated, miming shaking a baby violently, shaking and shaking and shaking. Gabriel's heart raced with anxiety just seeing her act it out. How could anyone do that?

"Of course not... no one would do that in front of a witness."

"So how do you compare a real case of Shaken Baby—if there is such a thing—with a fake one? With a bleed caused by a disease or an accident?"

How *would* you know? Gabriel slumped over and rubbed his temples. She was drawing him in again. Sucking him into her arguments. Making them sound reasonable.

"So what are you doing here?" he asked, putting further discussion of baby Alex or Shaken Baby Syndrome aside. "How did you even know where I was?"

"You knew where you were going before you left, remember? The Foegels. You knew from what Sky read."

"But how did you know where they lived? And how did you get here?"

"Google is your friend," Renata said obliquely.

Gabriel looked at her, waiting for her to explain clearly. Renata rolled her eyes. She looked at the front door of the house and then looked behind them, through the big living room window. She scanned up and down the street. Then she snuggled up closer to Gabriel and lowered her voice.

"I decided that somebody has to do something about it."

"About what?"

"About medical kidnap. It's even making it to the mainstream news. It's so common that they can't keep it hidden anymore. If we strike now, I think we can bring the whole structure tumbling down. We're at a tipping point."

"You want to... stop them from being able to take any more kids."

Renata nodded vigorously. "Exactly. We're going to expose what is going on, the corruption of the whole system. We have to get kids out from under their oppressors to tell their stories."

"We have to... what...?"

"You want to tell your story, right? Because you know that if people knew what was happening, they would be outraged. They would return you to your mom. If people could see the corruption, they would revolt against it."

Gabriel already knew that nobody was going to listen to him. "I've been trying," he said. "I even went to a court hearing of my case... but the judge wouldn't let me or my mom talk. She said that the judge has thrown her out before. They won't let us speak."

"Which judge?" Renata asked.

Gabriel was irritated by the segue. He scowled. "Dreyer."

"Oooh," Renata grabbed her chest as if shot. "Bad luck! He and Markey are golfing buddies."

Markey was Renata's nickname for Dr. De Klerk, Gabriel remembered. "Yeah, I figured. How did you know that?"

"Pssh. I've had them all at some point."

"Oh. So what am I supposed to do about Dreyer? I can't exactly get him to listen to me. Or get changed to someone else."

"My idea is bigger than one boy testifying in one courtroom."

"What, then?"

"I want to get kids away from their foster homes, to where they're safe to talk about what's going on. Get their stories told. If people can hear their stories from their own mouths, see how similar they are, how big the whole thing is…"

"Get kids away from their foster homes."

"Yeah. How about it, Gabe?"

"How about what? Me…?" Gabriel stared at her. "You want me to run away from the Foegels? And go where? Tell who?"

She was grinning, pleased with herself. "Why not?"

"Why—? Well, for one thing… I can't run!"

"You could do it if we planned it right. Not run, I don't mean. Just walk away."

"Where?"

"Did you ever hear of the underground railway?"

"I *am* black," Gabriel pointed out. "I couldn't exactly help hearing of the underground railway. It's the way that they got slaves away from their owners, to the north or Canada. So they could live as free people."

"So what if you and I started an underground railway for the foster kids? What's the difference? They're being kidnapped from their own homes and being treated as commodities, just like the black slaves. We get them out, give them a chance to tell their stories. Start an avalanche in the media."

"Where would they go? Where would they be safe to speak out?"

Renata had obviously not thought that far ahead. She meditated on the problem for a few minutes, leaning her chin on her palm. "Out of state," she said finally. "DFS is a state department Each one runs separately. If you suddenly showed up in California, they couldn't do anything without a new report, right? If you're not a criminal, they don't have to send you back where you came from."

"So you want me to run away to California with you?"

"It doesn't have to be California. You got somewhere you want to see?" She laughed.

Gabriel just sat there. She leaned over, looking into his face.

"Come on, Gabe…"

"So you ran away from your foster family."

She shrugged.

"What are you going to do? Where are you going to go? What's your plan?"

"I'm not stupid. I'm gonna stay below the radar and get whoever I can to come along. I don't need a foster family to survive."

"You can't just stop at McDonalds or a truck stop for something to eat. What are you going to do?"

She showed him her backpack. A ratty old army backpack. It looked like it was stuffed pretty full. "You think I'd leave without supplies? I got all the formula I could carry. Some ready-mixed, and some powder that you just have to add water to. Easier to carry that way."

"And your meds?"

"I've got my meds." She gave a little shrug. "The ones I need."

"Where are you going to stay?"

"Depends on how long I have to wait for you."

"I don't think it's a good idea, Renata. I'm sorry… I think my chances are better if I stay here, and do what I'm supposed to."

"So you're just gonna sit here and drink your nanobots and let DFS decide where you're going to live, what you're going to eat and drink, and what meds you're going to take? You know they're not going to send you back to your mom."

"They *could*."

"They're not going to. I've been around, Gabe. I know."

"Sometimes kids go back to their parents. I know. I've read it in the news. We just have to be patient."

"Judge Dread and Dr. Markey don't send kids back. Others might if they see through the wool DFS pulls over their eyes. But judges like Dreyer already know the score. They don't care if the allegations are true or not. They just care about money and power. And doctors like Markus De Klerk keep them fed."

"You really think so?"

"Didn't I warn you? I told you everything that was going to happen, didn't I? So why wouldn't you believe the rest?"

"I just don't... want to. I gotta believe that I'm going to go back to my mom if I just... try..."

Renata shook her head. She got up. "I'm gonna scram before your torturer—err, tutor—gets here. The fewer people that see me, the better."

"Where are you going to go?"

"I'll be around."

"You're not going... to California?"

"Not yet. I think you'll change your mind once you've had a chance to think about it. You're not dumb. I've got a couple of other kids to contact too."

Gabriel tried to envision what it was that Renata had in mind. "So you have other kids you think would run away... and talk about what happened to them. You think we could get the word out there about kids being taken away unfairly...?"

"Kidnapped," Renata questioned. "Language is powerful. Don't say 'taken away' or 'apprehended.' They were kidnapped. You and other kids that they just want to get foster care money for or put into research programs. The word is *kidnapped*."

Gabriel bit his lip. He stood up, following her to the front door. "So how do I contact you? If I change my mind?"

"I'll be in touch." Renata considered. "Go for walks. Tell Mrs. Foegel that you need to build up your stamina. I'll watch for you. You can't call me, and you can't tell anyone where I am."

"Nobody will ask."

"They'll be looking for me. It's not the first time I've escaped."

CHAPTER FOURTEEN

GABRIEL FELT SOMEONE WATCHING him and looked up from his schoolwork to see Heather standing in the doorway. He had been so lost in thought that he had completely lost track of time, and it took a minute to reorient himself. He could hear a kid's show playing on the television, so the younger kids were home from school now. He couldn't smell supper cooking yet, so it was still late afternoon or early evening.

Heather looked concerned, and Gabriel wondered whether he had been talking to himself or had an absence seizure. "Uh—hi. Sorry... I was thinking."

"Making any headway on that homework?"

Gabriel looked down at it. He had only written the first couple of lines of his essay. "No, not much. I got sort of... distracted."

"That can make it difficult! Let me know if you need any help with anything."

Gabriel wasn't sure why he would do that. She had already made it clear that she wasn't up to helping him with high school homework.

"It was nice to see your friend Renata," Heather said casually.

"Yeah. I was surprised. Didn't know that she was coming."

"I'm on a number of foster care email lists and newsletters."

"Uh... yeah? That's nice."

"They send out alerts, you know. When there is a missing child in the area. If a foster child runs away, sometimes a former foster parent knows where to look for them and can help out."

"Oh." Gabriel touched his pen to his paper like he was going to write more of the essay. But he couldn't even remember what the essay was supposed to be about. He just looked at the tip of his pen touching the paper. He could feel Heather's eyes still intent on him.

"Renata is a runaway. It's too bad we didn't know that when she showed up here. But I kind of wondered what was going on. Didn't you?"

"Sort of."

"You guys hadn't planned to meet...?"

"Last time I saw her, she was still in hospital. We didn't know when she would be getting out. I don't exactly have a phone or any other way to contact her. Or anyone else."

"If you want to call someone, just let me know. You can borrow one of the cell phones. But there are certain people that you are not allowed to call."

"Like my mom?" Gabriel looked up from his paper, not able to ignore the feeling of her eyes on him.

She nodded. "Like your mom. Did Renata give you a way to contact her? A phone number?"

"How would she get a phone?"

"She could have picked up a burner. Or borrowed a phone from a friend. She apparently took a good sum of money with her when she left."

Gabriel was shocked that Renata would have stolen from her foster parents. That was silly, though. He knew that she had stolen the backpack and formula, and whatever other clothes and sundries were in the backpack. Those were necessities. And the formula was hers; no one else would use it when she was gone. But stealing cash too seemed wrong.

"I didn't know she was going to run away. She didn't give me a number."

"Did she say where she was going to sleep tonight? Or where she was headed?"

Gabriel shook his head. "She wouldn't tell me anything."

"DFS is quite concerned about her. She has serious medical problems. And I gather from what they said… she could be a danger to herself or others."

"At the hospital, they said that she could get violent… but I never saw her act like that. I think… they just wanted me to stay away from her."

Heather walked the rest of the way into the room. She sat down on Gabriel's bed, looking at him intently. "We want to protect Renata. You need to tell me if you know anything. I know she wouldn't want you to, but you have to think about what is best, not about what she thinks you should or shouldn't do. You want the best for her, right?"

"Yeah."

"She seemed like a really nice girl." Heather smiled. "I can see why you like her so much. And she's pretty cute too, huh?"

Gabriel's face got hot. Sweat started to bead on his forehead. "We're just friends. Nothing like that. Just friends."

"That doesn't stop a girl from being attractive. Or a boy from being attracted."

Gabriel looked Heather square in the eye, ignoring how uncomfortable it was to do so. "I don't know where Renata is. I'm sorry."

"Okay." Heather got up off of the bed. "Thanks. If you do hear from her again, let me know. We need to get her back where she's safe."

Gabriel turned back to his essay without answering.

"Gabriel!" There was a squeal, followed by a thump on the mattress that made Gabriel jump, followed by a heavy mass landing in the middle of his chest. It was Josiah. Gabriel turned over, tumbling Josiah off of him, onto the bed.

Gabriel rubbed his eyes. "What are you doing here?"

"It's Saturday!"

Gabriel gave him a thumbs-up. "Yay. No school."

"Come watch TV with me!"

179

The previous Saturday, Gabriel hadn't been feeling well in the early morning and Josiah had recruited him as he came out of the bathroom. They had lain in front of the TV with blankets around them, eating sugary cereal, until almost noon.

"I was going to sleep longer. I'm still tired."

"No! Come watch cartoons!"

"Shut up!" Collin growled. He fished around beside the bed to grab one of his humongous shoes, and barely opening his eyes, fired it in Josiah's direction.

It hit the back of Josiah's neck, and he yelped. "Hey! Ow! Don't throw things!"

"Then don't wake me up. Get lost."

"Don't throw things at me!" Josiah challenged, not backing down.

Gabriel ruffled Josiah's head. "Did you already get your blanket?"

Josiah's eyes brightened, and he was instantly distracted from the futile argument with Collin. "Yeah. And I got the breakfas' out. Come and watch!"

Gabriel got up, pulling his blanket off of the bed and wrapping it around him like a robe. Josiah jumped down and hopped around. Collin watched them go with a baleful eye. Even though he seemed angry, Gabriel wondered whether secretly he wanted to be invited to join them. But he was too old and proud to ask to join them.

Gabriel was nearly comatose when Heather shuffled into the room, a bathrobe on, baby Alex in one arm and her phone in her opposite hand. "Phone call for you, Gabriel."

She handed him the phone, looking curious. Gabriel half-expected it to be Renata. Maybe she *had* bought a burner phone. And somehow got Heather's cell phone number. But it wasn't Renata. It was a cultured, older woman's voice that he couldn't place. A doctor or nurse from the clinic? A social worker or someone else involved with his case?

"Is this Mr. Gabriel Tate?" she asked formally.

"Uh, yeah. I mean yes. This is Gabriel."

"Gabriel, my name is Judge Deidre Whittaker. They call me Judge Dee-Dee. I realize that you don't know me, but I wanted to have a chat with you…"

"Um… okay…?"

"I understand that you are friends with a young lady named Renata Vega."

"Yeah."

"I heard a case involving Miss Vega some months ago… and I've been following her progress. Since your paths crossed, I've also looked into the details of your case and those of a couple of her other friends."

"You heard Renata's case? Custody?"

"No… it was actually her mother's case. Elena. I don't know if Renata told you about it?"

"You sent her to prison?"

The woman sighed. "Yes. As much as I would have liked to render a different judgment… I have to follow the dictates of the law. And there's no denying that Elena resisted arrest. When the police come into your home… even if you don't think that they have any right to be there, you can't assault an officer of the law. You can't interfere with the performance of their duties. And Elena fully admits that she did that."

"Renata didn't tell me much about what happened."

"It's on the public record… When the police came into her home to take Renata into custody, Elena tried to physically prevent them. As well as verbal assaults. She was a very angry woman. She didn't believe that they had any right to come into her home. No cause." There was a pause, and Gabriel didn't know if he was supposed to ask her something else. But then she went on again. "As it turns out, she was correct. They didn't have a warrant or just cause to enter the house. They were wrong to physically force their way into the home and lay hands on Renata."

"But you still sent her mother to jail."

"Elena chose to assault the officers rather than pursuing legal channels. I didn't really have any choice."

Gabriel let that sink in. He thought about Renata at home with her mother. The police coming to their door and then forcing their way in. Of course, Elena had fought back. What else would she have done? But the image of Renata at home with her mother didn't quite square with what he knew about Renata's history or what Renata had told him.

"I thought that Renata has been in foster care for years," he said. "But you just took her away a few months ago?"

"I didn't take her away. That was handled by another judge. I only heard her mother's case. Yes, Renata has been in foster care a number of times. Bounced back and forth between living with her mother or foster care or the hospital. Very disruptive for a child, I can't imagine it did anything for her mental health."

"Oh. I guess that makes sense."

"Word has it that Renata has run away again."

"Yeah, my foster mom told me. But I told her, I don't know where Renata is staying or where she is planning to go."

"She did come and see you."

"For a few minutes, yes. But I don't know where she is right now."

"Well, I hope that if you find anything out, you will report it. I wouldn't want to see Miss Vega get hurt."

"I don't know where she is," Gabriel repeated.

"Okay, Gabriel. Thank you for taking my call—"

"Wait!"

There was silence for a moment, and Gabriel wondered if she had already been pushing the end button on her phone and he was too late.

"Yes?"

"You said that you looked up my case when you heard that Renata and I were friends."

"Yes, I did. As much as I believe I did what was required by law by putting her mother in prison, I also feel like it gives me some responsibility in making sure that Renata is kept safe... I like to know who she is associating with." She hesitated. "You seem like a nice young man. I'm glad that the two of you connected."

He didn't really want to know her opinion of him as a friend of Renata's. "I wanted to know what you think of my case."

She made a noise that indicated she was thinking about it. A sort of a low hum. "I am sorry that this has happened to you, Gabriel. It must be very confusing."

"It was to start with. Now... I'm starting to get it."

She said nothing.

"Do you think they'll ever return me to my mom?"

"You shouldn't give up hope. Your mother seems to be very devoted. That works in her favor."

"But...?"

"But DFS and the doctors have built a pretty good case for medical abuse or negligence. If a judge is to believe the evidence..."

"Would you believe it, if you heard the case?"

"I don't know, Gabriel. I'd like to think that I would hear everybody out and be able to tease out the truth... But it isn't as easy as it sounds. And if you have any doubt, you have to err on the side of protecting the child."

"So you wouldn't send me back to my mom. Ever."

"I would want to make sure that you were safe and given the best care possible."

"What if my mom promised to take me to the mito clinic and follow the protocols? What if we said we'd do everything the doctors asked?"

"Gabriel..." She sighed a long, drawn-out breath of air. "You're almost sixteen. In two years, you'll age out of foster care, and you'll be able to decide for yourself what you want. Hopefully, by that time, you'll have a better picture of your mom as a whole person and be able to make your own medical choices."

In two years. Gabriel looked at the puddle of pills that he had laid out on the side table beside him to take when he was finished eating breakfast. Two more years of the protocol might just kill him.

"You think it's right for the clinic to experiment on foster kids?"

Her voice was a notch or two cooler. "Medical research is necessary. And some people have no hope other than experimental treatments."

"So that makes it okay to experiment on foster kids? Just like it was okay for the Nazis to experiment on the Jews in concentration camps? Medical research is necessary, so..." He couldn't believe that he was using Renata's line. But it just popped out. It wasn't right to conduct experiments on children in custody. He knew it wasn't, and Judge Dee-Dee knew it wasn't, even if she was fudging her answer.

"I'm afraid I have a conference call I need to take now, Gabriel. Thank you for taking my call. And do let someone know if you hear from Renata again or have thoughts on where she might go."

There was a click and the call ended. Gabriel looked down at the phone in his hand and the list of numbers on the screen. Recent calls. There were lots of calls with Matt Foegel. The DFS local office. The mito clinic. Dr. De Klerk. Judge Dreyer. They were all there, all the players. All within the last twenty-four hours.

Heather reappeared and put out her hand for the phone. Gabriel handed it to her and answered the question written on her face. "Just someone else wanting to know if I knew where Renata would go."

"Oh. Okay."

"Is there anything happening with my case right now? Any hearings coming up? Visitations?" He tried to keep his teeth from clenching. "Any changes?"

"No. You already know the date of the next hearing. Nothing else is happening."

Gabriel went for a walk.

Heather had raised her eyebrows at his announcement, but encouraged him with a smile. "By all means! Don't go too far, though. Just around the block for the first time. Then I know where to find you if you don't get back home."

"I'll stay close," Gabriel agreed.

He walked down the sidewalk to the city sidewalk and looked left and right. He remembered arriving on that first day, how he couldn't even make it that far. He had a lot more energy now, but he didn't know whether that could be attributed to the medications from the clinic or just the fact that he was able to eat more and was back on the medications that had been working for him before his hospital stay. He wondered whether the hospital had intentionally made him sicker by withdrawing meds and food so that the results at the clinic would look more dramatic. It was a thought Renata would have approved.

Gabriel walked down to the corner of the block. It was farther than it looked. He wasn't sure he was going to be able to walk all the way around the block. If a marathon runner could run dozens of miles, he should be able to push himself hard enough to get all the way around the block.

But that didn't mean he couldn't rest. Gabriel leaned up against the street light until his breathing was back to normal and then he started walking again. One step at a time, slow and measured. A steady pace. It didn't matter how fast he went, as long as he could get all the way around. It was a marathon, not a sprint.

He looked up from his feet and the sidewalk, scanning for some sign of Renata. Was she really that close? Sleeping under a tree or on a park bench somewhere, mere steps from where she had last been seen? Surely DFS would be combing the nearby streets for her. She had more energy than Gabriel, but she wasn't normal. Her energy was still severely limited by her mito, and she was still recovering from broken ribs and a punctured lung. DFS had to know that she couldn't cover a lot of ground after being spotted visiting Gabriel.

Gabriel didn't see any sign of her, but kept walking. He reached the next corner. There was a bus stop where he could stop and rest. The second corner meant that he was almost halfway around the block. That was the point of no return. The point at which it became shorter to go on than to go back. He was proud of himself for getting that far. His legs were feeling stronger, even without his braces. Gabriel bent down and rubbed his calves, feeling for an increase in muscle size or hardness. But the muscles were still skinny and soft, barely discernible under his fingers.

"Hey, stranger. Which bus are you waiting for?"

He looked over as Renata sat down on the bench beside him. "Where did you come from?"

She smiled, leaned over, and gave him a peck on the cheek. "I told you I'd be around."

"Where did you sleep?" He appraised her. She wasn't dirty or wrinkled. She was wearing the same clothes as the day before, but they still looked good. She smelled faintly of cigarette smoke, but that was the only difference as far as he could tell. "Are you staying with someone?"

"If I told you, someone might worm it out of you," Renata said. "Unless you're ready to leave. Have you changed your mind?"

"I got a call about you," Gabriel said, not answering.

"Yeah? Who called you?"

"Judge... I can't remember her name. Dee...?"

"Judge Dee-Dee? She's cool. Why would she call you?"

"Looking for you. Telling me that if I knew anything about where you were or where you were going, I should tell her."

"She's the one who put my mom in prison." Renata's voice was disconcertingly cheerful.

"That's what she said." Gabriel watched the street. "I asked her about my case."

"What would she know about your case?"

"She said she'd been following it because I was friends with you."

Renata frowned. "Oh? What did you ask her?"

"If they'd ever let me go back to my mom."

"They won't."

Gabriel didn't say anything. The bus drove up and pulled over, and Renata motioned for it to go on.

"So… what did she say?" Renata asked eventually.

"No."

She looked down, not saying anything. After a minute, she reached over and held his hand. She wove her fingers through his. "It's a bit different when a judge tells you, huh?"

"She thinks that I should just wait for two years until I age out." Gabriel sighed. "That's a long time."

"Yeah. So… what are you going to do?"

"I don't know."

They sat in silence for a while longer. She knew it wasn't the time to push him.

"I saw Dr. Seymour a few days ago," Renata commented after a while.

"Dr. Seymour? What about?"

"What do you think? I've been at the feeding clinic for years." She tapped the feeding tube under her shirt.

"Oh. Right. Well… what did she say?"

Renata looked at Gabriel and ran her thumb over the back of the hand that she was holding. He waited. She obviously wanted to tell him about it, or she wouldn't have said anything. He didn't know what to expect. Something about Renata? Or something about him? Whatever it was, it didn't sound like good news.

"I was in the office waiting, you know? They always make you wait there. Must be 'cause it's a *weight* clinic, huh?"

Gabriel smiled tolerantly at the pun, waiting for her to get to the point.

"Dr. Seymour was talking to someone in the next room, and I could hear, so I was listening in… It was your favorite nurse."

"Birch?"

"Yeah. They were really getting loud. Probably everyone in the clinic could hear them, or at least tell there was a fight going on."

"What was it about?"

"Bit—Birch was talking about seeing you at the mito clinic. Said that you were still losing weight, and maybe they should look at the herbs and supplements and diet that your mom had you on, to see if it would help."

Gabriel was floored. He looked at Renata's face in disbelief. "Birch thinks they should go back to what my mom was doing?"

"That's what she was asking. How about that, huh?"

Gabriel shook his head. "Unbelievable. If they did that... they'd have to admit that my mom was doing the right thing, and not putting my health in danger, wouldn't they? They have to admit that she didn't do anything wrong, and send me back."

"There's still the Munchhausen and other stuff. They could still say that she should have put you in the mito clinic too."

"I can't believe it!" Gabriel's heart was thumping so fast that it was making his head spin.

But Renata didn't look happy. She looked away from him. "Dr. Seymour... didn't agree."

There had been a fight over it. Gabriel had forgotten about that part. And Dr. Seymour was way above a nurse in influence with the clinic or the court. "Of course not," he growled. "She can't admit that someone might know more than she does, or have a better idea about something."

"She said that she's pursuing charges against your mom. She doesn't just want DFS looking into it and making recommendations. She wants criminal charges. She wants your mom sent to prison. No pleas or negotiation, hard prison time. She's pissed that they haven't done anything but investigate so far."

Gabriel swallowed. "No."

"Yeah. Sorry. I didn't know whether I should say anything. You already know that she doesn't want you to go back with your mom, so it's not really news..."

"What's wrong with that lady? What kind of person does that? She knows that my mom was trying to take care of me. Why is she doing this?"

"She's always gunning for parents. I dunno. Maybe *her* parents were abusive."

"So she's made it her life's mission to put everyone else's in prison?" Gabriel snorted and shook his head in disgust.

"The ones that she thinks are abusive, yeah. I've seen it before. Doesn't take much to set her off. She's put a lot of kids into DFS's hands."

"Is she the one who reported your mom?"

Renata shrugged. "I dunno. Lotta people have, over the years. I'm underweight, always sick, have psych disorders… people tend to think it's parental neglect."

Gabriel pulled his hand out of Renata's and held both hands over his face, trying to sort out all the emotions and facts. She sat beside him in silence. Gabriel thought about the phone numbers he had seen on Heather's recent calls list. Had Dr. Seymour been on the list? Heather said that nothing was happening with his case, but had clearly been in communication with all the players. What if they were building the case against Keisha? Trying to marshal the evidence required to have her arrested and put in prison? Gabriel couldn't bear it if she went to jail because of him. Because of his illness.

"I have to go," he said finally. "I have to go home and talk to my mom. Make sure she knows what's going on. She has to protect herself… maybe we should disappear together. Just take off, so no one can find us."

Renata nodded. "So you'll go with me?"

Gabriel's stomach was a tight knot. His heart was racing. His head was thumping. He still had to walk all the way back to the Foegels to gather his things. And then they would begin their journey. He hoped that Renata had figured out the details because he had no idea what to do.

"Let's do it."

CHAPTER FIFTEEN

WE'LL LEAVE TOMORROW."

Renata's instructions rang in his ears. She knew that returning to the house would sap his remaining energy. And then he would need to make covert preparations to go. Maybe even while everyone else was asleep. She gave him a short list of what to prepare.

"One extra set of clothes. Clothing takes up lots of space. You only need something to change into while you wash what you've been wearing, once it's actually dirty. All the money you can get your hands on. Cash, jewelry, electronics, anything liquid. Don't bother with credit cards. Grab the meds that you really need. Leave the rest. You'd better bring some snacks to keep your blood sugar steady if we don't stop for meals at the regular times. That's it. No extras. Travel as light as you can."

"I can't steal," Gabriel protested.

"You're entitled to your clothes and meds. That's not stealing. They're yours. And you gotta have something to carry them in."

Gabriel nodded.

"And I don't know if we'll be able to stop to get snacks everywhere along the way. If we're hitching or waiting for a bus, you're going to be out of luck."

"Yeah. I'll bring some snacks."

She looked at him, and he looked at her.

"You gotta have money," Renata said finally. "If you don't have money, we won't make it. I don't have enough for everyone. We can pool what we have, but you have to have something."

"Stealing is wrong. I can't do that. That's not the way I was raised."

"Then *borrow* it. You can send them money back to cover it when you're safe." Renata was annoyed, her voice blunt and clipped and her face set. And she was the one who knew what she was doing. She might be younger than Gabriel, but she had far more experience with running away. And so far she had remained at large, in spite of a big network of people looking for her.

Gabriel stared down at his hands. "I'll try, I guess. But it isn't like they leave their wallets and watches lying around."

"I'll bet I could find cash in the cookie jar. Look around. She'll have an emergency stash somewhere. And probably a coin jar for family pizza night. And there's an older foster kid too, right? He'll have something stowed away. Anyone who's been in the system long enough does. You never know when you might have to run."

"I only have a day to get ready. How am I supposed to find these stashes?"

"You're supposed to look. Now quit whining, Gabe. You're with me, right? Be a man and do a little work."

Looking through the closet in the bedroom, Gabriel found a backpack that wasn't being used. He didn't have a lot of clothes, but there were enough clean clothes to pack one full change in the backpack. In spite of what Renata had said, he put two extra pairs of underwear and socks into the backpack. He wouldn't be able to pack his meds or snacks until after supper, or Heather would notice. He turned his mind to liquid assets.

Gabriel looked over the dresser. Collin had a small music player and some big showy rings that were probably football trophy rings. Gabriel picked them up and stowed them in the front pocket of the backpack, feeling horrible. He knew how hard it was for foster kids to acquire any personal items, especially ones with value. Collin would kill Gabriel if he noticed before Gabriel left. But Gabriel wasn't as worried about that as he was about how Collin would feel about losing his precious possessions.

He looked carefully through Collin's drawers, checking underneath and behind everything, feeling all the socks for money rolls, and pulling out the drawers to look for anything taped behind or on the bottom. He came across a stash of blue pills, but no cash. Gabriel went back to the closet and looked through all the pockets of the jackets and pants that were hung up. He found little more than pocket change. He checked the toes of all the shoes.

After that, Gabriel looked around the room, trying to think of where else Collin might hide cash. There was no shoebox under the bed, but Gabriel looked under the mattress and hit the jackpot. There were a couple of catalog-size envelopes hidden there. Opening them up, Gabriel found wads of cash. There were hundreds of dollars, maybe thousands. Was Collin selling the blue pills? Or running some other shady business?

Gabriel took only one of the envelopes and put the other back. He also put Collin's music player and rings back on the dresser. He had more than enough cash to contribute to the venture. He'd have to keep track as he spent it, to make sure that he could pay Collin back when it was all over, and he could earn some money somehow.

Renata had advised Gabriel to have his breakfast as usual so he'd have something in his stomach, and then to go for another walk. That would give them at least an hour head start before Heather started looking for Gabriel. He dropped the backpack out of the window into the backyard so they would not see him leaving the house with it. Renata said she would scoop it up and then meet him around the corner, so there would be nothing suspicious about Gabriel's behavior if Heather watched him through the window. Heather was busy getting the kids ready for school and Gabriel didn't think that she paid much attention to him leaving.

By the time he got around the corner, his heart was going much faster than it had the previous day. He kept glancing around, sure that someone would see him. They knew that Renata had come to him. They were bound to be watching for her. He saw Renata coming this time, emerging from between two houses. She smiled, face lit up with excitement. She held his backpack out to him. Gabriel slipped his arms through the straps and settled it onto his back.

"You remembered everything?" Renata demanded.

"Yes."

"Got cash?"

Gabriel nodded.

"Good." She motioned down the block. "Let's grab the bus."

Walking with the backpack was going to tire Gabriel out a lot faster. But he didn't have far to go to the bus stop. And they sat down to wait.

At first, Gabriel was too excited and anxious to think about where they were going. He watched out the bus window for anyone who looked suspicious, making Renata laugh.

"I'm the paranoid one, you know," she said. "They don't even know you're gone yet. Nobody's looking for you."

"But they're looking for you," Gabriel pointed out. "Heather told them you were there."

"I know how to stay out of sight."

Despite her assurance, Gabriel still tensed up when a police car with flashing lights pulled up behind the bus. He put his hand on Renata's arm and covered the side of his face with his other hand, shading it from view through the window.

"Take it easy," Renata warned. "You'll attract attention."

"The police—"

"Chill. They're not after you."

The police car pulled around the bus, and Gabriel couldn't look at it. It turned its siren on, and the bus driver glanced at it but didn't slow down. The police car whipped past them and continued down the road. Gabriel blew out his breath.

"Whew. I was sure..."

Renata loosened his grip on her arm. Gabriel released her.

"Just take it easy. Even if someone stops us, you gotta act like everything is cool and you don't know what the problem is. They gotta be sure before they take you into custody. You bluff well enough, and they'll let you go."

Gabriel settled back against the seat, holding his hand over his pounding heart. "I don't know if I can do this."

"You can. You gotta be strong if we're going to make this work."

Gabriel nodded. "Yeah. So… what's the plan?"

"We've got a couple of other guys we're going to meet up with. But I figured we'd be too noticeable if we all traveled together. So we're traveling parallel until it's safer."

"I should call my mom. You have a phone?"

"You can't call your mom."

"To let her know that I'm okay, and that I'm on my way."

"You can't go back there."

Gabriel stared at Renata. "What?"

"You want to know where eighty percent of foster care runaways go? Back home or to the old neighborhood. That's exactly where DFS is going to be looking for you."

"I got out so that I could go back to her. And warn her about Dr. Seymour."

"Not yet. Not safe. You can't contact her directly. You can't go there. If she harbors a runaway, she'll go straight to jail."

"Renata! That was the whole idea! I want to go back to my mom!"

Renata glanced around, her eyes wary. "Lower your voice, Gabe. Look, eventually, we'll figure out a way to reunite you with your mom. When we're out of state, and this thing is blown wide open, then it will be safe. But not yet."

Gabriel slumped down. He couldn't really complain that she hadn't told him her plans. She had said that they would need to go out of state to be safe from DFS.

But Gabriel's plan had been to go back to Keisha.

At the end of the day, Gabriel wasn't sure that Renata had a plan. Their movements throughout the day had seemed random. Busing, walking, occasionally taking a cab or begging a ride from a likely-looking mark. Sometimes doubling back where they had just come from. Renata made Gabriel buy a cap to change his appearance and mandated clothing changes throughout the day. Jacket on, hat off. Hat on. A pair of sunglasses. New t-shirt. He was exhausted and kept falling asleep en route, then waking up groggy and unsure of where he was.

"When are we leaving?" Gabriel whined. "We've been hopping all over the suburbs like a grasshopper; when are we going to make tracks and actually get somewhere? You said we're going out of state, but we aren't getting anywhere."

"Not today." Renata shook her head. "They're going to be watching all the bus depots for the distance buses. Gotta give them a day or two to stand down before we use them."

Gabriel rubbed his eyes. "Then where are we going tonight?"

"Tent City."

"Where's that? What about a shelter?"

"We're close. We'll get a bite to eat first."

"Do you have a tent?"

"No. We'll put down a ground sheet and cuddle. Not supposed to rain tonight."

"Why not a shelter?" Gabriel didn't like the idea of sleeping on the ground, especially surrounded by a lot of homeless people. He had a lot of money in his backpack. What if they were mugged? A shelter seemed more protected, less of a danger.

"They get missing person flyers. It takes a few days before the new ones get buried. You don't want to be on the top of the pile."

"Oh." Gabriel followed Renata, not sure where she was going. "What would they do if they found us? Just send us back to our foster parents?"

"Yep. You run too much, though, and they'll put you in a secure facility. Running more than once or twice a year... not a good idea. You don't want to get locked up."

"Yeah, I think I've had enough of that."

Renata's eyes scanned the street. "Grocery store down there. Can we get something good for you to eat there?"

Gabriel nodded. It was time to refuel. The deli would have food that he could eat cold. And maybe a piece of fruit from the produce department, or a bit of peanut butter. Renata didn't need anything; she had her formula.

After checking the area out, Renata led the way into the grocery store. Gabriel quickly found what he wanted and got in line. Renata had already made him move a few dollars to his pockets and to bury the rest deep in his backpack, so no one would see them handling large amounts of money. They stood together, waiting for the line to move ahead. Someone pushed a cart in behind them, impatient to get their goods up on the conveyor belt. The cashier called for a price check and Gabriel sighed. The man in front of them turned around, rolling his eyes.

"Looks like we're here for a bit!"

Renata shrugged. Gabriel nodded. The man's eyes went slowly over them. Gabriel's face got hot. The man wasn't wearing a uniform, but he could have been a cop. Or he could be a social worker, or a foster parent, someone in the network who knew that Gabriel was missing, expected to be found traveling with a Hispanic girl. Gabriel adjusted his hat, pulling it down a little, and turned to scan the magazine rack beside him.

"You guys down on your luck?" the man asked. "You need more food than that."

"We just needed a couple things," Renata said, her voice light and unconcerned.

"Are you homeless?"

"Of course not. We're fine. Thanks."

"I could help you out. If you're new in town, you need to know where to go for help…"

"Why don't you leave her alone?" Gabriel demanded. "She told you we're fine. Just let it go."

Others were looking up from what they had previously been occupied with, listening to the conversation and watching to see if anything interesting was going to happen. Gabriel gulped. He knew what Renata was telling him now in her mind. Just chill. Keep cool and casual and don't attract attention. She had gone to all that work to make sure that they couldn't be tracked, and he was screwing it up by attracting everyone's attention.

"Sorry," Gabriel muttered. "I get grumpy when I'm hungry."

Renata laughed and the man gave a friendly smile.

"Understandable. Sorry, maybe I was pushing a bit. I just don't like to see anyone out in the cold, you know? Not when they could be warm and comfortable with full bellies."

"We'll be fine tonight." Renata smiled again. "It's nice of you to be so concerned."

The price check was completed, and the line moved again, with the man's groceries being scanned through. He paid, gave them another look and smile, and then left. Renata lifted her eyebrow at Gabriel, and their little stack of groceries was checked through. Outside, Gabriel had to find a bench and sit down for a minute, his legs shaking. Renata didn't sit down, but stood beside him, her eyes scanning the parking lot and nearby street over and over again in an endless loop.

"I'm sorry," Gabriel said.

"Don't worry about it."

"No, really, I'm sorry to cause extra trouble… people noticed us…"

"Can't change the past. You might have done us a favor, though."

Gabriel raised his head hopefully. "Really? How?"

"He was curious. He might have waited outside or followed us if you hadn't gotten in his face. But since you did, he wouldn't want to stick around. He wasn't anonymous anymore. If he stuck around watching or asking more questions, he could get beat up. Or we could call the cops on him for harassing us."

"You think he left? He didn't stick around to see where we went or what we did next?"

Renata hadn't stopped scanning the area. "I don't see him. I think you scared him off."

"Yeah? Good. That's what I meant to do."

Renata laughed and stopped her surveillance for a moment to smile at him and pat him on the back. "Good boy. So do you need to eat here or can we get settled first?"

Gabriel rubbed his burning leg muscles. "I can wait, as long as we're not going too far."

CHAPTER SIXTEEN

THE TENT CITY THAT had been set up in a grassy park was only a couple of blocks away. There were tents and shelters of every description, some of them just a tarp and rope, and some fancy high-end commercial tents. It was crowded and messy, and it stank. Old and young, singles and families, people milled everywhere. It was chaos.

Gabriel looked around in dismay. "I don't know…"

"What?"

"This is…" Gabriel trailed off. He couldn't think of an argument that would persuade Renata. "I never liked camping," he said finally.

She laughed. "Gee, woulda been nice to know that before we started!"

"I can't sleep here…"

"It'll quiet down in a while. It's not so bad."

"We can't just lay on the ground, with no shelter or anything."

"Sure we can. Groundsheet will keep us from getting too cold. And body heat."

"We need blankets."

"You've got a coat and an extra set of clothes, if you're cold. It's a nice enough night."

Gabriel shook his head stubbornly.

Renata rolled her eyes. "You're too tired to go anywhere else tonight. Maybe you'll get lucky, and the mission will be around handing out blankets."

Gabriel's stomach was growling. He put his hand over it. Renata put her backpack on the ground and opened it up. She pulled out what looked like a big garbage bag and laid it out on a free spot on the grass, covering up a litter of cigarettes, condoms, and other debris.

"Come on. Sit down. We'll have a picnic supper."

Gabriel reluctantly sat down on the plastic. Renata sat next to him. She pulled a bag of formula from her backpack. Gabriel got a pasta salad out of his grocery bag. He tried to focus on his own dinner and not to look sideways at Renata.

She nudged him. "Does this bother you?"

Gabriel bit his lip and slid his eyes in her direction. Renata coupled the tube on the formula bag with the one that she fished out between the button holes of her shirt. "No... it doesn't bother me. You need to eat too."

"You can look, I don't care. I know I'm different."

Gabriel nodded.

"Some people get all disgusted and grossed out," Renata said. "But it's just a tube!"

"It's okay," Gabriel repeated. "It doesn't bother me. I just didn't want to stare."

They sat up and talked for a long time after having their respective dinners. Gabriel wasn't ready to lie down for sleep yet. There was too much noise and chaos around him. He knew there was no way that he would be able to sleep through it all, even after all of the walking and riding they had done. The mission came around with blankets, and Gabriel took two for himself. He was exhausted by the time they finally lay down together. Gabriel was too self-conscious to cuddle up with Renata like she suggested. There wasn't much space on the ground sheet and whatever part of his body extended off of it froze. The encampment got quieter, but every time he started to relax, someone would start screaming again. Renata seemed calm and unworried.

"What if he comes over here?" Gabriel whispered as they listened to a German man shout. "He could be violent!"

"Shh. Just stay quiet and no one will bother you."

"Why is he yelling? What's wrong?"

"Probably schizophrenic. It's just like being back in the psych ward again, huh?"

Gabriel groaned. He got a bit closer to Renata, getting more desperate for her body heat. "I heard *you* yelling when I first woke up at hospital." He yawned. "Think it was you, anyway."

"Yeah?" Renata giggled. "I do go off, sometimes. Not my fault when the meds stop working."

"What if he comes over here?"

"Shh. He won't. Come here; you're cold." Renata put her arms around Gabriel, holding him close. Gabriel let his body melt against hers. She was warm, and his shivers gradually subsided. "Go to sleep," Renata whispered. "We have to get up pretty early. You gotta sleep when you can."

Morning came way too soon. It was barely even getting light out when Renata shook Gabriel awake.

"Come on," she encouraged. "We gotta move out."

"What? Why?" Gabriel rubbed at his eyes, looking around. Homeless people all around him were getting up, talking, and packing away their gear.

"Cops come by at five-thirty, everybody's gotta be on their way."

"Five-thirty?" Gabriel groaned. "I can't get up at five-thirty!"

"You're getting up now. Come on. Off my ground sheet." She pulled the ground sheet out from under him, rolling Gabriel off, and he was in the cold, wet grass. He jumped to his feet and pulled his mission blankets around him. He watched Renata swiftly fold the ground sheet in halves over and over again until it was small enough to put in her backpack. She left her blanket on the ground.

"Aren't you going to bring that?"

"I don't have enough room to carry it. They'll come by and pick up the discards later. Wash them up and redistribute them again. Just leave yours here."

"I need them! It's too cold."

"You'll warm up when we start moving. You can't carry them around all day. Leave them here so the mission gets them back."

Gabriel opened his mouth, looking for a good argument. Renata swore. He followed her eyes.

"Cops are here early," Renata growled. "Come on, time to move."

"We're already up. What are they going to do?"

"Are you forgetting there's an APB out on you? You want to get slammed right back in care? Maybe in a closed facility this time?"

Gabriel pulled his blankets closer. "No."

"Put them down and let's go."

Gabriel looked toward a couple of policemen who were making their way through the tent city. They didn't seem to be angry or mean; they were just telling people to clear out.

"I want to keep the blankets."

Renata tried to pull them away. "The point is to stay invisible, Gabriel. How invisible do you think you're going to be if they decide you're stealing the mission blankets?"

"I'm not stealing! They gave them to me."

"Just—"

"What's the problem?" One of the cops had managed to sneak up without Gabriel seeing him coming. "Time for you kids to move on." His eyes went over Renata and then took in Gabriel.

Gabriel could see questions in the cop's eyes. The man frowned at Gabriel, maybe trying to recall a missing person's bulletin that he had seen. Gabriel quickly shed his blankets, throwing them on top of Renata's.

"We're going," Renata said. "No problem."

"You kids in trouble?" The cop's name badge said Rusk. "Are you runaways?"

"We're discards," Renata snapped. "No one cares where we are. And we're leaving, so thanks for your concern."

Rusk frowned, his eyes piercing, trying to divine their secrets. "How about you show me what's in your bags," he suggested.

Gabriel picked his up. What if Rusk found his money? He was going to know there was something suspicious about a homeless kid with hundreds of dollars. Renata shook her head at Gabriel.

"How about we just move on?" she countered. "You got no *cause*. We don't have to show you anything."

Gabriel froze, holding onto his backpack, and he didn't open it like he had intended to. Rusk looked at Renata and back at Gabriel. "I'm sure I could come up with cause. I might think that your boyfriend here is carrying a knife, for instance."

Renata started to walk away. When Gabriel didn't follow, she tugged on his arm. "Let's *go*," she said in a low growl. "He's got no reason to detain us. Stay close."

Gabriel stuck with Renata as she worked her way deeper into the tent city crowd instead of out toward the street. Rusk didn't follow them. When Gabriel looked back, the cop was still watching them, but in another minute, they were lost in the crowd and could no longer see him. They made their way through the thickest of the crowd, and then out on the other side. Renata looked around and led the way to a McDonalds. Gabriel got a coffee, and they sat down. It was warm inside, and the chill from the early-morning air wore off gradually.

"So what is the plan today?" Gabriel asked. "Do we try the bus depot today?"

Renata nodded. "Yeah, I think we will," she agreed. "Maybe around noon, when they're not watching as close."

"Then what will we do?"

"Meet up with the other guys. Tomorrow maybe. Figure out how to get our stories heard."

Gabriel sipped his coffee, still too hot to swallow. "Who are the other guys?"

Renata nodded, conceding his right to know who else they were working with. "They're both mito," she said. "I thought I'd keep it all in the family. One boy, Ray, he's sort of like you. His parents wanted a second opinion. Dr. Seymour didn't like it and had him removed. Nick, it wasn't even the doctors who initiated it; it was DFS. They're a homeschooling family. I don't know how many kids, six or seven. They homeschool all of them, not just Nick because he couldn't manage the rigors of public school. So, you have seven kids home all day; things can get kind of messy. DFS decided that it was an unsanitary home environment, and that threatened Nick's health because he's medically fragile. So they took him away. His parents are scared to fight because they're afraid of all the other kids getting taken away too. So far, it's just Nick."

"So Nick, homeschooler, and... what was the first one?"

"Ray."

"Ray, second opinion. And they're both mito. In the research program?"

"Yeah, of course."

"Mito is so rare," Gabriel said. "People will have to see how there's too many of them just being taken out of their homes for no reason. They'll have to see that it's not in their best interest. DFS and the doctors are just trying to fill the research program up."

Renata nodded.

"What are they like? Ray and Nick?"

"Ray is pretty serious. Deals with lots of pain, so, of course, the first thing they do is withdraw all meds to make sure he's not addicted. Then drug him up so much he doesn't wake up for a week. He's from... I forget. Europe somewhere. Parents came here when he was little. Speaks three or four languages. Nick's more of a clown. Six siblings, you know, so things could get pretty wild at home. Since he couldn't really roughhouse, he sort of ended up the play-by-play announcer; he can be pretty funny sometimes."

"And they're together now? Did they know each other?"

"Yeah, they were both at the Children's at the same time. I wasn't there then but met them both separately. They split the day before yesterday. A day before you did. I'll try calling them once we're out of the area."

"And then we're going to meet up?"

"After I make sure they haven't been caught. We have to make sure we're not being lured into a trap."

Gabriel turned his coffee cup on the table several times. "You think that's likely?"

"Everybody's going to be after them, just like us. If they get caught, DFS wouldn't be above using them as bait."

"Once we get out of state, you think we're safe?"

"Well… I think so." Renata scratched at a dried-up ketchup spill on the table. "I don't know all the laws," she admitted. "But I haven't heard of them sending runaways back across borders. To tell the truth… I've never made it out of state before."

Gabriel swallowed too much coffee at once and winced at the burn. "How far have you gotten before? How long before you got caught?"

"I've been on the lam for a couple of weeks. But I didn't have anywhere to go; I just headed back to the old neighborhood."

"And that's where DFS looks first."

"Yeah. They didn't catch me right away. But eventually, enough people who knew me saw me and talked about it."

"So you knew not to do that this time."

"I've run away a lot of times."

"Why?"

Renata shrugged. "I like the freedom. I don't like being cooped up in one place… people monitoring me…" She took a quick look around to make sure that no one in the McDonalds was watching them.

Gabriel stared out the window. Renata had lots of experience running away. But she always got caught. He'd been depending on her expertise to keep them out of the hands of the authorities. But maybe he shouldn't.

"I never had a plan before," Renata said, reading the expression on his face. "I just took off. This time is different."

"You think we can avoid getting caught?"

"Yeah, sure."

"How about Ray and Nick?"

"Less likely," Renata admitted.

"Will just the two of us be enough? To convince people about the…" he had a hard time using her words, "…the kidnappings? All the corruption?"

"Hopefully enough that they'd do some research of their own. Check out other kids. There are already other stories in the mainstream media. But not the idea that it's a widespread conspiracy."

It was going to be hard to convince anyone of that. Gabriel still wasn't sure himself. He didn't believe everything that Renata said. Not one hundred percent. But the doctors and judges who were corrupt had to be stopped.

Gabriel wasn't normally an early morning eater. But they had been up for a while, and he was starting to get hungry. He didn't know what the schedule for the day was going to be, but he imagined it would involve a lot more walking around, and he'd better get some calories in.

"I think I'm gonna get a McMuffin or something. Are you going to eat?"

"Sure. Why don't you go order and I'll get set?"

Gabriel went back up to the counter and waited. It had been almost empty when they arrived, but people were starting to arrive now, all looking tired or grumpy, waiting to get their caffeine or sugar fix. When he got back to the table, Renata had her formula hooked up and one of the young McDonalds employees was talking with her. Gabriel put down his McMuffin on the table and was about to slide in when he realized that it was not a friendly discussion, but a low-toned confrontation.

"You can't do *that* in here," the employee whose name tag said 'Rhett' insisted.

"I'm eating. Exactly what everyone else here is doing."

"Not like *that!* You're disturbing the other customers. No one wants to look at that."

"Leave her alone," Gabriel told Rhett, trying to make his voice as hard as possible. "She's allowed to eat here just like anyone else!"

Rhett looked Gabriel over and apparently decided that the lightweight wasn't much of a threat to him. "If she wants to do *that*, she can use the restroom," he insisted, his nose wrinkling.

"She's not going to eat in the bathroom!"

Rhett stomped back to the front of the restaurant.

Renata rolled her eyes. "I told you!"

"I can't believe it! What an idiot!"

She smiled.

"These are the same kind of people who think that women shouldn't be able to nurse in public," Gabriel said. He sat down and started to unwrap his McMuffin. "It doesn't bother you if I eat by mouth here, does it?"

Renata laughed. "I dunno. All of that... masticating and slobbering... food that hasn't been properly pasteurized... it can't be very hygienic. It's disgusting."

Gabriel grinned and took a bite of his sandwich. When he was partway through, he took out his meds and assembled what he needed. His legs were already aching, so he added a couple of the Tylenol he had borrowed to the pile.

"No experimental drugs?" Renata double-checked, watching him sort everything out.

"Nope. Didn't bring them with me."

"Good."

Another employee walked up to the table. Not Rhett this time; he was hanging around at the front of the restaurant pretending not to watch them. This man, John, was apparently the franchise manager.

"I'm sorry. We're getting complaints," he said, motioning to Renata's tube. "I hate to do this, but I have to ask you to stop or to use the restroom; or we're going to have to ask you to leave."

"I'm not leaving," Renata said. "And do you think I'm going to eat in a bathroom? No way. This is how I have to eat. Deal with it. If I tried to eat by mouth, I'd be throwing up all over your table. Would you prefer that?"

"I understand that this is an unusual request. But we can't have you upsetting our regular clientele... We do have a rule about outside food or drink. It is not allowed."

"Oh, nice end-run," Gabriel said. "No outside food or drink? Am I allowed to take my meds?" He motioned to the rainbow of pills.

"Of course you're allowed to take your medication..." John conceded.

"They why wouldn't she be able to take her prescription?"

John's eyes went to the formula bag with its incomprehensible headlines and fine print. He looked back at Gabriel and avoiding looking at Renata and the tube snaking its way under her shirt. He turned his head to look back at Rhett, still watching from the counter, and shook his head.

"You have a nice day," he said, and walked away.

They killed time until noon, when Renata led them to the big bus depot. They looked at the departure boards and destinations, and each privately considered their own funds, before finally selecting a route.

"Should we go separately?" Renata wondered aloud. "The police bulletins have probably put us both together. We're less obvious if we go on different buses. You could take the twelve-thirty, and I could take the one-forty-five."

Gabriel shook his head. "No... I don't want to be separated. What if you didn't come? I wouldn't know what to do, or how to get ahold of the others. If we're going to get caught, I'd rather be caught together."

"Okay. As long as you know that it's riskier."

"Yeah."

"Let's at least go through the line separately and not sit beside each other on the bus. It's not much, but..."

"Yeah, okay."

Gabriel was about ready for bed. He hadn't slept nearly enough in the tent city. His head was pounding, and his eyes were drooping with fatigue. So he decided to do his best to sleep on the bus. He was sitting next to an old lady with wispy hair who smelled like baby powder. He was afraid that she would be the grandmotherly type who would talk his ear off for the whole trip, but she eyed him doubtfully and did not do more than smile a half-hearted greeting before burying herself in a brand-new paperback romance. With his backpack clutched in his lap, Gabriel leaned his head against the window and closed his eyes.

He awoke later with the sun in his eyes and looked around. They were in the middle of nowhere. No city in sight. No road signs. Barely any other traffic on the road. No gas stations. Gabriel was a city boy who hadn't even been well enough to go on school field trips to the farm. The city was all he knew.

Gabriel suddenly felt very alone and isolated. He was getting farther and farther away from Keisha. The hope of ever returning to her was fading fast. She would have no idea where he was, what had happened to him. If he contacted her and told her anything, she could be charged with harboring a fugitive. She was getting farther away, and he had no idea when he'd be able to see her again.

Gabriel sniffled and held back tears. He buried his face in his backpack and tried to regain control. The old lady patted him on the back. She didn't say anything to comfort him and didn't ask him any questions. She just patted him comfortingly, and when Gabriel was able to stop the sobs, she stopped and went back to reading her book.

CHAPTER SEVENTEEN

GABRIEL WAS STIFF AND sore when he finally got off of the bus. The old woman moved more spryly than he did. Gabriel exited without looking at Renata, not wanting to draw attention to their relationship and hoping that she hadn't seen his breakdown en route. Inside the depot, Renata moved to his side.

"How are you doing?" she asked. "Ready to stretch your legs?"

"Yeah, and I gotta eat."

"Grab one of your snacks to eat on the go. We can't stop here."

Gabriel sighed but did as he was told. "What are we doing now? Are we going to meet the others?"

"First, we gotta make tracks. Bus depots are too visible."

"Do you know where to go?" Gabriel looked around when they got outside the building. It was comforting to be back in a city again. All the open space on the road had freaked him out a bit. But it was weird being someplace so unfamiliar, not even knowing which way was home. Even the flowers and trees were different, like he had traveled to another country or another planet instead of just across state lines.

Renata cast her eyes around. "We'll just have to guess, until we can find someone to ask." She pursed her lips and looked up and down the street again, then finally motioned right. "This way."

Gabriel followed. "Why?"

"If you're not sure, go right."

Gabriel raised his eyebrows, not finding this particularly comforting. He had hoped that she had made some kind of observation that had led her to pick that direction. And maybe she had, but just wasn't telling him yet. He didn't like guessing. Renata was the one who was supposed to have a plan, and she didn't seem to know anything about the city that they had chosen to travel to.

"Who are we going to ask? About where we should go?"

"Who would *you* ask?" She countered. "Come on, Gabe. You're older than I am. More experienced. Use your thinker for thinking and contribute something."

"I don't think I'm more experienced," Gabriel countered. "You're the one who's run away a million times before."

"And been caught every time. So? Who would you ask?"

"I dunno. Someone homeless, I would guess."

Renata nodded. "Yep. That would be best. No one knows the city and where to go like the homeless."

"So we're just going to wander around until we find a homeless person? And then ask them… what? Where to go to sleep? I don't want to sleep on the ground again."

"No whining. We'll sleep where it's safe, and that's not usually the shelters. I'll find people to talk to, just give me a few minutes."

A few minutes was a lot faster than Gabriel had hoped for. He had envisioned wandering for hours, up and down tidy residential streets, unable to find their way to the neighborhoods where they could get help and not stand out. So he clamped his mouth shut to keep from whining and let Renata choose their course. She didn't always choose to go right, so she must be seeing some sort of signs that Gabriel wasn't. He tried to pay more attention to their surroundings. Renata was right; he needed to put some of his own thought and consideration into the process, instead of just asking her what to do all of the time.

He started to notice logic in her choices. Renata was staying away from the little residential streets. Choosing more commercial areas. Streets with cafes and urban parks and old brick apartment buildings. It was fascinating, but Gabriel found his energy flagging.

"Can we sit down for a rest?"

Renata looked around. She nodded. "As good a place as any." She didn't look for a comfortable green space or bus bench as Gabriel expected her to, but put her backpack down right where they were. Gabriel frowned. Renata picked up a discarded coffee cup from the gutter and placed it on the sidewalk. She sat down cross-legged, leaning against her bag, and looked at Gabriel with raised eyebrows. Gabriel reluctantly sat. The concrete was hard against his bony bottom. Renata dropped a few coins into the coffee cup. As people walked by them, she began asking for spare change.

Most of the foot traffic ignored them completely, walking by as if they were invisible. Some of them swore or called names. A few people, mostly middle-aged women, dropped a coin or two into the cup. Gabriel was uncomfortable, both physically and mentally. He had not grown up with much money. With only his father working on a soldier's salary and Keisha staying home to take care of Gabriel, they had lived in a poor area of town, in one of the few neighborhoods where blacks were not the minority, and no one thought it was odd that he didn't have a father around, because none of them had fathers around either. But Keisha had always insisted that they didn't take any kind of charity. Gabriel's medications and hospital stays were expensive. So were healthy foods that Keisha had to go out of the neighborhood to buy, while all around them kids lived on mac and cheese and their parents drank.

Renata elbowed Gabriel. "Smile!" she ordered through the side of her mouth. "You're scaring away the clientele!"

Gabriel blinked, and made an effort to smile at the people who were walking by. "Thank you, ma'am... have a nice day, sir... God bless... have a great day..." He fell into a rhythm, sending out well-wishes to everyone who passed, whether they paid any attention to him and Renata, or not. One woman gave them leftover donuts and sandwiches, somewhat dry, from meetings earlier in the day. Gabriel thanked her profusely, making her smile and blush pink. A young man stopped to give them coffee and

Gabriel thanked him too. They didn't try to tell anyone about Gabriel's allergies, or that Renata couldn't eat solid food.

Renata emptied the coffee cup at intervals, leaving only two or three coins at the bottom each time. Eventually, an older homeless guy who smelled strongly of beer approached them.

"This is my space," he confronted them. "You can't beg here."

Gabriel expected a fight from Renata, but she just stood up and picked up her cup and backpack. "Okay."

The man looked suspicious of her surprisingly compliant reaction. He frowned at Gabriel as he got up.

"You kids are new here?"

Renata ignored the question and grabbed Gabriel's arm, pulling him forward as if they were going to walk away.

"Wait!" the homeless man protested. "You kids don't know the ropes. Let me give you some pointers."

Renata looked back at him, stopping. Gabriel turned away and covered his mouth as if he were yawning, but really he was smothering a laugh. In a few seconds, Renata had skillfully turned the man from a potential threat into an eager advisor.

"I'm Les. You don't need to leave. You get a piece of real estate first, you hold it. Don't let anyone take it away from you. Okay?"

Renata played the naive newcomer. "Oh, okay. I didn't want to make any trouble..."

"No, you gotta stand up for yourself. Don't let anyone push you around. Unless they have a weapon. Then you make yourself scarce. Where did you two kids come from? I haven't seen you here before."

"No, we're new," Renata agreed.

Les waited for a moment, but there was no more information forthcoming. He looked at Gabriel. "You guys are boyfriend-girlfriend?" he guessed. "Maybe your folks didn't like that?"

Renata grabbed Gabriel's hand and didn't answer.

"Have you eaten today?" Les asked.

Gabriel picked up the bag of sandwiches and held it out to him. "You want some?"

Les pursed his lips and considered the offering. "Gotta watch my carbs," he said, eventually picking up one half-sandwich. Gabriel wasn't sure whether he was joking or serious. Les devoured it in a few bites. "Those are... not the best," he declared. "But food is food. You know where to find the Thirteenth Street soup kitchen?"

"Thirteenth Street?" Gabriel couldn't help asking.

"You got a real smart ass for a boyfriend; you know that?" Les said to Renata. He outlined where they could find the soup kitchen and when it was open. "And you're going to need a shelter."

"No shelters," Renata disagreed.

"Your money won't last long if you're renting hotel rooms. Sooner or later, you're going to need something free."

"Where can we sleep where the cops won't roust us?"

He looked at her, maybe revising his opinion on how naive she was. "You sleep rough?"

"Yeah."

Gabriel tried to catch Renata's eye. He had already told her that he didn't want to sleep on the ground another night. She ignored his signals.

Les suggested a few places where they might sleep. "But kids like you," he said, "you should find a youth shelter. That would be better."

Renata shrugged. "Thanks. You want another sandwich?" She gestured at the bag.

Les helped himself to another sandwich and a stale donut and nodded his thanks. "I'll see you kids around, then. Be careful."

They went on to scout out a couple of the locations that Les had mentioned. Gabriel was not happy about the possibility of sleeping out in the cold again. "We might not," Renata said, "we might find something else."

"Really? Where?" Gabriel demanded. It was getting late in the day, and he knew that Renata wasn't going to give in and stay at a shelter, where they might be recognized from a missing person's bulletin. "We could find a hotel, like Les said. Just one night. There's places that don't cost too much for just one night…?"

"I'm not wasting my money on hotel rooms. And they probably wouldn't rent to minors anyway."

Gabriel opened his mouth to argue further, and she waved him into silence.

"I'm gonna try touching base with Ray and Nick. Okay? See where they are."

"Okay. All right."

They sat down on a park bench, and Renata pulled out her phone. She looked all around, making sure that no one was watching them, then powered it on. She tapped a name and waited, phone to her ear, again looking around to watch for anyone who was showing too much attention.

"Ray. Hey, it's Renata. Where are you?"

Gabriel strained his ears, trying to hear Ray's part of the conversation, but the volume was too low to overhear it.

"You guys safe? No trouble?"

She listened for a while. Obviously, the answer was more than a simple yes or no.

"No, I've had it turned off," Renata's tone was clipped. "What have you guys been doing today? Are you up to travel?"

After some more consultation, Renata gave them instructions and checked the time. "I'll turn my phone back on in three hours." Then she hung up.

Gabriel was eager for her report. "They're coming here?" he asked.

"Yeah. They went a little further on, so they're going to double back. Should be safe to do that, the police won't be watching the reverse routes. It should only take them a couple of hours."

"Then what are we going to do?"

"I guess we're finding accommodations for four."

"Does that mean a hotel?"

Renata rolled her eyes.

"There's four of us," Gabriel persisted. "A four-way split of a cheap motel room wouldn't be so bad, would it? We'll have heat and privacy; we can make our plans and not get rousted by the police. Ray and Nick are going to be ready for something more comfortable too."

Renata sighed deeply. "Fine. We're going to look around a bit, see if we can find an abandoned building or somewhere else sheltered that hasn't been claimed yet. If you see a motel, you can ask how much. But only say it's for you, not for four. And... look older. You gotta be eighteen."

"Yeah, I'll try," Gabriel agreed.

He wasn't sure how he was going to look older. It was probably an attitude thing. Stand tall, act confident, project his voice... he wasn't that far from turning eighteen. He could pull it off.

The search didn't go well. The buildings that looked like they might be empty were locked up tight and usually had an alarm as well. Renata pulled herself up onto an old fire escape to gain entry into one old building and Gabriel just stood down below and shook his head. There was no way that he could climb around like a monkey. He didn't have the arm strength to support his own weight.

Renata pointed out one or two motels that looked promising, but the women at the check-in desks just looked down their noses at him and told him he'd have to find somewhere else to bed his girlfriend. Gabriel went into the next one angry. He shoved the door open with a bang and strode up to the desk, clenching his jaw and speaking through his teeth.

"How much for one night?" he demanded without preamble. No more being polite, it only seemed to tip them off that he was too young.

There was a man at the desk instead of a woman. Small, Asian, maybe Vietnamese. He had to look up at Gabriel, which was a good start. The little man opened his mouth to answer.

"And don't give me any crap," Gabriel warned. "I've been on my feet all day, and I just want somewhere to soak them and go to sleep."

"Yes, yes," the man said. He opened a drawer and pulled out a room key. "One night thirty dollar and fifty cent."

Gabriel snatched the key from him. He checked his pockets and started to count his money.

"How about twenty-eight... seventy-five?" he suggested.

The manager made a little shrug of acceptance and put a form on the counter. "You name, license plate number, and major credit card, please."

Gabriel slid it back. "I don't have a car or a credit card. You think I would be staying here if I did?" he barked. "I paid for the room. Good night."

He turned and walked back out of the motel foyer. His heart was beating wildly, but he couldn't restrain a grin. Renata was coming around the corner, watching for him. He held up the key.

"You just went ahead and got it?" Her voice was disapproving. "I thought we were going to talk about it."

"I paid twenty-eight," Gabriel said. "That's seven bucks a piece. I think that's pretty good for a warm room for the night."

Her lips tightened, but she nodded. "What room?" she asked. "I'd better leave and come back later. Don't want the manager to see more than one person going into the room."

"Room thirty-five. What are you going to do? You shouldn't be walking around here alone. It's not a nice neighborhood."

"Go ahead and let yourself in. I'll just go pick you up a burger and come right back. Won't be long. This is the knock..." She tapped a rhythm out on the wall of the building next to her.

A secret knock? Gabriel supposed that he should be happy it wasn't shave-and-a-haircut. He didn't attempt to talk her out of it.

"See you soon, then," he whispered. "Don't be long."

Renata gave him a kiss on the cheek and was gone. Gabriel gave a long sigh and went on to his assigned room. He didn't even bother to turn on the light, but fell into the bed and immediately fell asleep.

There were voices outside the room.

Gabriel rubbed his eyes and strained his ears to listen. He was safely out of sight. There shouldn't be anything to worry about. But he didn't like it. The two voices were male, and they were right outside his window. Not loud voices. That wouldn't have been so worrying. It was a quiet, covert discussion.

Gabriel sat up slowly. What was he going to do if they came into the hotel room? What if they were still there when Renata returned, and they harassed her? There was nothing in the room to use as a weapon. Even the lamp was screwed down to the bedside table to prevent theft. Or maybe to prevent lamps from being used as weapons.

If it had been two women, he would reassure himself that they were just the maids. And why couldn't two men just as easily be maids? But he knew that the lowered voices were not discussing which rooms might need towels. There would be no need to be covert about something like that.

There was another voice. Female. Gabriel got closer to the window to peer out through the crack between the curtains. Just as he tried to focus on the shadowy figures, there was a knock on the door.

Renata's knock.

He was reluctant to open the door to her with two other men standing there. But she was the paranoid one; if there were any need for caution, she wouldn't have used the special knock. Gabriel opened the door a crack. Renata pushed it open impatiently.

"Come on, don't leave us standing out here," she snapped.

Gabriel stepped back and watched the three of them file in. Renata found the light switch and flipped it on.

"Food is in there," she said, tossing a fast food bag onto the dresser.

Gabriel didn't look at the food, but at the two newcomers. One was close to his height, with deep-set dark eyes. The other was shorter, blond, with a sunny disposition.

"Gabe, this is Ray and Nick. Say hi."

The boys nodded at each other.

"I thought it was too dangerous for more than one person to come into the motel room at a time," Gabriel addressed Renata.

"Yeah. But these two half-wits think that they can get away with anything. They wouldn't wait and take things slowly."

Gabriel peeked out through the curtains. Now that there was a light on inside the hotel room, he couldn't see anything but the darkness of the parking lot, and the neon lights farther away along the street.

"I'm starving," Nick declared, grabbing the bag of food. "It's been hours since I had a bite. And nothing hot for two days."

He removed a burger and started to unwrap it. Renata got closer to him. "Not that one. No cheese. That's Gabriel's."

Nick passed it along and took another one out. He handed the bag to Ray. "I assume you've got your baby food," he said to Renata.

She didn't look offended, but Gabriel didn't like the remark. "It's not baby food. You should just be glad that you can eat solid food. It's not Renata's fault that she can't."

Nick looked at Gabriel, surprised. "Well," he drawled, "your new boyfriend is a little sensitive, isn't he? Don't go all mama-bear on me, Gabriel. Renny doesn't mind a little joke."

"It's okay Gabe," Renata assured. "Really. I'd rather he joked around than acted like he didn't even see it."

Gabriel wondered if that was a shot at him for looking away when she used her feeding tube the previous day. But she didn't seem to be angry. Ray and Nick sat down on the bed, and Renata opened up her backpack to get out her dinner.

"Since we have running water today, I'm going to go with the powder instead of the premix," she said, pulling it out with a flourish.

Gabriel watched her while he unwrapped his burger. She cocked an eyebrow at him, then retreated to the bathroom to get the water she needed. She came back and sat down on the bed as well, rigging up her tube. She leaned back against the headboard and patted the space next to her for Gabriel to sit. He obliged. Everyone let out a collective sigh as they started in on their dinners.

"The motel room is courtesy of Gabriel," Renata commented, as she was the only one without her mouth full. "We each owe him seven bucks for the warm digs."

"It's much appreciated," Ray said through a mouthful of burger. "As is the warm food. I never knew how cold you could get after two days sleeping on the ground without anything warm in your belly. I never knew how good I had it, sleeping in a warm bed and getting three squares a day."

"Amen," agreed Nick.

"Sometimes you have to put up with a little discomfort for your freedom," Renata said. "Just think about how much the blacks sacrificed to travel the underground railway."

"Was this whole underground railway thing your idea?" Nick asked Gabriel.

"Because I'm black?"

"Well, you are."

"No," Ray interposed. "It's a bat-crap crazy idea, and that means it was all Renata's."

Renata nodded her agreement. "You'd better believe it," she shot back. "And so far, it's working, isn't it? I mean here we are, the first four to ride the mito underground railway. Away from our foster families and medical research programs and safely out of the state. Just think about how many more need to be rescued."

"Crazy," Ray repeated. But he didn't seem to be in any hurry to go back to his old life.

"How are we going to get anyone else out?" Nick asked. "And what are we going to do now that we are out? We can't just keep on living here for long. Somebody's bound to notice and to squeal on us or kick us out."

"That's what we've got to discuss." Renata looked at the empty space on the dresser. "I was hoping there would be a TV, so we could start researching who to go to. Who around here does breaking-news, human-interest type stuff."

"Can't we just call all of them?" Nick asked.

"No. We have to be focused. If they only do local news, then they're not going to care about us. They have to have national connections, but we've got to make them interested enough to run the story. We have to offer them an exclusive. And the more people we call, the bigger the chances are that someone will just call the authorities and cause us trouble."

"I thought they couldn't do anything once we were out of state," Ray reminded her.

"Well… I don't think they can send us back. But they could decide to put us into foster care or something here. They still have to do something about runaways. If they get a fix on us."

"I don't like the sound of that."

"We'll have to find a library tomorrow," Renata said, redirecting the conversation. "We can do some research. Check the internet and papers and talk to the librarians. Then we'll sort out who we're going to contact, and how."

"She's crazy," Nick confirmed. He and Ray were both done their burgers. Gabriel was still working on his. Renata's bag was only half-drained. "So what are the sleeping arrangements? Don't tell me mommy and daddy get the bed, because we've slept more nights on the street than you have."

"More than me?" Renata challenged.

"Well, okay, maybe not more than you. But Gabriel's only slept out one night."

"And he's the one who got us a motel room," Ray pointed out. "It's because of him that you're not sleeping on the pavement tonight. Even the carpet is more comfortable than sleeping outdoors again."

Nick sighed, lying down crossways on the bed. "So mommy and daddy *do* get the bed."

"I'm taking a long, hot shower," Ray said. "And after that, I don't care where anyone sleeps. Good night."

They all watched him retreat to the bathroom, grabbing his bulging backpack on the way.

"If anyone wants to wash their clothes, do it tonight in the sink and hang them up to dry," Renata advised. "Don't know when you'll get the next chance."

"Aren't we going to stay here?" Gabriel asked. "It's really cheap. Why would we look for anywhere else?"

"We can't stay in one place. They'll turn us in. We have to keep moving. You got lucky on this motel. Chances are, we're not going to be somewhere warm with running water again for a while."

Gabriel put what remained of his burger on the table beside him and closed his eyes, frustrated.

"You're not going to finish that?" Nick asked.

"Go ahead."

"Sweet! Thanks!"

CHAPTER EIGHTEEN

G
ABRIEL LOOKED OVER RENATA'S shoulder to see how she was doing in sorting through the various news outlets and reporters who might help break their story. He saw garish fifty-point black headlines with exclamation marks and stopped.

"What are you reading?"

Renata jumped and turned quickly to look at him. "Don't sneak up on me like that!"

"Sorry, I didn't mean to scare you. But… what are you doing? That doesn't look like mainstream media."

She clicked over to another tab, but that one too seemed to be a tabloid. "No… I just lost track of what I was doing…" She closed several tabs. Gabriel noticed that her hand was shaking.

"Are you okay?"

"Yeah, sure. I'm fine. Why wouldn't I be?"

"You just took off on a tangent, huh?"

"Uh-huh. I'm a curious person; sometimes I follow a rabbit trail too far."

"And fall down a rabbit hole," Gabriel suggested.

She looked at him again, her expression tense. "I'm on it," she promised. "I'm not going to get distracted. What's important right now is getting the word out there. We have to tell our story. We have to get news of the corruption out there to the public so that more people will help us. We're going to get all of the kids out. The railway will be humming; it will be busy all the time, rescuing kids who have been kidnapped."

Her tone was frantic. Gabriel nodded reassuringly. "Sure. We'll get the word out there. We're going to help a lot of kids, Renata, by letting people know what's going on."

"Yeah." She was breathing heavily like she'd been running. "That's right."

Gabriel walked back away from her, giving her space. He caught Ray's inquiring glance and didn't know how to answer it. He just shrugged and went back to the periodicals to see what information he could find.

Eventually, they settled on a list of five reporters at five different news outlets. They were written down in priority order. It was time to make the call. Gabriel wasn't going to be the one to do it. They all talked back and forth and in the end, it was agreed that this was Renata's show, she would be the mouthpiece.

"You need to talk slow," Ray told her sternly. "Be focused. Follow the outline. If you start raving about Martians in tinfoil hats, you'll lose them. You have to stay… sane."

"It's not the Martians that wear the tinfoil hats," Renata muttered. "Yeah, I get it. Be calm and sane. Tell them the information without sounding like a crazy. I can do a pretty good impression of normal if I put my mind to it."

"Do that, then."

"Yes, sir!"

They made the call from the library, where there was a rare public pay phone. They all hovered around Renata to hear as much of the call as they could. The reporter that they had selected was a mother, which they thought would make her more disposed to be sympathetic toward children who had been torn from their families. As they expected, it took a while to get through to Kirstie Holt herself, but Renata refused to reveal her story to anyone else, and eventually made it through all of the gatekeepers to get to the reporter.

"Miss Holt?" Renata's voice vibrated with excitement. "I want to offer you an exclusive on the story of my friends and me, who were kidnapped."

She gave a little grin, listening to Holt's response.

"Not by Martians in tinfoil hats," she assured the reporter with good humor. "I'm talking about being taken away from our parents by a corrupt social services system."

Ray didn't like the humorous touch and looked at Gabriel with anxiety, his face pale and pinched. Nick laughed and nudged Ray.

"I know you've done stories on social services abuses before," Renata was saying. "That's why I thought you would be a good person to approach about medical kidnap. Kids being stolen away from their families for no other reason than that they have a disease. My three friends and I were all taken away from our families within the last year because we have mitochondrial disease, which is very rare. They wanted to use us for experiments being run by a mitochondrial research clinic."

There was tense silence as they all waited for some indication of Kirstie's reaction to this claim. Renata listened and gave them a little nod.

"We're all ready to meet with you, to tell you our stories. And we're not the only ones this happened to. The system is full of kids who were taken away without any reason other than that they were sick."

It sounded like the closer. Would Kirstie take it or not?

"Technically we are runaways," Renata admitted. "You would need to protect our identities."

Gabriel bit his lip. The whole thing sounded like a bad idea now. A stupid idea. Who was going to want to interview them? They would just end up being turned over to the police, or worse. Why hadn't they just kept running? Gabriel had enough money to get by for a few months, to get really far away and start a new life. Why were they staying around to talk to this woman, who would probably think that they were completely crazy?

"The public library," Renata said, giving the boys two thumbs up. "Downtown. Can we meet today?"

She settled up the details efficiently and hung up the phone. Nick gave a whoop as she put down the receiver. "You did it!" he cheered. "I didn't think there was any way, but you did it!"

He gave her a big hug and an exuberant kiss on the mouth. Gabriel froze.

Renata held her side, pale. "Ow. Take it easy there, Romeo. Damaged property, remember? Broken ribs."

"Oh, yeah." Nick's face was stricken. "I forgot! I'm sorry, Renny."

Renata breathed out in a whistle, obviously trying to control the pain. She grasped Nick's arm. "I gotta sit down."

Nick and Ray both supported Renata, guiding her into the nearest bench. Gabriel hovered. "Are you okay, Renata? Did he re-break it? What about your lung?"

Renata shook her head. "No," she said breathlessly. "Lung's still inflated. It will be fine. Just bruised."

Nick stood there, his hands over his head as if holding the top on. He clutched at his short blond hair. "I forgot," he repeated, agonized. "I just... it was just an impulse. I didn't mean to hurt you!"

"I know that, Nick," Renata said. "Just chill, please." She breathed a few times, in and out. "Kirstie Holt is going to be here in two hours. So we need to go over our stories and what we're going to tell her. There's lots to do; we can't just sit around here."

Gabriel wouldn't have guessed looking at Kirstie Holt that she had two children. She looked like she was barely out of high school, with a slim, girlish figure and fresh face. She had two men with her to handle the cameras and equipment. They both seemed entirely unaffected by her beauty or fame. He supposed that they worked with her every day and had seen her at her worst. The bloom would quickly fade.

He watched them set up with interest. He was trying to avoid thinking about the interview and all the ways that it might go wrong. He assumed that was also why Nick was running off at the mouth, joking and clowning around as if he didn't have a care in the world. Renata remained their spokesman, introducing everyone. She was quieter and more serious than usual. Which had the benefit of making her sound like a sane person instead of a conspiracy theorist. Gabriel was anxious about what was going to happen when Kirstie decided to look at their backgrounds and realized they had all been through the psych ward. At least, Gabriel assumed that Ray and Nick had also been through psych. Maybe they hadn't. Renata had said something about the Children's, not the psych ward.

"It's very nice to meet you all." Kirstie smiled over them. "I'm going to need to see some proof of your identities. I realize that you want to stay anonymous, but I do need to know that you are who you say you are. And I will need to look into your public records to verify what details I can."

They all exchanged glances. Renata nodded confirmation, and they each dug into their backpacks to get their IDs.

"We probably all have the same problem," Renata said. "You get kidnapped from your family, and you don't get to take anything with you. Including a wallet with ID. So all I have is my medical card."

"Then that will have to do," Kirstie said.

They were all in the same boat. They each had cards from DFS to cover their prescriptions and medical expenses. Ray happened to also have his birth certificate, but he was the only one.

"Now I want everyone to be relaxed and natural," Kirstie said. "We'll just chat and go over your stories. A lot will be cut out by editing, so don't worry if you find yourself rambling. We'll tighten it up. The more you can just be yourselves and share the truth about what happened, the better it will all come out."

They all nodded. Renata made Gabriel go first. He looked at her in a panic, shaking his head. Renata just crossed her arms in front of her chest and waited. The others were happy to have Gabriel go first. Kirstie smiled and invited him to sit down with her.

Gabriel was sweating, and his chest hurt. He didn't know how to sit, and the camera was uncomfortably close to his face. Kirstie gave him a reassuring smile that didn't help Gabriel feel any better and led in with the date.

"So tell me your story," the reporter encouraged. "Tell me what happened when you were first apprehended."

Gabriel took a deep breath and started to tell her about waking up in hospital and what had happened there. He told what he could remember of what had happened at the weight clinic, and everything since. Kirstie was a good listener, prompting Gabriel now and then to dig out a nugget of detail, but mostly just letting him relate his story.

After they had wrapped up, Kirstie shook Gabriel's hand. He hoped it wasn't too damp and clammy. "You did great, Gabriel. That wasn't so bad, was it?"

Gabriel nodded wordlessly.

After that, he was able to relax, listening to Ray's and Nick's interviews. He had only the briefest outlines about them from Renata, so it was all new. But also eerily familiar. Renata, interviewed last, immediately explained that her case was a little different because she believed that her mother *was* trying to harm her; but she believed that DFS had other motives for removing her. She explained that she didn't want to be part of the mito research experiments and that she believed that the unproven drugs were interfering with her other meds.

"What other meds are you on, Renata?" Kirstie had asked the boys too.

Renata showed no shyness about disclosing her private medical history. She listed several drugs by name and then faltered. "I don't remember them all. The doctors keep changing things around. I have paranoia, bipolar, OCD... right now it's under control. But sometimes I have a break and end up in hospital. That's where I met—" she caught herself quickly. "Some of the others."

"And is this all part of your mitochondrial disease, or something separate?"

"Probably part of the mito. There's no way to tell, but psychological problems are higher among patients with mito. So are developmental delays. You can't really tell where it came from, but you assume."

"So these experimental drugs could conceivably improve your psychological symptoms as well."

"That doesn't give them the right to force me into treatment," Renata growled. "No one has the right to control my body. Or my mind. They can't just decide how they're going to treat me without my input. Patients have rights—" Her voice was climbing higher and louder.

Gabriel looked at the other boys in a panic. If Renata freaked out, they were going to lose all of their traction. Kirstie would can the whole thing. Ray stood up and walked across to where Renata was sitting. He took her hand and leaned over to whisper something to her.

Renata coughed, then took a deep breath. She gave a little laugh. "I'm very passionate about patient rights," she explained, her voice calm once more. "When I see kids brought to the hospital and put under chemical restraints to keep them from making waves, it makes me furious. Some of them are hardly more than babies, comatose from benzodiazepines or antipsychotics. They don't have any diagnosed psychiatric disorder! The doctors do it just to keep them quiet!"

Gabriel could tell that Ray was squeezing Renata's hand, trying to rein her in. She looked up at him and nodded. "I know. I'm supposed to stay calm. It's just hard." She dabbed at the corner of her eye. "When you've seen the kinds of things that they do."

"I understand that. We are all sympathetic," Kirstie agreed.

"None of us are allowed to see our parents. DFS is supposed to be trying to reunite families, but we go weeks, even months without visitation. And then it is supervised to make sure that we can't say anything about our medical treatment. Nothing."

"But *your* mother is in prison. And you said you thought she was trying to kill you."

"I'm talking for the others," Renata said, and the camera panned back to where Gabriel and Nick were sitting. It took a huge effort for Gabriel not to put his hand up to cover his face, or to turn it aside. "How long was it before you guys got a visitation?"

The camera was on Gabriel and Nick. Everyone waited. Nick motioned for Gabriel to go first.

"Almost a month," said Gabriel. "And then only for ten minutes, because my mom noticed I had a rash from the protocol meds, and she wasn't allowed to talk about it."

He looked at Nick. "I haven't seen anyone in my family yet," Nick said. His voice was completely serious for once. "It's been two months. I was taken because they said the house was unhygienic and might be dangerous to my health. Just to mine, no one else's. And you know, they wouldn't want my mom to somehow bring the house to a visitation and make me sick, or something."

The attempt at humor flopped. The camera panned back over to Renata and Ray.

"It was twenty-four days before my first visitation," Ray said. "I've only had two, in spite of the fact that the court said I was to have weekly visits. Things just keep coming up each week that make visits impossible." He shrugged. "According to my social worker."

"That's a long time to go without visits," Kirstie agreed, probably thinking about her own children. "Especially when court-mandated visits are skipped. That must be very frustrating."

CHAPTER NINETEEN

WE HAVE TO GET a motel room tonight," Gabriel urged. They had been sleeping rough since the night at the motel, and while he was gradually adjusting to the discomfort and getting a few hours of sleep each night, it wasn't doing anything for his mito. He was tired all the time, and he thought the others were looking pale and worn as well.

"You think we should get a motel room every night," Renata pointed out, an irritated edge to her voice.

"But the broadcast is on tonight. We need to rent a motel room with a TV so that we can watch it."

Renata looked at the other boys, and they nodded agreement.

"We have to see how it goes off," Ray said. "Just because she acted like she believed us and was on our side, that doesn't mean she really is. We have to see what she says, and then figure out the next step."

For days, Renata had been repeating that they couldn't advance their plan until they knew how the broadcast went. She couldn't argue against her own words.

"Okay... but it will probably be the last warm bed for a while. Once it airs, people are going to be looking for us. We have to stay out of sight."

"We haven't broken any laws here, they can't do anything to us," Gabriel asserted. They had all repeated the refrain enough times that it felt like it had to be true. They all believed it. Except Renata, who didn't trust her own theory.

"Do you have somewhere in mind?" Renata asked.

"Paradise," Gabriel and Nick said in unison. Nick burst into a fit of laughter.

"Why?"

"Cheapest one with TVs and the right channels," Gabriel explained.

Renata frowned at Nick, who had to sit down on the sidewalk and lean against the low wall, he was laughing so hard. "And...? What else? I know Curly here hasn't researched the room rates."

None of them had an answer for him. Renata shook her head and addressed Ray. "You look the oldest. You rent it."

"No!" Nick wiped tears from his face. "No, let me do it, Renata. As penance."

"Right." Renata looked again at the three of them, trying to discern what was going on. "You're the shortest one. Ray is going to do it."

"Oooh...!" Nick drew out a whine of disappointment.

Renata pointed her finger at Gabriel's nose. "You tell me what else is at the Paradise. Why does Nick want to go there?"

"Because of the TV," Gabriel suggested. "Or maybe the free continental breakfast."

"Only one of us can go to the breakfast. And even if they load up a plate, it won't be enough for all three of you bottomless pits."

"The person that goes can fill up before taking a plate away," Gabriel said.

"Is that why you want to check in?" Renata demanded from Nick. "So you can pig out on breakfast?"

"Yeah." Nick tried to suppress another snicker and ended up snorting. "That's why!" He dissolved again into laughter. Gabriel was afraid Nick was getting hysterical. People were staring as they walked by.

Renata scowled at Nick. "Fine. You go right now and see if they'll give you a room. If you fail, we'll have to wait a few hours before Ray tries."

Ray turned away from Renata to hide his look of disappointment.

"But…" Nick started out.

"But what? I said yes."

"I don't know… if there's someone there yet. At the desk. They might not accept reservations until later."

"It's after three. All the motels have someone at the desk."

"But not the *right* someone," Ray said in a whisper to Gabriel.

Gabriel nodded, not looking at Ray. Being careful not to give Renata any sign. They watched Nick get to his feet and wipe his red face. Nick looked back once, pleadingly, and they all watched him start down the street. Gabriel couldn't help looking at Ray.

"I gotta watch this," Ray said and followed Nick.

"Watch what?" Renata demanded.

Gabriel followed Ray. Renata fell in beside him. They allowed Nick to get around the corner, and then followed covertly, watching him enter the lobby of the Paradise. Gabriel couldn't run, but he walked as quickly as he could to keep up with Ray. They both peered through the window, staying out of sight and squinting through the horizontal blinds.

"What the—?" Renata took up a place beside Gabriel and looked through the window.

They all saw Nick waiting as a young lady approached the desk, smiling and calling out to him. An apology for being away from the desk.

"Ooooh." Renata finally got it. She rolled her eyes. "Got his eye on chickie-poo, does he?"

Chickie-poo was blond, tall, and well-endowed. She wore heels and was too tall for the check-in counter unless she sat down, but she didn't. She bent over to deal with her customer, giving him an unimpeded view down her v-neck shirt. Renata made a noise of disgust.

"He'd better get the room. If I have to wait three hours because he had to take his hormones out for a walk…"

"Looks like he is," Ray said, with a note of disappointment.

The young lady handed Nick a key and Nick leaned on the counter and chatted for a few more minutes until her phone rang and she had to sit down and turn away to get it.

"You too?" Renata asked Ray.

"She's hot," Ray said. "I'm not supposed to notice?"

"No. And you?" Renata directed this at Gabriel.

"She's pretty," Gabriel admitted. "But... she's not really my type."

"Alive?" she gibed.

"Older," Gabriel said. "White. Out of my league."

"Oh. Well, she is all that," Renata agreed. Which didn't make Gabriel feel great, but at least it got her off his case. She'd be angry at Nick and Ray all night, but Gabriel hoped to stay on her good side and avoid her wrath.

Nick came out of the lobby, grinning and playing with the keys. He saw them all looking in the window and grinned even wider. "I told you I could do it."

"Was there someone at the desk?" Renata asked, her sarcasm so sharp that Gabriel felt Nick's pain.

"Yeah," Nick agreed. "Was there ever."

The segment was much shorter than Gabriel had expected it to be, considering all the time that had gone into the interviews. It was titled 'Medical Kidnap?' with a question mark, leaving it up to the audience to decide whether it was really a thing. The splash screen that they played before the segment and that appeared on the monitor behind Kirstie was a glowing purple picture of a mitochondrion. It looked like a bug. A trilobite. The editing of their interviews was so skillfully done, Gabriel couldn't tell where they had clipped the longer answers out. Everything sounded short and pithy and important. Their faces were blurred out, and their voices computer altered. Gabriel was sure that they were all still clearly identifiable to anyone who knew them. The hounds would be hunting them. He wondered if Keisha would see the broadcast.

"We would like to open the discussion up to you," Kirstie invited the television audience. "Our call in number is at the bottom of the screen. Call and let me know whether you find this story believable. Are children being torn from their parents for no reason other than to serve as human lab rats? Or are they misled, or misleading us, about the facts of their cases?"

"I didn't know she was going to do that," Gabriel whispered to Renata.

She nodded, not looking at him, her eyes intent on the screen.

Several calls followed. People who had a friend or a sister who had had a child taken away from them and put into experimental research programs. Some of them even in the mito program. Others pooh-poohed the idea. No social worker or doctor could ever get away with such a thing. No judge would ever be fooled or complicit. The system had all the proper checks and balances and could not be abused.

One motor-mouthed conspiracy theorist wildly expounded his own theories and Kirstie couldn't get a word in edgewise. His call was faded out and the program's theme music faded in, and they broke for commercial.

"What do you think?" Gabriel asked Renata. "Are you happy with it?"

"Not bad. I wish they hadn't cut that guy off, though!"

"Too much of a nut," Ray said. "He'd just make the whole thing a three-ring circus. You want people who sound reasonable and considered."

"I know. I just wanted to hear more of what he had to say."

Nick laughed and shook his head at Renata. "You're just as crazy as he is."

They continued to chat through the commercials, relieved that it had finally aired and they could now consider what to do next. Get more publicity? Confront the doctors? Go back for more kids and take them out through the underground railway, maybe. There would be people on their side now. Maybe people would reach out and help, just like they had helped escaped slaves.

The program resumed, and with a short summary, Kirstie went on to the next caller.

"I know those children," said a woman's voice, with a snap of anger in it. "They are not telling you the whole story."

Gabriel gasped. He looked at Renata and she mouthed 'Seymour' in disbelief. They were all glued to the screen, no more laughing and chatting.

"How do you know them?" Kirstie inquired.

"I have been involved with all of their cases."

There was silence for a long three seconds. Maybe the longest three seconds of Gabriel's life.

"Are you the one who reported their parents to DFS?"

There was a shocked murmur from the studio audience and some scattered clapping. Kirstie glanced at the audience with a quick shake of her head, and they fell silent. Seymour didn't answer.

"Are you the one who reported them to DFS?" Kirstie repeated.

"DFS reports are confidential. I have been involved with all of their cases and I know the facts. *Beep* is the ringleader." The broadcast must have been on an eight-second delay because they managed to bleep Renata's name. "She has paranoid delusions. She is very intelligent and very good at manipulating those around her. Even the medical staff have been taken in from time to time. She is the one who came up with this whole conspiracy theory. But there is no conspiracy. Only children being taken out of hazardous environments. Their parents are guilty of medical neglect or even abuse. *Beep* own mother is in prison. Do you think they put caring mothers in prison for no particular reason?"

"So…" Kirstie's calm, soothing voice took over. "Why don't you tell us the rest of the story? Why don't you tell us what the children have missed or obfuscated? And please, don't use their names, we need to keep minors' names private and we are dubbing them out of the broadcast."

"When you only hear one side of the story, of course it sounds unbalanced and crazy," Seymour snarled. "You are only hearing a fraction of the truth. Once you know the rest, it makes sense. You'll see there is no conspiracy."

"Again, I invite you to tell us the truth."

"Parents who cannot take care of their children properly have to be challenged. A mother who decides that her Google research of naturopathic bulletin boards is more valid than a doctor's years of research and training needs to be stopped. They must be stopped! They cannot be allowed to continue harming their own children!" There was passion in Dr. Seymour's voice. Pain. Gabriel couldn't help feeling a little sorry for her. She really did believe her side of the story, just like Renata did. And she really did want to stop children from being abused. Maybe it wasn't a conspiracy, but just... people who were misled or had misinterpreted the situation. Some people seemed more prone to draw the conclusions that would support their own theories and life views. Gabriel reached for Renata's hand. She pulled back from him, shutting everything else out to listen to the show.

However much Kirstie tried, she couldn't seem to draw any of the missing facts out of Dr. Seymour, and eventually cut the call off. They went to commercial again.

"This is getting real," Nick commented.

"It wasn't real when you were sleeping on the ground?" Gabriel snapped. "We've been dealing with the reality for weeks or months." He glanced at Renata. "Or years. It's time other people heard."

"What are you arguing with me for? We're on the same side, moron!"

Gabriel backed down. His emotions were running high, unable to process everything that had happened. He shrugged and settled back to watch a ketchup commercial as if it was the most interesting thing in the world. Renata glanced at him with eyebrows raised, then looked away again.

The show resumed, again with another sum-up of what had happened so far, and then another call. Gabriel half-expected it to be Seymour again, angrier than ever, but it wasn't. It was, however, another voice that he knew.

"I may get fired for this call," the woman said, voice unsteady, close to tears if she wasn't already crying. "But I have to set the record straight. I... was the social worker who apprehended one of the boys. And there have been others. I didn't agree with what we were doing, but I had my job to consider, and I went ahead and did what I was told."

"What was it you were told, and why didn't you want to?" Kirstie asked gently.

"I was told that—the boy—was being medically neglected, or that his mother had Munchhausen by Proxy, and he needed to be removed for his own safety."

"And you didn't believe it?"

"I was told to investigate. I did. I didn't find any sign that she wasn't doing everything she could for her son. No, she hadn't put him into the mito program at Lantern, but she was having good success with getting his health on track, getting his weight up, and keeping on top of his education. She did everything for him. She was a good mother!"

"Then why did you take him away?"

"I made my report of no findings to support the accusations. They told me to go back with the police and apprehend him. They said that my report was inadequate, that they had talked more with the doctors, and their finding was of medical abuse. They decided that without ever being in the home or speaking to the mother. They overruled my report, and sent me back to take him away."

"And you did?"

"It was that or lose my job and I couldn't lose my job. But I guess I should have. No job is worth giving up my ethical standards. I should have stood up for myself and refused." She sobbed slightly, but got herself back under control. Renata gave Gabriel's leg a quick rub to show her support. He just sat there with his mouth open, listening to Carol Scott's confession. "I thought that once they had him at the hospital for a few days, they would change their minds and see that he hadn't been neglected or abused. But they didn't. The first time I went back there, he was so drugged up they couldn't even wake him for me. It didn't matter what I said or did; they had already made their decision. They wanted him in the mito research study, and they were going to do whatever they had to to get him there."

"Who is 'they'? Who exactly do you think wanted him in the mito study?"

"I... don't know who was behind it. You'd have to go to someone over my head to find that out. I only talked with my supervisors."

"Do you think that senior DFS officials were involved?"

"I know they were."

"Doctors? Nurses?"

"I... I don't know which ones were or were not involved. I don't know who was in the know and who was just a pawn."

"Judges?"

There was silence from Carol Scott.

Kirstie pressed the point. "Is it your opinion that the judge in this young man's case or the judges in other similar cases were involved in a conspiracy? Do you think that they were misled or paid to look the other way?"

"I... I think that some of the judges have been misled by DFS or the doctors involved. And I think that one or two of them... know what is going on and are complicit."

Renata swore. Nick started to yell, unable to hold in his excitement over this revelation. Ray smacked him.

"Shut up! People are going to complain and you'll get us all kicked out."

"I don't care! Can you believe that she just said that? Somebody is on our side! Somebody who has been involved admits that the judges are corrupt! She said it right out!"

"Shut up!" Renata echoed. She was on the bed, and he was sitting on the floor in front of it. She kicked at Nick's head.

Nick flinched away, crying foul, but stopped shouting. Gabriel missed a line or two that Kirstie said and then they broke for commercials again.

"Holy crap!" Ray said. "It's breaking open. It's really working, Renata. You did it."

"Wish I had a laptop," Renata said. "They're doing online polls and comments. I'd love to answer some of them."

"Carol Scott," Gabriel breathed. "I didn't even think she had a soul. But now she's on our side."

"This is big," Renata said happily. "This is really big."

CHAPTER TWENTY

HE NEXT MORNING, THEY called Kirstie Holt from the library again. They got right through with no waiting and were talking to her within minutes. Everyone crowded around the receiver to be able to hear both sides of the conversation.

"Did you guys watch it?" Kirstie asked without preamble.

"Yeah, we did," Renata agreed. "I can't believe that Carol Scott called in. And Dr. Seymour. That was incredible."

"I agree. We're still getting calls this morning. We're getting great coverage."

"Do people believe us?"

"Some do, some don't. Those calls made a big difference. I think there are more who believe than not."

"Are you following up? What are you going to do next?"

"I'd like to pursue it, with your permission," Kirstie said. "I think we need to name names. The doctors, nurses, social workers, and judges who are involved. We will start an in-depth investigation, and where we can find evidence, disclose it to the public."

"Yeah," Renata agreed. "For sure."

"I don't want to put you guys in danger. We've already been getting calls this morning from DFS looking for information on where to find you."

"Don't tell them."

"We have the right to protect confidential sources, but where the safety of minors is at stake… I'm afraid we might be getting a subpoena."

"They can't do anything to us," Renata said. "We haven't broken the law."

"DFS can apprehend you just as easily here as back home."

"And do what? Put us into foster care? We'll just run again."

"They could put you in a closed facility. Send you back home and make sure you couldn't get away this time."

"They can't send us home. Not across state borders."

There was silence on the other end of the phone.

"Can they?" Renata asked, her voice small.

"There are interstate compacts. Not only *can* they send you home, they're *required* to within a limited timeframe."

The boys looked at Renata. She gave a little shrug, looking away. Ray swore under his breath. "So we're not safe here. And now that we've plastered ourselves all over TV, they know where to find us. Everybody's going to recognize us, even if they don't know our faces."

"We'll have to split up," Renata murmured. "Make it harder. I thought…" She shook her head. "You know what I thought. What about leaving the country?"

Kirstie's voice brought their attention back to the phone. "I really don't know if there are agreements with neighboring countries, but I would assume there are. And you'd have to be able to cross the border, which you're not doing without ID."

Renata sighed.

"I would suggest," said Kirstie, "that you stay away from the area where we conducted the interviews. If they do serve us with something that says we have to disclose what we know about your location, I don't want you to be there."

"Yeah," Ray agreed. "We'll move around."

"I need to know the names of all of the individuals that you believe are involved. So that we can investigate them. See who's taking orders and who is giving them."

"We'll call you back," Renata said. She pushed down the hang-up switch. They all looked at her in surprise.

"She could have told DCF where we were already," Renata said. "That was a warning. We gotta move, or we're sitting ducks, spending an hour talking on the phone with her while they close in. Come on."

Gabriel hated to lose the illusion of safety. It turned out they had never been safe, but now his heart was thumping hard like he was already being chased. If anyone identified them, there was no way for them to run away. Renata might be able to get away with one sprint, but none of them could handle any sustained activity.

A woman walking into the library with her two small children looked at them with a frown. Renata led the way out of the building, and the mother turned and watched them go.

"We need to go where there are other kids, so we don't stand out like a sore thumb," Renata suggested.

"Where do other kids hang out?"

They all glanced at each other.

"School," Gabriel pointed out the obvious. "DFS will never look there for us, and we can split up and blend in. Who's going to notice four more kids with backpacks at school?"

"Good call," Renata agreed. "I'll go ahead and call Kirstie back from the first one we hit. Then we'll need to go on and find another one to hide out at, in case her caller ID identifies where we are."

"If we call her from a school, won't they look at other schools?" Gabriel asked.

She looked at him. "Yeah… they might. Call from a fast food place? Then go find a school?"

"Double back," Ray said. "Don't give them a vector to follow."

"Aren't we all experts all of a sudden?" Nick jeered, shaking his head.

"We're going to have to be," Renata snapped. "You want to go back?"

"I'm getting awful tired of sleeping on the streets."

They all looked at each other.

"I thought that by now, we'd have somewhere more comfortable," Nick said. "We'd be able to stay in a shelter or something. This is just getting more and more ridiculous."

"You want to go back? So go back. No one is stopping you."

"Fine. Good luck."

Renata, Gabriel, and Ray watched Nick walk away.

"He'll be back," Renata predicted after he was out of sight.

"How is he going to find us?" Gabriel asked.

"He's got the phone, doesn't he?" Renata asked Ray.

"No. I've got it. He's on his own."

They stopped at a fast food restaurant and used the pay phone. Renata painstakingly gave Kirstie all of the names that she could remember of the players in the conspiracy. Gabriel watched the street outside for any suspicious people or vehicles. Renata was getting more and more wound up, and that worried him. Ray had split off. He had the other cell phone, so they would be able to touch base with him again when they needed to. Gabriel thought that Ray was probably going to search for Nick. The boys had grown as close as brothers during their flight. Letting Nick go back to foster care didn't sit well with Ray.

"All clear?"

Gabriel jumped at Renata's voice in his ear.

She giggled; a stressed-out noise, not happy. "Sorry, Gabe. Everything look okay?"

"Yeah. I don't see any problems."

"You want to get something to eat, while we're here?"

"You don't think they'll trace the call and show up?"

Renata grimaced. "You're right. Let's at least cross the street. We can watch from there." She gestured to a sub shop.

"Yeah, okay."

They walked together. Gabriel glanced aside at Renata. She was pale, and he thought she had lost weight since they'd gone on the run. She tried not to show any weakness, but she was just as sick as the rest of them, if not more so. When they reached the sub shop, Gabriel stood casually outside it, as if he were there for a smoke or some fresh air. But what he was doing was checking for discarded sandwiches in the outside garbage. There was one near the top that was not even half-eaten. Gabriel grabbed it and went into the shop. It was lunchtime, so there were plenty of people there. They settled themselves in a corner booth. Gabriel unwrapped the sandwich and Renata got her formula flowing.

Renata caught Gabriel's eyes on her. "What?"

"I haven't seen you take any of your meds."

"I take them through the tube, like everything else."

"Yeah, I know, but... when? I've never seen you take them. Are they already mixed into your formula?"

Of course, if that were true, that would mean she was still on the mito clinic protocol, because there would be no way for her to separate out individual meds.

"I just do it when you're not paying attention," Renata said with a wave of her hand.

Gabriel ate his sandwich, considering that. By the time he was finished, he was convinced that she wasn't taking her meds at all. That would explain why it was getting increasingly difficult to keep her on track, focused on their efforts instead of obsessing over new theories.

"Why don't you take them now?" Gabriel suggested. "Since we're eating anyway."

"I don't take any at noon. I already took my morning dose."

"When?"

"In the bathroom, this morning." She stared at him. "After my shower. Are you my mom now? You take your meds and let me worry about mine."

Gabriel hadn't yet taken his lunch-time pills, so he did. Renata watched him lay them all out and her suspicious expression softened. She patted his arm, then checked her tube.

"Are you getting enough?" Gabriel asked. "You look like you're losing weight."

She hesitated. "I gotta find a source for more. It's prescription. That means I gotta find a doctor."

"We'd better do that, then. Will a walk-in clinic do it? They're so busy; they might not figure out you are a runaway. Even if they do, you still need to eat, right? They can't deny you food."

"DFS will have put a flag on my prescription card. As soon as I use it, they'll know."

Gabriel thought about his prescriptions. He always had to wait for the pharmacist to dispense it. Half an hour, an hour… In that time, the police could be there to apprehend them.

"What about some kind of off-the-shelf formula? Baby formula or Ensure or something?"

"It'll make me spew everywhere. The kind I need is only available by prescription."

Gabriel finished swallowing his pills. "How much should you be eating?"

Renata fiddled with the formula bag, frowning. "Four times a day," she said. "I've only been eating three."

It was no wonder she was losing weight.

"We'll just have to try," he said. "I'll be lookout. We'll make sure there's no cops around when we pick the prescription up."

"I don't know…"

"You can't starve yourself. You have to eat."

"Yeah… I guess."

Gabriel watched the restaurant across the street. "I haven't seen any police or anything; I guess they didn't trace the call."

"Or they haven't forced Kirstie to tell what she knows yet," Renata agreed. "Sometime in the next few days, though."

Hanging around the school was a good idea. They were completely invisible. No one looked at them twice. Gabriel enjoyed being around the other kids, watching them horse around or gossip in little groups, doing normal teenage things. He had not been at public school for months, and it was comforting to see that everything was still the same as it ever was. Other kids were still going to school. They had no idea of what it was like to be kidnapped and used as a guinea pig and not allowed to see your family anymore.

They had talked at first about splitting up so that they would be less visible, but no one was looking at them when they were together, so in the end, they just stayed together. Renata didn't seem happy. Gabriel watched her, wondering what was bothering her. Not like there weren't enough options. They had plenty to be worried about. But usually, Renata kept upbeat, almost manic.

"You okay?"

She looked at him. "I forgot what it feels like. Being here. So... lonely and isolating..."

Gabriel frowned at her. He found it energizing, exhilarating. He missed the noisy crowds. "There are lots of people," he pointed out. "It's not lonely."

"It is when you're the only kid with psychiatric illness. You think other kids want to hang out with you? Or their parents tell them that they can't. Afraid that I'm contagious. My mom always said that public school was the best place for me. Lots of opportunities for socialization. Role models. Learning to be normal." She hugged herself, looking bleakly at the swarms of students.

Gabriel had never seen Renata as an outcast. She was friendly and outgoing, cheerful despite the paranoia. But he watched her withdraw into herself now, avoiding meeting anyone's eyes. Afraid of being rejected. He pictured her mother telling her that she had to go to school to learn to be normal. What a cruel thing to say to someone who had no control over her mental illness. Gabriel put his arm around Renata, pulling her closer into a comforting hug.

"It's okay. You don't have to worry about what anyone else here thinks. They're just our cover. Do you want to go somewhere else?"

"I know... I think it's the safest place to be right now, though."

Gabriel rubbed her back. "If you're sure. We should probably leave before school lets out to go to the clinic anyway, get you some more formula."

She nodded, looking cheered by this. "Yeah, you're right. The clinic will get busier after school."

Renata's bleak expression faded when they left the school, but at the clinic, she was clearly anxious. Her head swiveled back and forth, looking over everyone in the waiting room, checking the doors, checking on the nurses, and starting over again.

"Do you want me to stay in here?" Gabriel asked. "Or should I watch outside, in case… someone shows up?"

Her eyes went back and forth. "Stay here, in the waiting room. Then if you see someone, we can find a back door…"

"Okay. I'm sure no one will show up. They don't have any reason to report you for anything. But just in case…"

"Who knows how many people are in on it," Renata said in a hoarse whisper. "These guys could all be hooked into the mito clinic by computer. They could have people on the lookout for us already. We were on TV; they know we're in the area."

Gabriel nodded. "Well, I'll watch. You don't need to worry."

She squeezed his hand briefly and didn't say anything. It was another hour before they called Renata in. He could see by the way that the nurses were watching Renata's increasingly-frantic pacing that they were nervous about her. Once a nurse took her down the hall, Gabriel turned back to watch out the window. He didn't really expect to see the police or anyone who wanted to apprehend them, but Renata's anxiety made him jumpy.

There were no police cars. No one whose clothing and bearing screamed 'social worker.' There was a young doctor who walked in and talked with the nurse at the reception desk. He apparently didn't work there; she didn't seem to know him. He only talked to her for a couple of minutes before leaving again without ever entering the back offices. He stopped and looked around the waiting room briefly before walking out. Gabriel thought that the man's eyes paused for an instant longer on him, but that was probably just because Gabriel was staring at him. Gabriel watched him walk back out to a rust-red station wagon in the parking lot. He sat in his car talking on the phone for several minutes before driving away.

Gabriel watched the other cars in the parking lot, looking for anyone who was watching the clinic. There were a lot of cars, but he didn't see anyone who was just sitting there, and everybody who came into the clinic seemed to have a reason to be there.

Looking out into the parking lot again, Gabriel jumped at a light touch on his shoulder.

"All clear?" Renata asked.

"Yeah, looks like it. Did he give you the prescription?"

Renata nodded. "No problem. Wants me to find a local gastroenterologist, but he gave me a repeat prescription anyway. Let's scram."

There was a drug store right across the parking lot from the clinic, but Gabriel eyed it uneasily. "I think… we should go somewhere else. If someone does report us… that's exactly where they'll expect us to go next."

Renata agreed. It was a commercial area. Lots of strip malls. It wouldn't be hard for them to find a smaller pharmacy farther away. Renata ducked into the back alley to change her t-shirt so that she wouldn't be wearing the same thing if they made a report on her. She went into the pharmacy by herself so that they wouldn't be observed together. Gabriel was getting tired with all the precautions. He again stood lookout. His eyelids were beginning to droop, which probably wasn't a good idea for a guard. Renata was in and out quickly.

"Okay, let's go. They said they'd have it ready in an hour."

Gabriel nodded.

"I'm not going to go back today," Renata said. "If they're going to send someone to pick me up, it will be in the next hour. They can't leave someone here twenty-four hours a day until I show up. I'll pick it up tomorrow. If they try to stall me…" She shook her head. "I won't hang around. Sooner or later, they'll just have to hand it over. They can't refuse to give me my prescription, and the police or DFS can't be here waiting all the time. Right?" She looked at Gabriel for reassurance. Her eye sockets were getting hollow with all of the worry and the weight that she had lost.

"Right," Gabriel agreed. It was a good plan that ensured they wouldn't just walk back into a trap when they came back to get it. "Can we… take a nap or something?"

Renata laughed. "Sure, old man. But I want to watch to see if anyone shows up, so we need to stay close by."

Gabriel looked around. There wasn't anywhere remotely comfortable, but at that point, he didn't need comfort. He just needed to lay his body down. They crossed the street together, and he lay down on the sidewalk. Renata sat down with a cup for change. For all intents and purposes, they were invisible. Renata could watch to see if anything went down at the pharmacy.

Renata poked Gabriel awake. "Shh," she warned. "Take a look."

Gabriel opened his eyes. He couldn't see from his supine position, so he sat up, head still fuzzy with sleep. It took him a moment to focus on the activity across the street.

There was a police car in the parking lot. It didn't have its lights or siren on and was just cruising through. In another minute, it disappeared into the alley behind the pharmacy and didn't come back out.

"He's there," Renata breathed. "Waiting for me."

Gabriel couldn't find any other explanation. They continued to watch. Gabriel knew nothing was going to happen, because Renata wasn't going to go over there to get caught, but he was fascinated anyway.

Renata pointed to a minivan that passed the pharmacy twice and then pulled into one of the parking spaces in front of it. No one got out. They just sat there, in the vehicle, waiting. Gabriel's heart beat a rapid rhythm, and his breathing got louder and faster.

"I don't believe it," Gabriel said.

Who was in the van? A social worker? One of the doctors from the clinic? Somebody who expected to be part of recapturing Renata. Renata's head turned back and forth, and Gabriel looked to see what else she was watching.

"Looking for a phone I could borrow," Renata whispered. "I wonder what would happen… if I called Kirstie. Do you think she would come? What would they tell her if she did?"

"Nothing. They'd say it was all confidential and none of her business."

Renata snorted. "Too true," she agreed. She turned back to look at the parking lot, entranced. Still, no one got out of the van, and the police car didn't reappear.

"How long has it been? Since you dropped off the prescription?"

"Half an hour."

"They were quick."

"Yeah. Scary quick."

A red station wagon wove through the parking lot, looking for a space. Gabriel watched it idly at first, then frowned.

"What is it?" Renata asked.

"That car. You see it? The station wagon. It was at the clinic."

"Somebody else who needed a prescription filled."

"Why would they come over here instead of going to the one that was closer? No… it was a doctor, not a patient."

"A doctor?"

"Yeah. He was there when you were in talking to your doctor. He talked with the nurse, then left again and called someone on the phone. He didn't work there."

"That's weird."

"I know. And now he's here."

"You're sure it's the same car?"

"Look at it. Do you think I'd make a mistake?"

"No… I guess not." Renata hesitated, her whole body tense. "Okay," she decided. "I'm going to try calling Kirstie. Tell her what's going on. You…" Renata patted her pockets, and came out with her cell phone and held it out to him. "You see if you can get a video. They might be gone before she can get here, or she might not be able to come. But if we can get a video of what's going on…"

Gabriel nodded, taking it from her.

"But no phone calls," Renata warned. "It can be traced. We don't want to give anyone our GPS location."

"Won't they know that when you tell Kirstie that you're here?"

Renata shook her head. "The pharmacy isn't going to go anywhere. But the phone is going with us and will keep broadcasting our location."

"Oh. Yeah, okay."

Renata got up and walked briskly away. Gabriel stood up for a better vantage point and started the phone video recording. He wasn't holding it very steady, and nothing much was happening. But he hoped they'd be able to do something with it.

In the end, the suspicious vehicles all left, including the police car. Kirstie didn't make it there in time to see them. Renata promised to get the video to her soon, but Gabriel didn't know what value the low-quality video would have.

"We're getting a lot of pushback from everybody that we've contacted so far," Kirstie advised when they called her back. Gabriel and Renata both cuddled close to the phone to hear it at the same time. "But they can't keep us from public records, and that includes grant applications by the Lantern Clinic for research studies. We're getting a team to collate the statistics and see what they can come up with—number of kids with mito, number of kids being treated at the clinic, how many of them are in foster care. That one's a bit harder, but we're hoping to get some help from Carol Scott."

"She hasn't been fired?" Renata asked.

"She's been suspended with pay. Which means that she doesn't have access to current records, but she's putting together what she can remember. The number of kids that she has apprehended that have gone into the program, the number she's heard of from other social workers or seen in the news."

"I know some too," Renata offered. "I mean, besides the four of us."

"Skyler," Gabriel suggested.

"Yeah." Her eyes got distant. "Man, I'd like to break him out."

"Renata," Kirstie warned, "you can't suggest to me that you're planning to break the law. I'd be ethically bound to report it."

"I didn't say I was going to break him out, just that I'd like to."

"I know. But I need to stop you before you say anything that I'd have to repeat to the police."

"Yeah, okay. I'm not going to say anything like that. I'll try to put together a list. I bet I know at least ten of the kids who went into the mito program this year. Maybe fifteen."

"Out of how many?" Kirstie asked.

"Forty," Gabriel said. "That's how many they need to provide for the study." He looked at Renata. "How do you know that many of them?"

Renata shrugged. "I've spent a lot of time in hospital this year. And I'm friendly. I talk to people. If I see someone new in the program, I find out who they are. What their story is."

"Fifteen," Gabriel repeated. "If Carol knows another five... we'll have the names of almost all the kidnapped kids. I mean... half of them have to be kids whose parents agreed to put them into the program, right? Some parents would try anything."

He had seen how desperate Keisha sometimes got to find some way to help Gabriel. The mito clinic had been tempting at first. She was excited to find someone that specialized in mitochondrial disease instead of just having a passing knowledge of it. But when she had looked more deeply into the program and realized that they were testing potentially dangerous, experimental drugs, she had decided to turn them down. That must have been when Dr. Seymour decided to report her. Up until then, she had been waiting for Keisha to put Gabriel into the program voluntarily.

"Do you really think there are that many cases of medical kidnap?" Kirstie asked Renata, her skepticism carrying over the line.

"There's a lot more than that. That's just the kids that got put in the mito clinic."

"Well, I'll do my best to find all of the ones being treated at Lantern. I'm getting a lot of calls from my superiors, so we must be stepping on some pretty important toes."

"We already knew that," Renata said. "Judges and big famous doctors."

Kirstie sighed. "We've probably been on the phone too long. You guys should clear out. Head to a new location."

CHAPTER TWENTY-ONE

THEY WENT BACK TO the pharmacy early the next morning to pick up Renata's prescription. It was a chilly morning and Gabriel wanted to move around to get warmed up. Instead, they had to lurk around the parking lot, looking for any suspicious vehicles. Gabriel shivered, crouching behind a van, looking for the rust red station wagon, or a police vehicle, or anything else that set off alarm bells.

"Black van with an antenna." Renata pointed.

They watched it. A couple of minutes later, a man climbed out and went into the coffee shop. They circled around to make sure there was no one else still sitting in the van.

"Courier truck," Renata whispered, nodding to a brown van.

"What's wrong with a courier truck?"

"They're owned by the feds. Good cover vehicles."

So they waited for the courier to make his deliveries and pull back out of the parking lot. Gabriel rubbed his arms, waiting for Renata's verdict.

"Okay," she said finally. "In and out."

"I'm coming in with you this time."

She didn't object. They hurried purposefully toward the doors and took one quick look around before going in. Renata grabbed Gabriel's hand and squeezed it, then let it go. She led the way to the prescription counter in the back of the store. There was no one visible.

"Hello?" Renata called.

An older man with wire-frame glasses came out of the back room and looked at them. "Oh... hello. How can I help you?"

259

"Renata Vega," Renata snapped.

"For a pick-up?" he asked pleasantly, moving at a leisurely pace toward the shelf lined with white prescription bags that had been prepared and not yet picked up.

"Yeah."

He looked over the bags and frowned. "Vega with a V?"

"Yes."

He shook his head.

Renata leaned forward over the counter. "I can see it right there. The box."

"Oh, I didn't realize it would be a case lot…" He bent down to pick up the box and looked at the white piece of paper taped to the top. He froze.

Gabriel and Renata exchanged a glance.

He knew.

"I'll just need to clear this…" he said.

"You don't need to clear anything. It's ready and I'm here to pick it up."

"I don't think it has the right codes on it. Your health care corporation…"

"I gave my card yesterday. Just give me my food. I can't eat anything else. If you withhold my formula, you're withholding necessaries of life. You're forcing me to starve."

"I'm not withholding anything, miss," he said, his voice kind. "I just need to check on the coding… it will only take a few minutes. If you want to come back in half an hour…"

"Give it to me," Renata ordered. "It's paid for. You can sort out your coding issue later."

He hesitated, holding the box in his hands.

"Just give it to her," Gabriel ordered, using his toughest voice.

The pharmacist nodded. He removed the white note from the box, crumpled it in his hand, and brought the box over to Renata.

"Thanks."

They retreated as quickly as possible. Gabriel opened the door for Renata. She stopped before exiting, looking around for any waiting vehicles. Then they walked away.

In spite of the fact that they had only walked, Gabriel was breathing like he had just run a race. They ducked into the alley behind the strip mall to rest for a moment.

Renata was pale and sweating. "I don't know how far I can carry this."

Gabriel grabbed the box. "We'll trade off."

But it was much heavier than he had expected. He didn't know if he could even carry it to the end of the alleyway. Certainly no farther than that.

"Oof. We'll have to hide it. Get some help, or carry one can at a time."

Renata obviously didn't want to part with it. She moved to take it away from him.

They both heard the car engine.

"Get down!"

Gabriel didn't know who said it first, or if they both said it at the same time. They both ducked down behind a big garbage bin, out of sight. A car made its way down the alley. Slowly, like it was lost. Gabriel tried to quiet his breathing. As if the driver of the car would have been able to hear him. Renata clutched his arm. The weight of the box grew and grew in Gabriel's arms, and he had to crouch lower and put it down on the pavement. Ever so quietly, ever so slowly. The car stopped. They both stayed frozen.

"Come on…" Renata whispered urgently, willing the car to drive on.

"Shh."

The car started to move again. Gabriel peeked around the corner of the bin. Renata pulled at him, but he couldn't help himself. He had to see. It would be some soccer mom or a senior citizen who had taken the wrong turn. He only needed a glimpse to reassure himself. Then they would both laugh at how silly they had been.

He caught a glimpse.

A streak of rust-red paint. He gasped and fell back, falling hard on his butt. A stab of pain ran from his tailbone up his spine.

"What?" Renata demanded. "What is it?"

"It's him. The doctor from the clinic. The one with the station wagon."

Renata swore. They waited. Eventually, the doctor made it to the end of the alley and continued on. But he was still going to be out there, patrolling the streets looking for them. He knew that they had to be close by, and if he knew about them, then he knew that they couldn't run away. Neither of them had the physical stamina to run.

Gabriel started to shiver again. But he didn't want to get up and walk around anymore. He didn't want to do anything but sit there on the ground, safely hidden behind the garbage bin, until all danger was past.

"He's gone," Renata said.

"Not far. And he'll be back. And the cops too. Everybody. We're not going to be able to get away."

"We can do it," Renata reassured him. She put her arms around him to warm him. "You got another shirt in your bag? You'd better put it on."

Gabriel obeyed, shaking violently. He remembered getting hypothermia at school over recess one day, outside playing in the snow like the other boys. It felt like that. Numb inside. Shivering as he started to warm up. Unable to control the shaking of his body. Renata held him again, and rubbed his arms, trying to warm him back up.

"We'll leave the formula here," she said. "You take one can in your backpack, and I'll take one in mine."

"What are we going to do with the rest? We can't carry it around with us, and we don't exactly have a cupboard to put it in."

"We'll... we'll get a locker. At a gym or the bus depot. We can store it there. We'll take a few trips, and we can leave everything there that we don't want to carry with us all the time. That's a good idea anyway, right?"

Gabriel nodded. Maybe they could even get more clothes. Blankets. Other comforts that they didn't have the space or strength to carry with them.

"Come on," Renata encouraged. She opened her backpack and used a set of keys to split the tape on the formula box. "We'll get ready, so when it's safe, we can just go."

Apparently, a couple of homeless kids renting a locker at the bus depot was nothing to raise eyebrows. The man reeled off the list of items that could not be kept in a locker in a monotone. He handed them a key, hardly even looking at them. They unloaded everything they could from their backpacks to make room for formula, hoping to be able to carry all the remaining formula back in one trip. Going back to that back alley repeatedly felt like a very dangerous thing to do. Gabriel scanned the inside of the terminal for anyone suspicious once they were done with the locker.

Renata took out her phone to call Ray. The forced cheer in her voice was plain to Gabriel and he wondered whether Ray heard it as clearly.

"Hey, Ray! How's it going?"

Gabriel and Renata leaned their heads together so that Gabriel could hear him too.

"Renata, where are you?"

"Just wondering whether you found Nick," Renata said, deflecting the question. "Are the fab four back together again?"

"No..." Ray sighed. "I mean... what I mean is... I found him, yeah, but I couldn't convince him to stay with us. He's going back home."

Renata swore. "Oh well, I guess he wasn't cut out for it. So you want to meet? You can fill us in on all the details."

"Renny... I'm going to go back too."

"What?"

"I'm sorry. But I agree with Nick. We all thought that once we got here and told our story, we'd be safe. They'd roll out the red carpets, and everything would be okay. I never thought we'd still be running and sleeping on the street. I thought we'd at least be able to stay at a shelter and be safe there. But that was all just fantasy. There's nowhere for us to go."

"You can't do this, Ray. Come on. We need your help."

"If you and Gabriel don't want to go back, that's fine. This was your show from the start. But you don't need me. You can do this on your own." His voice carried a tone of finality. He wasn't going to be talked out of it.

"We need to put together a list of all the kidnapped kids in the mito clinic," Renata said urgently.

"Go ahead. You know them better than I do."

"I need your help!"

"Sorry, Renata. I really am. Maybe we'll run into each other again sometime. You'd better not call me at home. You wouldn't want them to trace your number."

"No!"

"Bye Renny, Gabe."

Gabriel was speechless. He couldn't answer. Before Ray hung up, there was another noise. Ray said politely: "Oh, sorry sir. I didn't see you..." and then he was gone.

Renata blew. She screamed with wordless fury and launched the phone across the terminal. Gabriel heard it smash, heard the broken pieces scattering across the floor.

"Renata, it's okay—"

But she was not to be consoled. She shoved Gabriel away from her. "No! No, no, no! Damn him! Why did he have to do this to me?" She screamed again, sounding like an enraged animal.

Everyone in the terminal was looking at them with interest. There was no reason for them to pretend they didn't see such an open display in public. Gabriel saw a security guard striding toward them.

"Renata. We have to get out of here."

She started to rant at the top of her lungs. Gabriel could barely tell what she was saying. Some of it didn't even sound like real words, a garbled mess in the middle of her meltdown. Gabriel had a split second to decide whether to stay with her, or whether to walk away before the security guard got there. But he couldn't run and he couldn't abandon Renata to her fate.

"What seems to be the problem here?" the security guard asked in a neutral voice as if this kind of thing happened every day. And at the bus depot, maybe it did. Gabriel had heard once about how some mental institutions, when they wanted to be quit of a particularly difficult patient, would put him on a bus with a one-way ticket out of town. The patient would be left at the destination with no money, nothing but the clothes on his back, and no possibility of getting gainful employment. So maybe that sort of thing was par for the course when you worked security detail at a bus depot.

"If you just give me a minute, I'll get her out of here," Gabriel said.

"Yes, sir..."

The security guard didn't back off, but stood there, waiting. Gabriel tried to touch Renata. He tried to hold her hand or find some way to calm her. But she wasn't having any of it. She continued to scream and rant, sounding truly insane. Gabriel didn't know what to do.

"Ray's right. We don't need him," Gabriel told her. "This has always been your operation. It doesn't matter, Renata."

Whenever he approached her, she shoved him back or hit him. The security guard gave Gabriel a minute or two to sort her out, then became active again. "Miss? I'm going to have to ask you to leave. Can you do that?"

She swore at him, then went back to her deranged ranting.

"Miss, if you don't leave, I'm going to have to put you under arrest and call the police. If you don't want to spend a night in jail..."

Renata launched at the guard, both fists flailing. Gabriel couldn't follow the progress of the fight. They moved too fast for him to see what was going on. He saw the security guard's nose blossom red and knew that Renata had punched him in the face.

Renata's frenzied attack could last only a minute or two. She didn't have the energy in her muscle cells to maintain it.

The guard had her on the floor and was attempting to force her hands into white plastic restraints.

"She has broken ribs," Gabriel said, "be careful, please!"

The guard didn't look up at him, intent on getting her under control. "Come on, miss. Don't fight me. Just take it easy now."

Renata was restrained. She lay on her belly, panting. Gabriel was worried about her ribs and about her feeding tube. He didn't think they should have her lying on her stomach.

"You should turn her over."

"Prone is safer. I'm calling the cops. If you don't want to be here when they get here, you'd better make yourself scarce."

"She has broken ribs and a feeding tube. You should put her on her back."

He looked at Gabriel briefly, then flipped Renata over. She didn't try to kick him, but lay there floppy and lifeless, eyes shut. The guard checked her pulse and leaned in close with his cheek in front of her mouth to listen for her breathing.

"She's okay."

Gabriel nodded. The guard sat back on his heels and pulled out a phone to call for ambulance and police. Gabriel touched Renata's face to reassure her. He didn't know whether she was unconscious or just exhausted.

"Do you have to call the police? She didn't really do anything wrong. I mean… other than punching you in the face," Gabriel added, feeling his own face heat up.

The guard dabbed at his bloody nose with a tissue. "I have to call them any time I put someone in restraints. She could try to sue me."

"She just… she had some bad news; that's all."

"That was more than just bad news."

Gabriel looked around. "Can I put her bag in our locker?"

"Go ahead."

Gabriel picked up Renata's backpack. "Can you... not tell anyone we have a locker here...?"

"Not anybody's business but your own."

"There are people... after us..." Gabriel trailed off at how paranoid it sounded. "Really... it could cause us real trouble."

"Go put your stuff away."

The policeman who answered the call drove Gabriel to the hospital when the ambulance refused to let him ride along. Gabriel sat in the front seat and tried to avoid answering any of the persistent officer's questions.

At the hospital, he was allowed to sit by Renata's gurney in the emergency room. They didn't send her directly up to psych.

"What's her name?" asked the admitting nurse.

"Uh... I don't know. We just met."

She glared at him, then looked at the paramedics. "Did she have any identification?"

"Nothing."

Gabriel had stashed anything that might identify her in the locker.

"Jane Doe, then. What do you know about Jane's medical history?" she shot back in Gabriel's direction.

"Uh... not a lot. She said she had broken ribs. I don't know if they're fully healed yet. And she needs this," Gabriel put one of Renata's cans of formula on the little side table. "She has a tube thingy."

The nurse took a look under Renata's gown, even though the paramedics had already filled her in on the fact. She made some observation aloud that Gabriel assumed identified the brand or type of feeding tube, and wrote it down. She looked at the can of formula and made another notation.

"This is prescription. Where is the prescription label?"

"I don't know."

"We can't give that to her without a new prescription being issued."

"Well, she can't have anything else. If you give her a different one, she'll be sick."

The nurse scribbled something down. "What else?"

"What?"

"Medical history. What else do you know?"

"Umm…" Gabriel wasn't sure how much he should reveal. "She has something called mitochondrial disease. I don't know if you know what that is…?"

"Of course, I know what that is."

One of the paramedics looked up, frowning. "There was a program about that on the TV the other day…" His eyes widened as he looked from Renata to Gabriel. "Wait… that was you, wasn't it? You were both interviewed on the show. By Kirstie Holt."

Gabriel looked down at Renata's hand, interweaving his fingers and hers. "I don't know what you're talking about. We just met."

"Yeah, I'm sure it was you!"

"What is her name?" the nurse asked the paramedic.

"They were anonymous informants; their names were never given. But the show will know. If they don't want to get sued, they have to do their background checks."

"Well, we'll have to have the police follow up on that."

"She has a psychiatric history too, doesn't she?" the medic aimed this at Gabriel.

Gabriel shrugged. "It's all part of her mitochondrial disease."

"Yeah, she did. Paranoid delusions and some other stuff. Sees conspiracies everywhere. That's what the whole show was about. This big conspiracy to kidnap kids with mito and force them to have medical treatment."

"Well, of course they need to be treated," the nurse said.

"It wasn't like that…" Gabriel protested weakly.

"Do you know what meds she's on? Antipsychotics?"

"Umm… no." There had been nothing in Renata's bag. She had lied to him about taking her meds. "I think… she's been off them… for a few days."

"But you don't know what."

"No."

"If you know her name, you'd better tell us so that we can access her medical history. If we give her the wrong treatment or something that she's allergic to, it will be on your head."

"She said she responds to meds the wrong way… I forget the right word… paradox?"

"Paradoxical. But which meds?"

"I don't know… benzos…"

"Benzodiazepines. Is that it?"

"I don't know," Gabriel said helplessly. "I don't think so."

"Then give me her name."

He just shook his head, staring down at his hands.

The nurse grunted. "I'll talk to the police officer. He can make the calls to Kirstie Holt's station manager."

They were screwed.

Gabriel sat there with Renata until the paramedics transferred her care to a doctor, and then he was kicked out. "We'll have to transfer her to psych. No visitors."

Eventually, Gabriel found a phone that he could use and placed a call to Kirstie. On answering, she obviously already knew what was going on.

"Oh my goodness, Gabriel. Are you all right?"

"Yes. But…" he found himself choking up. "I don't know what's going to happen to us."

"It will be okay. They'll take care of Renata. And you'll be okay. It will all work out."

"You said that once they have us in custody, they have to send us back. Across the line."

"I'm seeing whether there is anything I can do from here."

"Like… what?"

Gabriel saw a movement out the corner of his eye and turned his head. It was the cop. Watching him. Gabriel supposed that he was under orders to detain Gabriel if he tried to run.

"There are a few clauses in the interstate compacts. Not very extensive… about the sending state being required to ensure that the child is not being sent back to a situation where their safety is at risk…"

"Then they can't send us back! Renata was right!"

"Well, they have to do some more research to figure out what the requirements are. I gather no one has ever used the safety exception before, so they're not sure what to do. Right now, they have three days to send you back, unless they can use that clause."

Gabriel nodded, even though she couldn't see him. "Okay. Thanks."

"Are the others boys with you too? Ray and Nick?"

"No. They decided to go back voluntarily. That was sort of what set Renata off in the first place."

"Oh. Well, I hope that doesn't throw a wrench into the works. Can we say that it is dangerous for you and Renata to return when Ray and Nick have gone back voluntarily?"

Gabriel's gut tied itself into a knot. "They could be wrong. Isn't there enough evidence to show that we would be in danger? We don't want to be put back into the mito program. It's experimental. They shouldn't be able to force us. It just made me sicker."

"I know. We'll stay on top of it, okay? But we don't have long to convince them. Only three days."

"Yeah." Gabriel watched the cop, who was pretending to stand around casually, but was watching Gabriel. "There's a cop here. Are they going to arrest me?"

"They won't arrest you. But they will put you into care. They have to, knowing that you are a runaway from another state."

Gabriel let out a sigh of exasperation.

Kirstie swore suddenly. Her voice carried shock and fear that sent Gabriel's already-tight stomach into spasms.

"What? What is it?" he demanded.

"Gabriel… this has just come across my desk. The police haven't made a public statement yet."

"What?"

"They found Nick's body."

"What?" Gabriel's voice screeched upward. He grabbed at the wall for support. The cop took a few steps closer to him. Gabriel didn't know whether he thought Gabriel was going to run or if he thought Gabriel needed help. Black spots grew in front of Gabriel's eyes until he couldn't see anything around him. He clutched the phone tightly against his face.

"Nick's body? How could that be? What happened to him?"

"There aren't any details yet. The police will be making an announcement in an hour."

"Are you sure it's him? It could be someone else."

"I saw Nick's ID. I have his full name. And the description matches. We can't make it public yet, because the family hasn't been notified."

"*His* family or his foster family?"

"I don't know how it usually works."

Gabriel pulled at his hair. "What happened? How could they get to him?"

"Don't jump to any conclusions, Gabriel. We don't know what happened yet."

"There's been a doctor dogging Renata and me... they must have put someone onto Nick too. What about Ray? Can you call him and warn him?"

"I don't have Ray's number. Do you?"

Gabriel thought of Renata's smashed phone. "No. Renata might remember, but she's not awake yet. Can't they..." he tried to think of some suggestion, but was at a loss. He yanked on his hair again, tears of pain and frustration welling up in his eyes. "Kirstie..."

"I'm going to come to the hospital," Kirstie decided. "You need someone with you, and when the police announce Cause of Death, we might need to put together a spot. Can you hold it together until I get there?"

"O-okay," Gabriel agreed, sobbing.

"Okay. Good boy. I'm going to get a crew together, and I'll be over soon."

CHAPTER TWENTY-TWO

A SOCIAL WORKER SHOWED up before Kirstie got to the hospital. The police officer continued to hang around but didn't approach Gabriel directly.

"My name is Kelly Lassiter, Gabriel," the social worker introduced herself, putting out her hand to shake his. "How are you doing?"

She was an older woman, with a typical social worker blazer and skirt suit, and her gray-streaked hair pulled back from her face. Her hands were unusually large and her grip too firm. Gabriel tried to stay in control of his emotions.

"I'm… okay."

"Why don't we find a quiet room to talk in?"

Gabriel shook his head. "I don't want to talk. And I'm waiting for Kirstie Holt."

"Ah yes, we've been hearing all about your interview with Miss Holt."

"I'm not going back. There are people trying to kill us! They already got Nick."

Lassiter's eyebrows went way up. Gabriel could see her reevaluating him, adding a 'psych?' notation to her mental file on him.

"*Who* already got Nick?"

"I don't know. They sent someone after us; they must have sent someone after Nick and Ray too. We didn't stay together so that we wouldn't be as visible. But somebody got to him. They found his body!"

"Well… we'll have to wait to find out what happened, won't we?"

"You can't send me back. If I'm in danger, you can't send me back."

"At this point, I don't think there's any evidence that you would be in danger. I think you children have misinterpreted the facts."

"Nick is dead. How can I misinterpret that?"

"We don't know what happened yet. There could be a perfectly logical explanation."

"There is."

"He *was* sick," she pointed out.

"Not *that* sick. I just saw him."

Kirstie arrived with her crew, causing a stir and making everyone around sit up and take note. Kirstie spotted Gabriel and hurried over to him. "Gabriel! Are you okay?" She didn't shake his hand, she put her arms around him and gave him a tight squeeze. "This must all be so hard for you. Are you really okay?"

She pushed him back and looked at his face. Gabriel was crying in earnest now and tried to wipe the annoying tears aside. He nodded, choking out, "I'm fine."

"Good." Kirstie kept one hand on Gabriel's arm and looked at her wrist on the other. "The police are giving an update in fifteen minutes. Then we'll know more." She looked around and pointed out to her crew where she wanted to set up for the spot. She looked at Lassiter.

"Kirstie Holt," she introduced herself.

"I know who you are. Kelly Lassiter. I'm Gabriel's social worker. Temporarily, anyway."

Kirstie gave her a keen look. "We are trying to block the return of Gabriel to his home state. For reasons of personal safety. You understand that?"

"The press doesn't generally override DFS," Lassiter sniffed. "At the moment, we don't see any danger in returning Gabriel to his home." She looked at Gabriel. "You are not claiming that you were abused by your foster family, are you?"

Gabriel thought of Collin's bullying and how Gabriel had stolen hundreds of dollars from the older boy. That wouldn't go over well if Gabriel were returned to the Foegels.

"It's called medical abuse," Gabriel said instead. "If they can use 'medical abuse' to take kids away from their homes, then it should apply to foster care too. I don't want the Lantern Clinic's mito treatment. It's experimental, and it makes me sick. I shouldn't have to be sicker, just because Dr. De Klerk wants to make money on me from the drug companies."

Kirstie was busy giving her crew directions, but she laughed softly at Gabriel's words. "You tell'em, Gabriel."

"Putting you in a treatment program does not qualify as abuse or a threat to your personal safety," Lassiter maintained. "Unless a real threat is revealed in the next two days, you will be returned to your foster family, or wherever your DFS deems it appropriate to send you."

Gabriel shook his head and looked away from her. It was far more interesting to watch Kirstie get ready for her spot. He was tired of listening to the social worker. The minutes counted down, Kirstie was in position, and they had performed all of their sound checks and lighting checks.

"Okay," Kirstie touched her ear, listening to her radio earbud. "I've got the feed now. They're just getting ready for the announcement."

Everybody was silent, waiting. Gabriel held his breath.

"They've confirmed that Nick was one of the boys in our feature. He's saying..." Kirstie shook her head at Gabriel. "They're saying that it appears he died of natural causes."

"Natural causes?" Gabriel echoed.

"They will still need to do an autopsy, but they are not treating it as suspicious. No apparent foul play."

"No!"

Kirstie's hand dropped away from her ear. "I'm sorry, Gabriel. It looks like it was just his time. His body couldn't hold up any longer."

"The guy that has been following Renata and me is a doctor. He could make it *look* like natural causes. Give him an injection or something. No one would ever know because he was sick. No one would look for it."

"A doctor wouldn't kill Nick, Gabriel," Kirstie said. "It would be breaking the Hippocratic oath."

Gabriel stared at her in disbelief. "I'm pretty sure murder is against the law. But that doesn't stop people from doing it." Gabriel had another thought. "Maybe it was one of the drugs on the protocol," he said. "Can anyone tell that? Maybe sudden death is one of the side effects. They wouldn't want us to know that."

"Nick wasn't taking the Lantern Clinic's protocol anymore," Kirstie said. "None of you were."

"Withdrawing meds suddenly can cause problems," Lassiter chimed in, reminding Gabriel of her existence with a start. "There are a lot of medicines that you have to taper off slowly, under a physician's guidance, or they can cause problems. Maybe it was *quitting* that killed him."

Kirstie shook her head at Lassiter, frowning. "It's a natural death, Gabriel," she repeated as if he might believe her when she said it this time. "You're just going to have to accept it."

"What about the doctor who's been following us?"

"Where did you see him?"

"At the clinic where Renata went to get her prescription refilled. And then at the pharmacy when she went to pick it up. Not right next door. Farther away. The next day."

"Maybe he's a pharmacist. Maybe he's a drug rep. He could be those places legitimately. It could just be a coincidence."

"And it's a coincidence that Nick died, too."

"Well, yes. I can't see a common thread that binds the two together. I don't think they are related."

Kirstie prevailed upon the hospital to put Renata in a private room, which meant that Gabriel could sit with her again. Gabriel didn't know whether Kirstie paid for the room or just traded on her celebrity status, but he didn't care either way. He was happy just to sit there waiting for Renata to wake back up. Since she had only exhausted herself and hadn't been given any sedatives or antipsychotics, he was hoping that she would wake up soon. The bed looked so soft and comfortable after so many nights sleeping on the street. He felt like just climbing in and snuggling up with her. Even the chair was more comfortable than anywhere he had slept recently, other than the motel the night Kirstie's program aired.

The social worker had agreed to leave Gabriel at the hospital rather than taking him off to foster care immediately. Probably something to do with the fact that there was a cop outside the door to make sure that they didn't run off again, and they didn't have security like that at the usual foster home.

There was a tap at the door, and Gabriel turned his head sleepily to see who it was. The doctor looked vaguely familiar. He gave Gabriel a little smile and walked up to Renata's bed. "Any change?" he asked.

Gabriel studied him. He was pretty sure it wasn't the same doctor who had been around to see Renata earlier. Why would he come around again so soon without any urgent reason? Yet Gabriel had seen him before.

As the doctor put his fingers on Renata's wrist to feel her pulse, Gabriel flashed back to it. The doctor who had visited the clinic while he was waiting for Renata. The doctor in the red station wagon. Gabriel was on his feet in an instant, his lethargy gone. "Leave her alone!"

The doctor looked at him, eyebrows raised, as if he didn't have any idea what was wrong. He put on his stethoscope and listened to Renata's chest.

"I said leave her alone!" Gabriel insisted. But what was he going to do, fight the man?

The doctor slid Renata's gown to the side to expose her feeding tube. He inspected it. Gabriel's head spun. The doctor reached into his lab jacket pocket and came out with a syringe and a vial of something. "Just a little something to keep her quiet," he assured Gabriel.

"You're not her doctor! You can't give her anything!" Gabriel ran toward the door. Except he couldn't run, so it was more of a walk. A slow, deliberate walk, while the menacing doctor stood over Renata and prepared to give her some kind of medication through her feeding tube. Gabriel started to shout before he reached the door. "Help! Officer! Help me! He's going to kill her!"

The policeman opened the door and looked at Gabriel in irritation. Gabriel turned back toward the bed, gesturing. "He's going to put something in her feeding tube! He's not her doctor! He can't give her anything; she could die! They already killed Nick!" Gabriel felt like he couldn't get any air. His voice kept getting higher and screechier. He knew that he should stay calm, should explain it quietly and coolly so that the cop wouldn't think that he was a lunatic. But he was in a panic. In the time that it took for the cop to understand what Gabriel was saying and believe him, the doctor could squirt something down Renata's tube and walk out the door. He'd be gone before Gabriel even managed to convince the cop that it was serious. Gabriel started walking back toward the bed. "Stop him! You have to stop him! He doesn't even work here!"

"Sir, if I could get you to step back...?" the policeman drawled, reaching toward his hip and motioning the doctor to get back from the bed.

The doctor looked at the policeman calmly, raising his eyebrows. "There is no problem here. I'm not sure what the boy is so hysterical about. Maybe I'd better give *him* a sedative next!" He moved again toward Renata's feeding tube.

"Get back!" the cop snapped out. This time, the doctor froze.

He took a step back. Gabriel reached Renata's bedside again and grabbed the end of the tube, pulling it farther away from the doctor and putting his finger over the end. He knew it probably wasn't sanitary. Renata would get angry because she'd have to get the tube sterilized, or a new one put in or something, but he wasn't leaving anything open for chance. The doctor couldn't put anything into the tube while Gabriel's finger was over the end.

"Back. Another three steps. Right to the wall," the policeman ordered the doctor. Gabriel watched the doctor think about it and then obey. The doctor and the policeman stared at each other, gauging each other's movements.

"Put down the needle," the policeman said.

The doctor displayed it. "No needle. Just a syringe. I couldn't do more than squirt you with it."

"Put it down anyway."

The doctor put it down on the windowsill beside him. The cop grabbed the doctor's identity badge, pulling it off of the lab coat with a snap. He looked at it, eyes narrow. "Dr. Glover. The kid's right. You're not a doctor at this hospital."

"I have privileges at several hospitals. I just grabbed the wrong badge."

"You're the girl's doctor?"

Glover's eyes went back and forth, not answering immediately. "I'm treating her."

"What's in the syringe?"

"A sedative. To keep her calm."

"She looks pretty calm now."

"She's not supposed to have anything," Gabriel insisted. "She reacts to things the wrong way. You give her a sedative, and she's going to be bouncing off the walls. If that's what it is." He looked at the doctor. "If you were really her doctor, you'd know that."

"Turn around and put your hands on the wall."

The doctor obeyed slowly. The cop used his foot to pull the doctor's feet back farther, and then patted him down. He brought the doctor's hands around behind his back and clipped a pair of handcuffs over his wrists.

"This is a mistake," Glover protested.

"If it's a mistake, I'll be the first to apologize. I need to be sure."

"You can't go around arresting doctors at the hospital for no reason."

"I think I have cause at this point. Let's get it straightened out."

He escorted the doctor out of the room. Gabriel fell into the seat next to Renata's bed, letting his breath out with a sigh. He was still holding onto Renata's tube and couldn't let it go quite yet. The danger was past, but he just couldn't relax his guard.

He could hear the policeman talking to the nurses out at the desk. They must have confirmed that Glover didn't work there because the doctor did not come straight back in.

"Knock knock?"

Gabriel looked back at the door. Kirstie stood there, Officer Mills beside her, his extended arm barring entry.

"Yeah, come in," Gabriel invited.

The cop let her in and resumed his guard post. Kirstie sat on the edge of Renata's bed.

"I hear you had some excitement."

Gabriel watched Kirstie tap the screen on her phone and lay it on the rolling table between them. The big red dot obviously indicated that it was recording their conversation.

"Can this be off the record?"

"I don't think so. We need to get this information out to the public if you want to be able to take these guys down."

Gabriel closed his eyes and leaned his head back, exhausted. "I'm not sure… I want to do this anymore."

"You've already started the ball rolling. You can't exactly stop it at this point."

He sighed. "Okay. Fine."

"So the doctor in the red station wagon wasn't just a paranoid delusion."

"No." Gabriel rubbed his stiff neck. "Did you find anything out about him?"

Kirstie looked like the cat that swallowed the canary. She perched there on the hospital bed, with a self-satisfied smile. Gabriel's heart pounded. Maybe it was good news. Maybe it was real progress, instead of more people being convinced he was paranoid.

"What?" he demanded.

"Glover is a junior doctor from the Lantern Clinic."

Gabriel gripped the arms of the visitor chair and leaned toward her. "He's from the Lantern Clinic? De Klerk sent him?"

"We don't know who sent him. He says nobody did; he was just there to help treat Renata—forget the fact that he doesn't have any privileges to do so. He says was just trying to help her."

"What was in the syringe?"

"They are having it analyzed, which will take forever. But the bottle that it came out of says that it's a high-protein feeding supplement. Just formula."

Gabriel frowned, thinking about it. Why would a doctor come all the way from the Lantern Clinic to feed her? She already had her prescription, which he would know from their visits to the walk-in clinic and the pharmacy. He wasn't trying to treat her. He was trying to harm her.

"What kind of formula?" Gabriel asked. "She could only tolerate one kind."

Kirstie picked up her phone and tapped through a few screens to remind herself, then put it down carefully between them and waited a moment before speaking again. "It is a high-protein egg and dairy based formula. Used for tube-fed patients who need to gain weight."

Gabriel swore under his breath. His eyes found Kirstie's. "It probably would have killed her."

"How?"

"The dairy would make her throw up. She could choke to death throwing up when she was unconscious. I don't know what the egg would do to her, or any of the other ingredients. You should ask her mom."

"I will when we can get access to her. It's a good thing you were here. If Renata had been alone and he just walked in and put it down her tube and walked back out... they would think it was an accident."

"Like Nick...?"

"Because of Dr. Glover's involvement, they *are* going to take a closer look at Nick's death as well. But from what you've said,

Glover was following Renata. He couldn't be both places at the same time."

"De Klerk could have sent more than one guy! Hundreds of people work there. Has anyone found Ray yet?"

"Not yet. And he hasn't returned to his foster family."

"He could be in danger. Why aren't they looking?"

"They are looking. They've been looking since you guys ran away."

"He could already be dead."

Kirstie nodded, her eyes sad. "We'll just have to hope for the best. And focus on you and Renata, and keeping you guys safe. Has she been awake at all?"

"No. But she's been more restless..." Gabriel gave Renata's arm a gentle shake. "Hey, Renata. Are you ready to wake up now...?"

She stirred a little and didn't open her eyes.

"Renata... wakey, wakey."

"Mmmph. Leave me alone, Gabe."

Gabriel flashed a smile at Kirstie. "You don't want to wake up? You've got a visitor."

Renata opened her eyes and rubbed them blearily with one hand. She scowled at Kirstie. "What are *you* doing here?"

"Renata!" Gabriel was shocked by her reaction. "Kirstie's been helping us."

"I didn't ask for any help."

"Uh... yes, you did."

"She's probably the one behind it all." Renata's eyes were dark and hollow. "She's the one who masterminded the whole thing."

"No... she's helping us. She got it on TV and everything, remember? And she just came to tell us about the doctor. You know, the one who was following us. In the red station wagon."

"Yeah, she knows all about him, hey?" Her tone insinuated that Kirstie was behind it.

"Renata. What's going on?"

Kirstie put her hand on Gabriel's arm. "It's okay, Gabriel. It's just her illness. She can't help it."

"But… I don't get it. She knows you're our friend. She knows you've done what she asked you to."

"And she thinks that the mother she loves tried to poison her. She can't choose what thoughts come to her."

"Don't talk about me like that! I'm right here!"

"I'm sorry," Kirstie said.

"Do you want to hear about the doctor?" Gabriel asked, trying to focus Renata on what had happened.

"Not with her here." Renata continued to stare at Kirstie with suspicion.

"It's time for me to go anyway," Kirstie said pleasantly. She tapped her phone to stop the recording and picked it up. "You know how to reach me if you need me," she told Gabriel. "I'll try to keep you updated as I hear any details. Okay?"

"Okay. Thanks."

Kirstie walked out. Renata watched her go, then turned her eyes toward Gabriel. He was afraid that she would turn her suspicions on him now. That their friendship would be ruined by her illness and her choice to stop taking her meds. But she seemed to be okay once Kirstie was gone. Renata took a careful look around the room, her eyes returning again to Gabriel.

"I don't remember what happened. How did we get here?"

Gabriel related the missing details to Renata the best he could, trying not to focus on her meltdown or the depressing details of Ray's disappearance and Nick being found dead.

"I need a phone," Renata said. "I need to call Ray to warn him, make sure he's still okay. Where did you put my phone?"

"You sort of launched it… it's broken."

"We can fix it. Probably just the screen is broken, it will still work."

"It shattered. I didn't bother to pick up the pieces. I can call from the public phone if you give me his number."

She looked at him for a minute, not answering. "What else happened?"

"The doctor that has been following us…"

"Yeah?"

283

"His name is Glover, and he's from—"

"The mito clinic."

Gabriel looked at her in astonishment. "How did you know that?"

"I've been going there longer than you. I probably don't know everyone, but I know a lot of them. Glover... he's kind of creepy. So he was trying to find us, to bring us back?"

Gabriel shook his head. "He came in here, while you were unconscious. He tried to put something in your feeding tube, but I wouldn't let him."

It wasn't exactly like Gabriel had wrestled with Glover, but he didn't need to tell Renata all he'd been able to do was scream for help.

"What was it? Poison?"

"Pretty much. A high-protein formula. Eggs and dairy."

Renata called Glover a very uncomplimentary name. "He was there last year when I had an anaphylactic reaction to a vax because they didn't check to make sure it was safe! He knew eggs would kill me!"

"He was going to do it with me right there watching."

"He probably had plans to take care of you too."

Gabriel thought about that. Would Glover poison Renata and just walk away, assuming that Gabriel wouldn't continue with the fight against medical kidnap? Would he leave Gabriel there to potentially call a nurse and save Renata? Both scenarios seemed pretty unlikely. Glover *must* have had plans to deal with Gabriel too.

"De Klerk is trying to kill us," Gabriel said. "I can't believe that the money is that important to him."

"It's not just the money now. His reputation, his whole life is at stake."

"Yeah. You do think it's De Klerk, though? Kirstie said it could just be Glover acting on his own. That's what he's saying. He just wanted to help you."

"Help me into the next world, maybe." Renata struggled into a sitting position. "Definitely De Klerk. We gotta call Ray. And we gotta get out of here."

"There's a policeman guarding the door."

She looked toward it. "Will he let you go make a phone call?"

"Probably not now. He can't keep an eye on you and watch me on the phone at the same time."

"He doesn't need to guard me if I'm still asleep." She promptly settled back, closing her eyes. "And they've already got the psycho doctor, so I'm safe to be left alone for a few minutes."

Gabriel leaned over her. "I need the phone number."

"Oh, yeah." She whispered it to him and made him repeat it back.

Gabriel went out to where Mills was standing guard. Or, more accurately, sitting guard. "I have to make another phone call."

Mills peered back into the hospital room and saw Renata lying still, apparently asleep. As Renata had predicted, he left her alone and followed Gabriel out to the phone. Gabriel didn't know what Renata's plan was, and didn't know what he would do himself after that. But Renata had been right so far. He'd have to trust her.

He went to the phone and dialed the number that Renata had told him. It rang and rang, eventually giving him a 'this party is not answering' recording.

Gabriel stared at the phone. Did that mean that they had gotten to Ray too? Gabriel closed his eyes, remembering Ray's last words, as they both hung up that last call. 'Oh, sorry sir. I didn't see you...' Who was he talking to? Had he just bumped into someone on the sidewalk? Or was it another doctor or hired gun who had been sent to take care of him?

How had they managed to track Nick and Ray down? Had the boys called their social workers or foster homes and trustingly gone with the helpful party who had arrived to pick them up?

"Are you done?" Mills asked, getting a little closer.

"No..." Gabriel looked at the phone. He needed to give Renata as much time as he could. He pressed the hang-up switch and dialed another number instead. Kirstie answered after a couple of rings. Gabriel could hear the sounds of her car in the background. She was probably driving back to her office to put the story together.

"Gabriel. Long time, no see. What's up?"

"I got Ray's number from Renata."

"Oh, that's good. Hang on, let me write it down."

He pictured her rummaging in her purse for a pen and paper while barreling down the highway. He winced. "I can call you back with it later."

"Oh no, not a problem. I'm ready."

Gabriel gave it to her slowly, half-expecting the sounds of a crash. But everything was fine.

"Did you try calling him?"

"Yeah... but there was no answer. I figured maybe the police could track the phone or something."

"You could just give it to Mills. He'll pass it on to the appropriate department."

"Oh... yeah..."

"Don't worry, Gabriel. There are lots of reasons that Ray might not answer his phone. He's probably fine."

"The last time we talked to him... something happened... he apologized for running into somebody, for not seeing them. What if it was someone...?"

"You can't spend all your time fussing over what might have happened. You don't know. You guys did your best to look after each other, but this thing is way too big for you. And... he's probably just fine. You're probably worrying over nothing."

"It's not nothing. Nick is dead, and Glover tried to kill Renata. I'm not just being paranoid. I'm not 'misinterpreting.'"

"I've never said that to you."

"Okay... I guess not... but I'm tired of people treating me like my opinion doesn't matter."

"You have a right to be. You've been through a lot."

Gabriel really didn't have anything else to say to Kirstie, but he kept her on the phone anyway, asking her about the update that they would broadcast and anything else that might keep her talking. Mills was starting to shift back and forth, obviously uncomfortable with having left Renata's room for so long. He looked over his shoulder toward the hospital room. Gabriel tried to think of something else to ask Kirstie about. She was saying something in his ear now, but he had no idea what it was. Mills walked back toward the hospital room. As he drew up even with the door, Gabriel stepped away from the phone, pulled the fire alarm, and walked into the open elevator.

The doors closed. It was quiet in the elevator, the alarm bells muffled and far away. Gabriel didn't have to press any buttons; it was programmed to go automatically to the ground floor when the fire alarm was triggered. Mills wouldn't be able to use an elevator after he realized that Renata had escaped. He'd have to use the stairs. Gabriel couldn't run, but at least the elevator gave him a bit of a head start. When the doors opened in the lobby, he started moving with the crowd. A sea of patients and visitors flowed out of the lobby into the street, with lots more behind. There were a few hospital workers trying to keep things calm and organized, but they were primarily ignored. Gabriel got to the edge of the mass and kept walking. He kept his eyes peeled for Renata, but she still surprised him, stepping out from behind a building and tapping him on the shoulder.

"Pulling the fire alarm?" she questioned. "I'm having a bad influence on you."

She had apparently had time to get her street clothes on, which meant that they didn't look like hospital patients and could walk away without being challenged. As long as Mills didn't spot them.

They stopped at a bus stop and waited on the bench for the next bus.

CHAPTER TWENTY-THREE

RENATA AND GABRIEL WAITED in line, their backpacks growing heavy, weighing them down. But Gabriel kept an image of a cot fixed in his mind and managed to stay strong. When they got to the woman checking everyone in, she paused in her routine speech and stared at them.

"Aren't you those two runaways…?"

Renata and Gabriel had decided to try out an alternative approach. Renata sighed and shrugged. "On TV? Yeah, but they said nobody back home wants us after we caused so much trouble, so we can just suck it up and see what it's like out in the big cruel world." She sighed again, rolling her eyes. "Tough love, you know?"

The woman looked liked she was trying to suppress a smile. She replaced it with a grumpy scowl. "You'll be expected to follow the same rules as anyone else," she said, handing them each a thin blanket. "There's no celebrities here."

"Yeah, okay," Gabriel agreed, sounding as depressed as he could. A cot for the night. A blanket. It was going to be heaven, no matter what the rules were.

"Find a spare locker, put your bags and the contents of your pockets in it and lock it up. No personal objects in the sleeping room."

They followed the rest of the group to the wall of lockers and picked two that were side-by-side. Gabriel removed his evening dose of meds and put them in his pockets. Renata took out a bag of formula she'd already mixed, not sure whether there would be anywhere sanitary to mix it at the shelter. They exchanged satisfied smiles.

"Easy as pie," Renata said.

They were herded like recalcitrant animals into the dining room. Which was more of a sit-on-the-floor-and-use-your-elbows room. One of the supervisors noticed Renata's formula and pounced.

"No outside foods or supplements," she growled, reaching to take it from Renata.

Renata jerked it back. The woman pursued.

"You think I can put your beef and potatoes in here?" Renata pulled up her shirt.

The woman stared at the tube, her mouth open. She didn't reach for the formula again.

"So I can keep it?"

The woman walked away without saying anything else. Gabriel waited for his plate while Renata hooked herself up.

He was surprised to find that there was a TV in the sleeping room. It was a large flat-screen, mounted up in the corner by the ceiling. Most of the room had a pretty good view of it. People who came into the sleeping room sat or lay down and immediately looked up at the TV as if mesmerized. It looked like television was an excellent choice of sedative to use in a shelter.

The one downside of sleeping at a shelter was, of course, not being able to stay with Renata. Boys and girls had separate sleeping rooms. There was a family room for women with little kids, but he and Renata didn't qualify as family. They didn't have any family anymore.

The volume on the TV wasn't quite loud enough, but when everyone was still, Gabriel could make most of it out. It was weird, lying there in bed, watching TV, just like he was relaxing at the end of a normal day. It had been a long time since he had just watched TV.

The cot wasn't comfortable, but it was easier on his bones than the ground. Lots of people coughed or had occasional outbursts, but mostly they just watched TV.

Later in the evening, Kirstie Holt was on. There were some cheers and whistles from the men. She was a good-looking newswoman and obviously popular. Gabriel focused on the TV, trying to block out any other noise.

Kirstie had on a sad, serious face. She recapped the previous program about medical kidnap. "Many of you felt that this was just paranoid delusions. Others were aware of similar stories, but didn't know whether to believe them or not."

Nick's picture was displayed in the corner of the screen, his face blurred as it had been on the show. Then they removed the blur so you could see his whole face. There was a lump in Gabriel's throat. Poor Nick.

"One of the boys on the segment was Nick Meredith. Sadly, his body was discovered today. At this time, Cause of Death has not been determined. Foul play was originally not suspected." The picture of Nick was replaced with a picture of Renata, her face still blurred. "An attack was made on one of the other children when a doctor from the Lantern Clinic attempted to inject her feeding tube with a substance she was highly allergic to." Kirstie waited a few seconds to let this sink in. "The Lantern Clinic denies any complicity in the murder attempt and says that Dr. Glover was acting on his own. One of the other boys is missing, and this network is doing what it can to help with the search."

She looked down at her paper copy, her face composed. She looked back up. "This network has been served with an injunction prohibiting us from reporting anything further on the story." She sat there for another minute. "It would appear that we have stepped on some important toes. We will be appealing the gag order and will keep you updated on our progress."

Then they went on to the next story. Gabriel closed his eyes.

They had failed. Renata had thought that once they got the word out, the conspiracy would crumble. The doctors would go to jail. The Lantern Clinic would be shut down. The corrupt judges would be disbarred, or whatever it was they did to judges. No more kids would be taken away from their parents to be experimented on.

But instead, they had bombed. They had put themselves into the line of fire and the courts had just shut the story down.

Nick had been killed and maybe Ray too. Renata had barely escaped with her life.

They hadn't gotten anywhere.

CHAPTER TWENTY-FOUR

THERE WAS ONLY ONE thing that Gabriel wanted to do. He wasn't sure what he would do after that.

"You'll get her in trouble," Renata warned. "They're going to have her phone tapped, and they'll know as soon as you call her."

"I just have to... I can't keep running and never have the chance to talk to her again."

Renata made a wide shrug. Gabriel picked up the receiver and dialed the familiar number. He waited while it rang, afraid she wouldn't answer.

"Hello?"

Keisha's voice gave Gabriel a thrill. He had missed her so much.

"Mom. It's me."

"Oh, Gabriel!" Her voice broke. "Baby, are you okay?"

"I'm okay, Mom. I am."

"When they said on TV that one of the boys was missing, I didn't know if it was you. Nobody would tell me anything. You're all right? Really?"

"I don't know what to do. Nothing has changed... we didn't make any difference."

Renata scowled at this. But she had to know it was true. She'd seen Kirstie's report in the women's sleeping room too.

"Mom... what should I do? Should I just come back? If I go back to the program, I'll still be able to visit you... If I just go back and do what they tell me to..."

Keisha was silent. Gabriel waited for her to tell him to go back. If she said to go back, he would. He would take the pills that made him sick. He'd toe the line. So that he'd be safe from harm and be able to see his mother.

"Gabriel, you can't give up. You *are* making a difference. People know what's going on now. Other moms are coming to me… I don't want you to go back."

Renata was staring at him, waiting for some sign of what Keisha was saying.

"You want me to keep trying," Gabriel echoed.

"I want you to be safe… but I don't think you'd be safe if you go back, either. You *are* helping. I'm proud of you."

"Okay." Gabriel sniffled a little. "I guess… we'll keep trying…"

"Be safe, sweetie."

"I will."

"You can't call me again, though. I have to report this call after we hang up, or they'll charge me with harboring a fugitive."

"Yeah, okay. Sorry."

"No, I'm glad you called. I needed to know that you were still alive."

"Okay. Bye, Mom."

"Bye, sweetie. I love you. And Dad does too."

Gabriel hung up. He stood there looking at the phone for a long time before turning to look at Renata.

"She says we're making a difference… other moms are calling her."

Renata's eyebrows went up. "They are?" Her voice rose. "Then maybe… the underground railway is still a possibility. If there are others who want to help…"

Gabriel nodded.

"We'll need to set up an organization," Renata went on. "Burner cell phones… people can't know more than one or two others in the organization, to prevent one person from ratting us all out." She spoke rapidly, bounding on ahead. "We'll need passwords and signs to recognize helpers by… the underground railway had songs that were escape instructions…"

"That might be going a bit overboard," Gabriel laughed.

Renata scowled. "Do you want it to work, or not?"

They worked hard, getting phones at different convenience stores so that no one could identify them as the same lot, making short, cryptic calls to those that they thought might help out. They didn't talk about Nick and Ray and the very real danger they were still putting themselves in. If they gave themselves away, another hired gun might show up to take care of them.

Renata saw spooks everywhere, paranoid of every car with tinted windows or extra antennae, but so far Gabriel hadn't been able to identify any more real threats.

They stayed at the shelters for a few days, getting caught up on sleep, but never going to the same one twice in a row. They had become invisible like the rest of the homeless.

But one morning, Gabriel waited for Renata outside the shelter the next morning, and she didn't come out. He waited until everybody had cleared out, growing more anxious by the minute. He finally went to one of the workers to inquire.

"Have you seen my friend, Renata? She was here, but she hasn't come out... is she sick in the bathroom or something?"

The woman looked at him like she'd never seen him before and didn't know what he was talking about. Then she nodded. "We had a disturbance last night. One of the women had some kind of meltdown, and she was taken by ambulance to the hospital."

"Was it Renata?"

"I don't really know names. I think I've seen you two together. Young girl."

"Yeah. What happened?"

The woman looked around as if expecting someone else to fill in the details. "I don't know, exactly... She attacked another woman, said she was watching her, involved in some plot to kill her... a real break from reality... she was very wild..."

Gabriel sighed. It had been bound to happen sooner or later, with Renata off her meds. He'd seen how paranoid she had been getting. Nothing he said to her helped.

Running the railway was going to be up to him.

CHAPTER TWENTY-FIVE

GABRIEL WATCHED THE BUSES coming in and finally saw the one he was expecting. He walked over to the arrivals door and waited for the passengers to disembark and sort out the luggage. A few people came in through the doors and then he saw the tow-headed ten-year-old. He waved.

"Sky! Over here."

Skyler looked around for a minute, ignoring Gabriel; then Skyler walked over to him.

"Everything go smoothly?" Gabriel asked.

"Yeah. Good. Where do we go from here?"

"Come on." Gabriel turned and Skyler followed. It was a complicated trip, never in a straight line. Walk, bus, surface train. Making sure no one could follow them without being seen. They arrived in a residential neighborhood and again walked. They were both tired, moving slowly and taking frequent rests. They finally reached the safe house and Gabriel knocked on the door.

"Hello?" the intercom beside the door inquired.

"I have a package for you. It needs to be signed for."

"Someone will be right down."

"If it wasn't safe," Gabriel told Skyler, "they'd say they weren't expecting a package."

Skyler nodded. The homeowner opened the door and looked at the two of them. Then she scanned the street behind them.

"All clear?"

"All clear," Gabriel agreed.

She motioned for them to enter. Gabriel let Skyler go in first and brought up the rear. They went up the stairs to the living room. A man and a woman were waiting there. The man had sandy hair that had probably once been light blond like Skyler's. The woman was short and frail-looking. Both jumped to their feet on seeing Skyler and hurried over to hug and greet him.

Gabriel hadn't ever seen Skyler smile before, but he did now. Their words of greeting all overlapped each other, parents and child who hadn't seen each other for months. It was a few minutes before they broke apart. The woman looked at Gabriel.

"Gabriel... I can't thank you enough! I didn't think we'd ever be able to be together with Sky again." She stepped closer and gave him a hug. Her shampoo smelled fruity, like strawberries.

"I'm just glad we got him out," Gabriel said, unable to suppress a huge smile over the successful extraction. "Now, you've got everything you need? You know where you're going?"

"We have all our new identification. Enough meds to last until we get established and can find a trustworthy doctor. We'll be far away from here."

"You have new ID for me?" Skyler asked, looking up at them.

"Yes. We have everything we need, thanks to Gabriel's connections."

"Does it say boy or girl?"

Skyler's mother laughed. "It says boy. Which will make us even harder to trace."

"Perfect," Gabriel said. "Renata will be happy to hear that we got you out next time I see her. She was always really concerned about helping you."

"Tell her thank you," Skyler's mother said, squeezing Gabriel's hand. "I hope she's feeling better soon."

Gabriel returned the squeeze. He didn't know how long it would be before Renata was released or managed to escape yet again. He didn't know if she'd ever be stable enough to help with the underground railway that had been her vision.

But as long as there were kids being stolen from their parents because of their medical conditions, Gabriel was going to keep working on getting them out.

Did you enjoy this book? Reviews and recommendations are vital to making a book successful.
Please leave a review at your favorite book store or review site
and share it with your friends.

Don't miss the following bonus material:
Sign up for mailing list to get a free ebook
Read a sneak preview chapter
Learn more about the author

Sign up for my mailing list and get Diversion, Breaking the Pattern #2 for free!

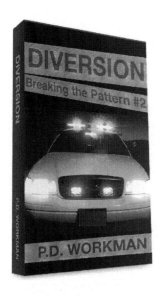

"fast-paced and intense, with a great climax and conclusion!"

SIGN UP AND GET IT FOR FREE!

Preview of EDS

Katt let herself into the house and immediately turned on the TV. After finding the remote and turning to the right channel, she headed into the kitchen to pull together a snack. She had timed everything perfectly so that she had five minutes before her show came on. She danced around the kitchen, tossing her blond hair and sweeping her long arms out like a ballerina before deciding that was a bad idea if she didn't want to risk smashing into something.

An apple, peanut butter, some milk because milk was important to build strong bones. If anyone needed to build strong bones, it was Katt. She pulled open the fridge and grabbed the big milk jug. It was full and it was heavy. Katt's mind was already on her next movement, two steps over to the fruit bowl. She wasn't thinking about bracing herself properly or pulling the milk jug out straight or about sliding one hand under it for extra stability. She just put her hand through the handle and jerked it off the shelf.

There was a loud pop in her shoulder and Katt yelped and let go of the milk jug. There wasn't even time to swear as the jug fell and she realized that it was going to hit her foot. She was still reaching for her right shoulder with her left hand when the jug hit her foot. Katt gasped with pain.

"Ow, ow, ow!"

She hopped on her left foot, grabbing her injured right foot with her left hand while her right arm hung loosely at her side. Then she swore. Not again. How could she be so clumsy? The

301

pain in her foot was worse than when she stubbed her toe on the iron frame of her bed. But she decided she'd better stop jumping up and down, or she was going to fall and break her tailbone too. Standing on one foot, she leaned against the central island of the kitchen, probing the bones of her right foot delicately. She was slender and her skin was so fair that the veins showed through the skin, and in the right light she could just about trace the bones beneath the skin without an x-ray. Almost without thinking of it, Katt transferred her grip to her right shoulder and eased the joint back into place with another loud pop. She rolled both shoulders and returned her attention to her foot.

The small bones in the top of her foot didn't feel right. Unbelievable. It was like the boys at school said, all they had to do was look at Katt and she'd break a bone. Katt put her foot down, and balanced on the heel, not laying it flat on the floor. She bent down and used both hands to pick up the milk jug, which miraculously had not popped its top and hadn't leaked a drop onto the floor. One less thing to worry about. She put it back into the fridge and opened the freezer to take out an ice pack. They were all arranged in the door of the freezer waiting for her.

Walking on her right heel, Katt minced through the kitchen, grabbing an apple from the fruit bowl, but abandoning her plans for peanut butter and milk. She settled herself carefully into the easy chair just as the opening notes of her show started to play on the TV.

Katt raised the footrest and carefully arranged the ice pack over her foot, settling back to watch her programs.

"I'm home," Karina called out to Katt as she walked into the kitchen through the garage entrance and put her purse down on the counter. "How was your day?"

Karina rubbed her back with long, slender fingers as she went into the living room to greet her daughter. She instantly took in the ice pack on Katt's foot.

"Uh-oh. What happened?"

Katt looked at her with luminous blue eyes. Her face was even paler and more angelic-looking than usual. Her wispy hair was tousled by the wind outside. Karina automatically gathered her own dark hair, pushing it behind her ears and back over her shoulders.

"I dropped the milk jug," Katt said, apologetic.

"Anything broken?" Karina bent over Katt's foot and pulled the now-warm ice pack away for a look. The foot was obviously swollen; the skin pulled tight. "Oh, damn."

"I'm sorry, Mom. I didn't mean to. I just wasn't paying any attention when I picked it up…"

Karina returned the ice pack to the freezer and retrieved a cold one. She handed it to Katt to replace, knowing that Katt would tolerate the pain better if she were the one laying the ice pack over the injury. She went back to the garage and grabbed a pair of crutches, hardly even having to look to lay her hands on them. She took them over to where Katt was sitting.

Katt eyed the crutches and sighed. "Can we have dinner first?"

She was probably more concerned about watching the rest of her show than she was about eating, but it was a valid request. They both knew the menu in the hospital cafeteria sucked and that they would be waiting for at least a couple of hours before getting the foot set. They had to eat something at some point. It might as well be in the comfort of home.

"Fine, all right," Karina agreed. "I'm just going to make mac and cheese. We'll want to get over there before the evening rush."

Katt looked at her watch and didn't say anything. They were probably going to get there right in the middle of the evening rush, but Karina wanted to remain optimistic. Maybe there would be a lull, and they could get in and out in good time.

"How was school?" she asked, as she moved back into the kitchen to get started on cooking supper. "And how much homework do you have?"

EDS, Medical Kidnap Files #2 by P.D. Workman is coming soon!

About the Author

FOR AS LONG AS P.D. Workman can remember, the blank page has held an incredible allure. After a number of false starts, she finally wrote her first complete novel at the age of twelve. It was full of fantastic ideas. It was the spring board for many stories over the next few years. Then, forty-some novels later, P.D. Workman finally decided to start publishing. Lots more are on the way!

P.D. Workman is a devout wife and a mother of one, born and raised in Alberta, Canada. She is a homeschooler and an Executive Assistant. She has a passion for art and nature, creative cooking for special diets, and running. She loves to read, to listen to audio books, and to share books out loud with her family. She is a technology geek with a love for all kinds of gadgets and tools to make her writing and work easier and more fun. In person, she is far less well-spoken than on the written page and tends to be shy and reserved with all but those closest to her.

~ ~ ~

Please visit P.D. Workman at pdworkman.com to see what else she is working on, to join her mailing list, and to link to her social networks.

~ ~ ~

If you enjoyed this book, please take the time to recommend it to other purchasers with a review or star rating and share it with your friends!